SL BEAUMONT

Death Count

A Kat Munro Thriller

Contents

Also by SL Beaumont

Shadow of Doubt

The Carlswick Mysteries series

- The Carlswick Affair
- The Carlswick Treasure
- The Carlswick Conspiracy
- The Carlswick Deception
- The Carlswick Mythology
- The Reluctant Witness (novella)

Chapter 1

Kat Munro twisted in her seat and looked behind. A dark shape took form as it approached from the gloom at speed, its headlights bearing down on them. She sensed Gabe ease their car towards the edge of the bitumen to allow the other vehicle to pass. A frown creased the skin between his eyes for a moment, and his long slender hands gripped the wheel. The breeze tossed his hair as he turned his head to look at Kat, and a warm smile lit up his handsome face. But instead of passing, the engine of the car behind them roared, and it closed the distance like a lion tracking its prey. Kat felt fear clutch at her throat. Had she been seen? The drive into town for extra supplies in Gabe's convertible now seemed fraught with danger.

"What the…" Gabe began, glancing in the rear vision mirror.

Kat looked across at him as she felt the car accelerate and gather speed.

From the back seat, Felicity hiccupped and giggled, twin dimples forming in her cheeks. She toed off her shoes and kicked her long legs up onto the seat.

Kat peered behind once more; her heart was thudding fast in her chest. The other car was keeping pace with them and was so close that she could make out the outlines of those in the front seat.

The light breeze, scented with the aroma of the wild honeysuckle growing at the side of the road, whipped her hair around her face.

"Gabe, slow down," Kat said, pushing the strands aside.

A bend in the road was fast approaching. Gabe changed gears, slowing the car as they entered the corner, but then sped up as they exited the turn. Their pursuers fell back for a moment before catching up to them again. Kat gripped the edge of her seat, terrified. A second tighter bend loomed in front of them when the other vehicle made a sudden move to pass and clipped the back of their car. The convertible shuddered from the impact and hit the loose gravel at the side of the road. It began to spin, with Gabe fighting to control it.

"Hey," Felicity shouted as she was tossed around on the back seat, too drunk to comprehend the danger they were facing.

The next images came into Kat's mind in a series of flashes.

The slide into the low stone wall, the car sailing through the air before hitting the ground in a field and rolling twice… Felicity's cries of pain… men approaching the vehicle and pulling a dazed Gabe away from the wreckage… thick and cloying smoke, blood, and flames.

Kat's screams rang out as she looked at her arm, draped over the side door of the car, and saw her bloodied hand hanging on to her wrist by a flap of skin and tissue.

Kat bolted upright. The room was dark, the bedsheets twisted. Her breathing was coming in uneven gulps, and her heart was racing. She glanced at the bedside clock, 4:30 a.m.; there would be no more sleep for her tonight.

Chapter 2

The rain which had been threatening as Kat hurried from her flat to the tube station had started falling while she was underground. As she rode the escalator up from the platform to the entrance hall, she could see that the road outside was slick with rainwater. Kat paused at the small hole-in-the-wall coffee shop at the station entrance. After a night of broken sleep, she'd need all the help she could get to make it through the day without dozing off at her desk. The barista began to prepare her usual coffee, a small skinny cappuccino when he saw her approach.

"Better make it a double," she said.

"Sure thing. I thought we'd seen the last of the rain, Kat," he said in his soft Irish accent, tossing his head to flick his long hair out of his eyes.

"Yeah, me too. Isn't it still supposed to be summer?" Kat replied, tapping her bank card against the payment reader and marking one square on her frequent coffee card with the stamp sitting on the counter. She slipped the cards back into a side pocket on her cross-body bag and loosened the tie holding her umbrella, dangling it at her side as she reached for her coffee with her free hand.

"All set?" the barista asked.

Kat nodded. "Thanks." She took a sip of the hot liquid and sighed. "That's just what I needed."

She joined the crowds heading out onto the street and braced for the rain. Fortunately, it had eased to a sprinkle, but at the entrance, she pressed the button on her umbrella's handle, watching as it unfurled over her head. She hesitated for a moment, making sure she had everything balanced before joining the groups of office workers waiting for the walk light to turn green.

At the signal, Kat crossed the busy road before hurrying along the block to her office. To her left, the River Thames was flowing dark and fast. A commuter ferry crawled along the water towards Westminster, its windows steamed up from the passengers crowded inside out of the rain. Even with an increasing proportion of the population working remotely, thousands of people still commuted into the city each day by road, rail, and ferry.

Kat rounded the corner leading to her office building's main entrance on a quieter side street. The lower levels had a red brick façade, retained from the days when the building had been a grain store. Sprouting from behind the walls, four stories up, was a modern steel and glass structure.

A dark grey Audi sedan pulled up on the pavement opposite the entrance to the building. Two men alighted from the back seat. One, dressed in a dark suit, bent his head and spoke with the driver, while the other, dressed in jeans and black leather jacket, leaned against the car, his eyes sweeping the surroundings. He had a half-smile on his face listening to the banter between the driver and the other passenger, but he didn't participate. He glanced up and caught Kat's eye at the same moment a bicycle courier veered onto the footpath.

The cyclist headed straight towards Kat but swerved at the last moment and only just avoided hitting her. He thrust an envelope at her as he passed.

Kat leapt sideways, knocking her left elbow hard against the brick wall of the building. The envelope floated to the ground, and her coffee cup went flying from her grasp, hitting the footpath with a liquidy thud as the lid popped off, splashing coffee on the cuffs of her trousers and shoes. She watched as the brown liquid ran across the gently sloping footpath and into the gutter.

"Watch where you're going, you arse," she called to the lycra-clad rear end.

"Sorry," he called over his shoulder as he continued down the street.

Kat crouched down to pick up the now empty cup and continued to curse the reckless cyclist. A large pair of feet clad in shiny polished boots stepped in front of her. She looked up to see that the guy who'd been leaning against the car had crossed the road and had his hand out, offering to help her up. Kat ignored his hand and stood. Somehow she was still holding the umbrella above her head, and he had to take a step backwards to avoid being hit. Kat felt a sharp stinging sensation above her left elbow.

"Are you okay? Can I get you another coffee?" the man asked.

She glanced at him for a moment, registering the steely blue of his eyes. His hair, damp from the rain, looked as though it was overdue a cut, and he had several days of stubble across his jaw. She was aware that her left hand looked awkward, but his gaze didn't leave her face, for which she was grateful.

"No, thank you. I'm fine."

"You dropped this," the man said, bending and retrieving the envelope from where it had landed on the footpath.

"Thanks." Kat snatched the paper and shoved it into the side pocket of her bag. She stepped around him and retracted the umbrella before pushing through the revolving door into the building. The last thing she wanted was some stranger feeling sorry for her.

Kat dumped the empty cup into a rubbish bin in the foyer and fumbled in her pocket for her pass. The strap of her bag pulled on her neck, sending shooting pains down her arm. She winced, and retrieving her pass, held it against the electronic reader at one side of the entry barrier. The low gates opened with a quiet swish. She walked through and across the marble floor to the stairwell. She climbed the single flight of stairs to the first floor and entered an ample open plan office space. There were clusters of desks grouped in pods of four. The brick walls of the converted warehouse were reinforced with steel beams, and polished wooden floors gleamed. Glass-fronted meeting rooms ran the length of the back wall, and the senior partner occupied a magnificent corner office with a view across the river. Kat wove her way among the desks. Two of her team were already seated behind their computer screens and glanced up to greet her. Nathan, an Australian accountant, who looked more like a surfer with his messy blond hair than a number cruncher, saluted her with one finger to his temple.

"What happened to you?" asked Shamira, a petite dark-haired woman sitting next to him.

"Bloody cycle courier. I dropped my coffee and banged my arm," Kat said.

She let the umbrella drop to the floor beside her desk and

pulled the bag's strap over her head with extreme care, before dumping it on her chair.

Shamira jumped to her feet. "Are you okay?" she said, concern showing in her deep brown eyes.

"Yeah, I just need to fix my hand."

"Do you need me to help?" Shamira asked, glancing at Kat's left hand and frowning.

Kat shook her head. "Nah, I'm all good."

Kat grabbed her bag and headed back towards the stairwell, where the bathrooms were located. She closed the door and placed her purse on the counter, wincing as she removed her jacket, pulling her right arm out first and easing the fabric over her left. Kat hung it on a hook by the door. She felt a trickle down the back of her arm and twisted in front of the mirror to look. Sure enough, there was a tear in the thin fabric of her shirt sleeve, and a bloody graze ran down her arm to just above her elbow where she'd hit the wall. Cursing and letting out a shaky breath, she undid the buttons on the chiffon blouse before releasing the suction that held her left hand in place, eased it off and laid it on the counter. The door burst open, and Shamira entered the bathroom as Kat pulled her arm out of the torn sleeve.

"Oh, Kat, please let me help," she said, reaching for the box of tissues on the counter.

Kat relented as Shamira pressed a wad of tissue to the graze with one hand and pulled open a drawer under the counter. She removed antiseptic cream and several large Band-Aids. She worked quickly, cleaning and covering the graze.

"Thank you," Kat murmured, stepping forward and picking up the prosthesis and turning it over. Fortunately, the attachment didn't appear damaged. The hand was very lifelike, with a soft texture resembling skin made from a sturdy silicone material.

"It looks so real," Shamira said.

"It should look close to the real thing for the amount it cost," Kat said, putting it down again and easing her arm back into the shirt sleeve, fastening the buttons using one hand, with practised ease. She ran her hand over the stump of her wrist, feeling for any pain or sensitivity. Finding none, Kat reattached the hand, sensing the silicone pads suction onto the end of her arm, and eased the flesh-coloured stretchy sock into place over her forearm. She flexed the fingers of the prosthesis as the synapses fired.

Shamira held out her jacket. "You have a tear in the sleeve of your top," she said.

"I'll just keep my jacket on, I have a meeting shortly anyway," Kat replied. She met Shamira's eyes in the mirror. "Thank you. I hate this."

"I know, sweetie, but it's okay to let someone help you from time to time," Shamira replied, helping her on with the jacket and giving her a quick hug. "On the bright side, it looks like we have to go shopping at lunchtime."

Kat smiled, and together they walked back to their desks.

"You've gotta see this," Nathan called in his broad Australian accent as they rounded the corner. He was leaning his wiry frame against the windowsill and peering through the window.

"What is it?" Shamira asked, rushing to join him.

"Looks like Stephenson got lucky," Nathan replied with a grimace.

Shamira hit him lightly on the arm. "Nate."

"You have to agree it's gross. He's so old."

"He's not that old," Kat said, joining them at the window. "Although it's the first time since he moved back from the States that I've seen him with anyone."

Together they looked down to the street below and watched as their manager, Charles Stephenson, gave the woman in his arms a long deep kiss.

"I think I might lose my breakfast," Nathan added, holding a hand to his stomach and performing a fake heave.

Charles Stephenson was a solid middle-aged man with thick cropped sandy hair and a severe side parting. They watched as the woman reached up and rested her hand on his cheek for a moment before turning and walking away. She looked younger than him from a distance, dressed casually with her dark hair pulled into a high ponytail.

"There's no way a man closing in on fifty could pull a woman like that," Nathan said.

They continued looking until Kat saw Stephenson smile as he glanced up and spotted the three of them watching through the window. With a final glance at the woman's retreating figure, he turned, and whistling made his way into the building.

"Well I think it's sweet, just shows that there is someone for everyone," Shamira said.

Kat and Nathan snorted with derision.

"Are you sure you're an accountant? I could've sworn I heard a romance novelist speaking for a moment," Nathan teased as Stephenson strode onto the floor thirty seconds later.

Shamira shook her head at Nathan and sat down at her desk.

"Morning all," Stevenson called as he walked across the

room to his office. "Kat, I see our clients have arrived. Can you organise coffee and show them to the meeting room? I'll join you in a moment."

"Sure, boss," Kat said before looking across at Shamira and Nate. "I'm so glad I spent all those years studying just to arrange coffee for our clients," she said, rolling her eyes. She went to grab a notebook and spied the envelope that the courier had dropped lying on the floor by her desk. She scooped it up and turned it over. It was addressed to her. Kat frowned, opened it, and eased out a single sheet of paper that contained a typed message.

'Stop whatever it is that you think you're doing, or you'll be sorry.'

Kat dropped the page onto her desk as though it were poisonous and took a quick step backwards.

"What's up, mate?" Nathan asked, leaning over and reading the note.

Kat grimaced.

"Are you still looking into..." he began before Kat interrupted him.

"Of course not."

"Really?" He didn't sound convinced. "I thought you'd let all that go."

Kat shrugged.

"Kat, don't just shrug this off, this is serious," he said. "Someone has just threatened you."

"I know, which just makes me think that I'm onto something."

"You need to be careful," Nate said.

Kat nodded and headed out to the reception area.

The two men from the Audi were standing to one side of

the reception desk. They hadn't seen her yet. Kat realised that she didn't know their names or even why they were there. She ran her hand through her long mane of dark auburn hair.

"Good morning. I'm Kat Munro," she said, approaching them with her right hand outstretched, wishing she hadn't been quite so short earlier.

"Detective Inspector Hugo Greenwood," the man in the suit replied with a warm smile, accepting her handshake.

The second man nodded. "DS Adam Jackson."

"Can we get coffee in meeting room one please?" she asked the receptionist, who smiled and nodded. "Cappuccinos?" she asked the two men.

"Please," Greenwood replied. He had a wise, weathered face and reminded Kat of a school headmaster.

"Detectives, this way," she said, holding out her arm to indicate the meeting room's direction.

"Do we get to see you perform your coffee juggling trick again?" DS Jackson murmured as he walked past her.

Kat rolled her eyes at his back. "Everyone's a comedian," she muttered and thought she heard him give a low chuckle.

She followed the visitors through into the meeting room where Stephenson was waiting. The spacious room contained a long wooden conference table and eight chairs. At the centre of the table sat a tray with a pitcher of water and several glasses. A wall-mounted screen dominated one end of the room above a long, low cabinet. The windows on the far side of the room commanded a picturesque view along the river towards Tower Bridge.

"Gentlemen, good morning," Stephenson said, stepping forward and shaking their hands.

"Charles," DI Greenwood said. "It's been a while. How's

business?"

"Very good. Yourself?"

"Busy, which sadly doesn't say a lot about the state of business in this country," DI Greenwood said.

"Indeed."

"In fact, we're completely backed up investigating other financial crime cases at present, but fortunately I'm able to engage independent experts, such as you, to help fill the gap," Greenwood continued.

They all sat down at one end of the long boardroom table.

"Kat, I should explain, DI Greenwood is head of the Met's new Financial Crimes Unit. Hugo, Kat Munro is one of my best analysts."

Kat smiled. Stephenson had managed to get the firm registered on the police database of forensic experts and had been touting their expertise to the country's various police forces and the Serious Fraud Office. Hence, she wasn't surprised that the two men sitting opposite her were police officers. She hadn't realised that their firm's services had actually been engaged to work with the new Financial Crimes Unit. No wonder Stephenson was looking so smug; this was something of a coup. Many of the larger accounting firms with specialist forensic units had been chasing the business. It was interesting that Stephenson had succeeded as a relative newcomer. She wondered how he'd pulled it off.

"Let me introduce DS Adam Jackson. Adam is heading up the homicide investigation." DI Greenwood's smile was warm as his eyes flicked across the table to Kat, resting momentarily on her left hand before looking away. DS Jackson's stare was assessing, but once again, his gaze never left her face. Kat moved her left hand to rest in her lap and sat forward, picking up her pen with her right.

"Homicide?" Stephenson's smug expression was replaced with one of concern.

"You may have seen in the news a few days ago that a security guard was found dead at the offices of Capital Investment Partners and one of the directors was missing," DI Greenwood began. "We've had our eye on CIP for a while, nothing major, just a couple of anomalies that the firm easily clarified. But when the missing director, Henry Smyth, also turned up dead yesterday, we decided to reopen our case and look deeper into the company. One death is tragic, but two unexplained deaths related to a firm that has been on our watch list warrants further examination, which is where Adam's investigation and mine intersect."

"The security guard's death is being treated as suspicious. He was found in the lobby atrium of the CIP office, having fallen from the second floor. We know Smyth accessed the building that same evening before he disappeared. And now he's been found dead at his apartment in central London," Adam explained. "An apparent suicide."

"Ah," Stephenson said.

"So how can we help? We don't usually work on murder cases. I'm assuming that you would like us to look into the firm's business affairs or those of Henry Smyth?" Kat asked.

"Both," Greenwood replied. "We would like a high-level independent review of CIP's business, using only publicly available information. We need a legitimate reason to take another look at them, but we don't want to show our hand at this stage. I'm not convinced that the directors have been completely forthcoming with everything that they've told us to date."

Adam cleared his throat. "For the record, I'm not sure what bean-counters can tell us that I couldn't find out from half an hour in an interrogation room with each of them."

Kat raised her eyebrows at the remark.

Greenwood laughed. "You'll have to excuse Adam. CID detectives don't usually have the pleasure of working with specialists in forensic accounting. Charles, I thought you could explain what it is that you do better than me."

Stephenson beamed. "Of course." The door opened, and the receptionist, a plump middle-aged woman, entered carrying a tray of coffee, which she rested on a side table before placing a cup in front of each person. Kat let her pen drop and sat back. This would take a while, especially once Charles warmed up. She murmured her thanks for the coffee and took a sip, savouring the caffeine hit that she'd missed out on earlier.

Stephenson looked thoughtful and stroked his chin for a moment before speaking. "Forensic accountants are the detectives of the financial world, DS Jackson. The word 'forensic' means being suitable for use in a court of law, so we apply rigorous processes to gather and analyse data. We are highly skilled in the areas of information technology and computer analysis. We have a deep understanding of accounting, tax, banking, and financial systems. We are familiar with legal concepts and proceedings, as we are often called upon to give evidence in court as expert witnesses.

"Our job is to sift through company records, business financials, and supplier relationships, looking for anomalies that investigators like you can examine and use to provide prosecutors with ample information to build a strong case. A forensic accountant is a chess player in this business; it's all about attention to detail and thinking several moves ahead of the criminals.

"Let me give you an example, DS Jackson. You may recall the case of City Build Construction last year. The Board of Directors engaged us after they became suspicious of the activities of the Chief Financial Officer. We did a deep dive into their records going back five years and discovered a number of fraudulent transactions. A case was built on the information in conjunction with the Serious Fraud Office, and we provided the expert witness testimony to the court. The CFO was ultimately convicted of embezzling £1.5 million from the company."

Kat smirked as DS Jackson held his hands up. "Okay, you've convinced me. I appreciate as well as anyone that you need properly gathered evidence to make any charges stick," he said.

DI Greenwood nodded. "Thanks, Charles. Now, Kat, if you can begin your analysis of the firm using any information that's in the public domain. And then look into the financials of Henry Smyth."

"Okay," she said, scribbling a couple of notes on the pad in front of her.

"We'll get Smyth's bank accounts to you once we have access to them," DS Jackson said, looking across the table at Kat. He glanced at his watch. "I'm meeting the deceased's parents at his apartment in half an hour. They have something they'd like to discuss. Would you like to come? It might give you a better feel for the type of people we're dealing with."

Kat looked at Stephenson, who was already nodding, eager to do whatever was necessary to secure the business.

DI Greenwood stood and extended his hand to Stephenson. "Great to be working with you again, Charles."

"Likewise," Stephenson replied, pushing back his chair and rising. He accepted Greenwood's handshake. "We must have lunch soon."

"I'll just grab my bag and meet you in the foyer," Kat said to DS Jackson as they filed from the meeting room. He nodded and followed DI Greenwood through the reception area and down the stairs.

Stephenson couldn't keep the grin off his face as they walked back into the office. "I don't need to explain to you what an enormous opportunity this is for our firm," he said. "Do whatever they ask. You can have Nathan and Shamira, but let me know if you need more resources." Kat nodded. "Well then, get to work." Stephenson strode towards his corner office, bouncing on his toes as he walked.

"He is such a buffoon," Shamira said, watching as Stephenson passed while Kat dropped her notepad on the desk. "But those two in your meeting weren't. Nate wants to know who the guy in the leather jacket is." She fanned herself with several sheets of paper.

"Nate wants to know, or you do?"

"Both, I think he and I just might come to blows," Shamira replied, pulling a face at Nathan.

"Bring it on, girl," Nathan said.

"I don't think he's your type," Kat said with a smirk.

"Someone's called dibs already," Nathan stage-whispered to Shamira.

Kat laughed. "Those two are police detectives. We've got a new assignment, with none other than the Financial Crimes Unit."

"Ooh," Shamira said. "No wonder Stevenson is looking so pleased with himself."

Kat scooped up her bag and threw the long strap over her head and across her body. "I'm heading out with them now. I'll fill you in on the details later. In the meantime, pull up what you can on Capital Investment Partners."

Chapter 3

DS Jackson rocked from one foot to the other as he waited for Kat in the foyer and watched Greenwood get in the back of the car they'd arrived in earlier. He glanced at his watch. How long did it take to grab a bag? He pulled out his phone and scanned through his emails, looking up when he heard Kat approaching, the heels of her shoes echoing on the marble floor. He studied her as she exchanged pleasantries with the security guard, smiling at something the older man said. She was tall with an athletic build and had thick auburn hair tumbling over her shoulders. She had a pretty face, with a light dusting of freckles across her nose. His eyes flicked to her hand. He was dying to know her story. He'd known immediately when that stupid cyclist had almost crashed into her that it was false. He'd come across plenty of amputees in his time. Still, he'd been struck by how naturally she moved her limb, as well as her fierce independence. He knew he couldn't ask about it; he would have to wait until she offered.

"Sorry to keep you waiting, DS Jackson," she said, still smiling as she joined him. It was a genuine smile that went from the soft curve of her lips to her eyes.

"No problem. And call me Adam," he said, sliding his phone

back into his pocket. He walked towards the revolving doors exiting ahead of her, guessing correctly that she would repel any act of chivalry.

Out on the street, Adam raised his hand and hailed a black cab from a queue further down the road. It eased to a stop, and he opened the door, climbing in the back ahead of Kat, who followed pulling it shut behind her. Adam gave the driver the address of Henry Smyth's apartment and sat back, turning his body on the bench seat to look at Kat.

She sat straight, stiff almost, looking out of the side window as they merged with the traffic along the Embankment. He studied her, surprised at the sudden display of tension when it hit him that her rigid posture wasn't from nerves. She was in some discomfort. She was holding her left elbow and shoulder away from the seat.

"Were you hurt this morning?" he asked.

Kat swung her head around as he spoke and looked him in the eye. She lifted her prosthetic hand from her lap and turned it over. "This?"

Adam raised an eyebrow.

"Yeah, my hand was chopped off when I hit the wall earlier, but it's okay now, I heal quickly." She held his gaze for a moment before looking out of the window again. The taxi turned and crossed London Bridge.

"That's a relief; we wouldn't want you bleeding all over the cab," he replied, refusing to allow her to embarrass him. He'd seen similar flippant reactions from former army colleagues, injured in Afghanistan. He guessed that any further inquiry into her well-being would be rebuffed.

He saw the corners of her mouth twitch upwards. "I'm surprised that you agreed to bring me," she said. "After all, bean-counters are next to useless in a criminal investigation, right?"

"You have me there," he conceded with a shrug. "We have different skill sets, that's all."

"Ooh, diplomacy. Now that's unexpected."

He studied her for a moment. "Don't get too used to it. I'm a tactless Neanderthal most of the time." A voice in his head reminded him that was exactly how his soon-to-be ex-wife described him. He stroked his bare ring finger and was startled when Kat laughed.

"Fantastic, we're going to get along just fine," she said, looking back at him, her smile carrying to her eyes and lighting up her face.

Adam grinned back at her, realising that he'd just passed some sort of test, and was surprised to find that he was pleased that he had.

"Is here okay?" The taxi driver's voice came over the intercom as he pulled into a loading bay on a busy street at one end of a six-level red brick apartment building. It was a new block built to blend in with the older buildings and surrounding warehouses.

"Thanks." Adam held a credit card against the contactless reader before opening the door and climbing out. Kat followed, slamming the door shut behind her. The taxi roared away as Adam consulted his phone and looked up at the building. "Smyth had the penthouse."

"Very nice," Kat said.

Adam turned a full circle, taking in the surroundings. At street level, the modern purpose-built building housed a dry cleaner, real estate agent, and a small café. Across a narrow cobbled lane, the muddy Thames swirled and wound its way towards Tower Bridge. He walked to the building's main door and pressed the intercom for the top floor apartment. After a few seconds, a strained voice answered.

"DS Jackson, I have an appointment with Mr. and Mrs. Smyth," Adam said.

"Come in, detective."

The door buzzed as it was unlocked remotely. Adam and Kat entered the building and waited for the lift. When the doors opened, a tall, stooped elderly gentleman with thinning grey hair, and kind but sad eyes greeted them. He shook Adam's hand as he introduced himself.

"Alfred Smyth. I'll take you up."

"Good to meet you, sir. I'm sorry for your loss," Adam replied, showing his warrant card. "This is my colleague Kat Munro." They stepped into the lift, and the doors closed.

Kat too shook Mr. Smyth's hand and murmured her condolences. Mr. Smyth looked tired, and a little defeated, but nodded and gave her the ghost of a smile. He tapped a card against an electronic reader, and the lift rose.

The lift opened into the apartment, and they entered a large reception room with floor-to-ceiling windows facing the river. Deep brown leather sofas and armchairs were grouped around a grand fireplace on one side of the room, and a square wooden dining table which seated eight filled the space by the windows. A small older woman, with soft white hair curling around a weary, grief-stricken face, waited for them.

"Dear, the police are here," Mr. Smyth said. "DS Jackson and Miss Munro."

Adam stepped forward and shook her hand. "We're so sorry for your loss, Mrs. Smyth. I understand you have some further information for us."

"Yes, detective, this way. I've made tea." Her voice was flat, and every step seemed like an effort. She turned and walked to an opening on the right-hand side of the room. Adam indicated for Kat to follow while he trailed behind admiring Henry Smyth's minimalist taste. The only exception appeared to be the tall bookshelves along one wall which overflowed with books.

Mr. Smyth noticed Adam's interest. "Henry would be horrified if he could see what they did to his books," he said, pausing and shaking his head.

"What do you mean?" Adam asked.

The older man sighed as a wave of grief washed over his face. "Henry was meticulous. There was never anything out of place. He'd been that way since he was a boy. Someone ransacked this place before we got here. His study was the worst."

"Ransacked? That wasn't in the attending officer's report. Is anything missing?" Adam asked.

"Hard to tell. We've tidied as best we could," Mr. Smyth replied.

"Did you tell the police?" Kat asked.

"We're telling you now," Mr. Smyth said. "We don't want to cause trouble. The firm sent someone over to pick up his laptop and any sensitive business documents, so perhaps they were a little overzealous."

Adam raised his eyebrows. "Capital Investment Partners sent someone? Before or after the initial police response?"

"Before, I believe. We arrived as Henry's body was being removed, and the police officers were still here gathering the things they needed. They said they had all the items and forensic data they needed and that since it wasn't a crime scene that we were free to tidy up. No one has been since."

They moved into a modern kitchen, all gleaming stainless steel appliances, and granite benchtops. Adam's eyes settled for a moment on the extensive wine rack nestled beneath the windows along one wall. A teapot and white china cups with matching saucers sat on a tray at one end of the breakfast bar. Mrs. Smyth waved her hand, indicating that they should sit down. She poured the tea and offered them lemon slices, sugar, and milk from matching dishes. Adam watched as Kat perched on a stool and admired the view across the river in one direction to St Paul's Cathedral and the other around the curve in the river to the Tower of London.

"It's something, isn't it?" Mr. Smyth said. "You should see it all lit up at night."

Kat murmured her agreement, and thanks for the tea. When she reached for her cup, Adam noticed Mrs. Smyth's eyes widen a fraction before a look of sympathy settled on her face. Kat did not indicate that she saw the reaction. Given her response in the taxi, she wouldn't take any form of pity at all well, he supposed.

"Is this Henry's only property?" she asked.

"No," Mrs. Smyth said. "He has a lovely big cottage in the Cotswolds and a ski chalet at Chamonix."

"Was he a collector? Books, wine?" Kat said.

Mr. Smyth gave a sad smile. "Yes, he was always quite the collector and more so once he could afford it. That bookshelf will be worth thousands and thousands of pounds; there are many first editions. As for the wine," he followed her gaze to the wine rack, "I'm not sure, but some are pretty old."

"What did he do before CIP?" Kat said.

Adam glanced at Kat. Perhaps Stevenson had been correct

when he said they were financial detectives if Kat's careful conversational questioning was any indication.

"Investment banking," Mrs. Smyth said.

"Did he have a partner?" Adam asked.

"No one special that we were aware of," Mr. Smyth said.

"We are, were, very proud of our Henry," Mrs. Smyth said. "He worked hard at school and Cambridge. He got a blue for rowing. And he was one of the most successful equities traders at the International Bank of Commerce before he started Capital Partners with those people." Her voice wobbled with barely concealed emotion.

Mr. Smyth put a hand on his wife's arm. "The business was very lucrative right from the start, but it wasn't enough for the others. They just kept pushing. Henry was tired and stressed the last few times we saw him. Something was bothering him, but he wouldn't, or couldn't, talk to us about it."

Mrs. Smyth picked up a small picture frame sitting on the bench and passed it to Adam. Henry Smyth stood between his parents in the photo holding a glass of champagne and wearing a wide, dimpled grin. He was a handsome man, broad-shouldered with short wavy brown hair.

"That was at his sister's wedding last year. The last time we saw him happy," Mr. Smyth said.

"They've said that it was a drug overdose, a deliberate one," Mrs. Smyth added, removing a lace handkerchief from her pocket and dabbing her eyes. "I'm sorry."

Kat put her cup back on its saucer and placed her hand on the old lady's arm.

"Henry liked to party, but drugs? That wasn't his style," Mr. Smyth said. "But he had seemed so out of kilter lately that we thought maybe it had all gotten too much for him and he'd decided to take his life. But we don't believe that any longer."

Adam hid his surprise. "And what changed your mind?"

Mr. Smyth stood up and retrieved a book from a drawer in the kitchen. He sat down again and placed the well-worn copy of Kipling's *The Jungle Book* on the bench. It fell open at the centre binding. Tucked into the fold was a piece of paper.

"May I?" Adam asked.

"Please." Mr. Smyth pushed the book towards him.

Adam pulled a pair of thin disposable gloves from his pocket and prised a handwritten note from the book with care. He laid it on the counter. Kat leaned closer.

Dear Mum & Dad,

If you are reading this, then something has happened to me. Perhaps I'm paranoid, but I think I'm being followed. Someone has been in the apartment, and the others have been making decisions without me, which makes me nervous. Don't believe everything they tell you about me; I've been naïve. I love you. I'm sorry, but I must leave.

HS

"Yes, this does put a different complexion on things," Adam said. "Where was the book?"

"That's the thing. I know that Henry left it for us to find because it was here, in the kitchen, on the shelf with his cookbooks. Henry had a very particular filing system for his books, and a childhood favourite most definitely does not belong in the cookbook section," Mrs. Smyth said.

Kat leaned across and read the letter. "By 'leave', do you think he meant to go away rather than take his life?"

Mr and Mrs. Smyth exchanged glances, and Mrs. Smyth gave a delicate shrug.

"May I take this?" Adam asked, producing an evidence bag

from a pocket and tucking the note inside.

"Of course." Mr. Smyth nodded. He looked as though he were about to say something else, but didn't.

"We should have the pathologist's initial report and findings this afternoon, which may give us some more answers," Adam said, standing.

"Do you think it was them?" Mr. Smyth blurted out.

"Them?"

"Those bastards he was in business with."

Adam shook his head. "We have no evidence of that, sir, but we will most certainly look into Henry's death from all angles."

Mr. Smyth visibly deflated. "Thank you."

"May I see the rest of his apartment before we leave?" Adam asked.

"Certainly, this way."

Chapter 4

Adam was deep in thought as they waited for a taxi outside the apartment.

"You think he was killed and staged to look like suicide, don't you?" Kat asked.

"I'm not sure of anything at this stage. But it will be interesting to compare the writing in this note, with the 'suicide note' that Smyth left," Adam replied as a taxi pulled up.

"He left a suicide note?" Kat said.

"Well, someone did."

They climbed into the back of the black cab, and Adam gave Kat's office address to the driver.

"Who found him?" Kat asked.

"The cleaner. Smyth had been dead a day. Unfortunately, it seems she called the firm before the police," Adam replied.

"Really, how strange? Did she say why?"

"That was what she'd been told to do by someone at the firm. Her English wasn't good, and she was distraught, so the uniforms didn't get much from her. We'll need to interview her again."

"What happens now?" Kat asked.

"Well, I'll drop this off with the crime scene team for analysis, and then I thought I'd head over to Credit Investment Partners. It's time I introduced myself to Henry's partners. They were unavailable when I was there a couple of days ago looking into the circumstances surrounding the security guard's death."

"Can I come?" Kat asked. "It might help with my report for DI Greenwood if I had a feel for the other people involved."

Adam hesitated for a moment and considered her suggestion, then smiled. "Why not? Sorry, mate," he called to the driver. "We have a change of destination. London Wall."

The driver pulled over and swung the taxi around.

"How did the security guard die?" Kat asked.

"Broken neck. He appears to have fallen to his death from the second floor."

"Appears?"

"There are some anomalies that we're following up."

Several minutes later, the taxi dropped them outside a shiny glass-fronted tower. Kat craned her neck to look up. The structure was modern and sleek, nestled between two other towers, one with a three-story nineteenth-century façade, the other an ugly 1960s building, which was in desperate need of refurbishment. Above the revolving glass doors, the name 'Capital Investment Partners' stood out in tall silver lettering.

They walked through the entrance into the busy foyer. Groups of people sipping take-out coffee purchased from the small café by the front window, gathered around the clusters of comfortable chairs dotted about the space. A collection of tall indoor plants with shiny leaves separated the seating areas from the reception desk and the elevators. A four-level atrium surrounded the ground floor on three sides, and Kat looked up to the second floor and shivered. No one could have survived a fall onto the marble floor.

Adam strode to the security desk, pulling his warrant card from his jacket's inside pocket to identify himself.

"I'm here to see Roger Chen, Mary McFarlane, and Eduardo Diaz," he said to the attractive young woman wearing a smart black jacket, a headset and mouthpiece, seated behind a tall counter.

"Hello again, officer," the receptionist said, smiling. "As I told you the other day, you need to make an appointment to see the partners; they are busy people."

Adam shook his head. "Not this time. Tell them it's regarding the murder of Henry Smyth," he said.

The low-level hum of chatter from those in the foyer ceased. Kat felt, rather than saw, heads swing in their direction.

The receptionist looked shaken. "One moment, please." She spoke into her headset in a soft voice.

She looked up at Adam a few seconds later. "They will see you now. The eighth floor," she said, pointing towards a bank of glass-fronted elevators.

"Thank you." Adam flashed a smile.

Kat followed him to the lifts very aware of the attention that they had attracted. She slipped her left hand into her pocket, then checked herself and pulled it out again.

"You certainly know how to make an entrance," Kat murmured as she followed him into the lift.

The doors closed and the lift rose at speed to the eighth floor. An efficient looking woman with a hawk-like nose and her hair pulled into a tight bun waited to greet them.

"I'm Avery Willis, Mr. Chen's executive assistant. This way, please," she said.

She ushered Adam and Kat into a large meeting room with opaque internal walls and windows with a view over London

Wall to the building opposite. The end wall contained a bank of computer screens displaying all manner of financial indices, and directly opposite was a large painting which Kat could only assume was a Banksy original. Two men and a woman, all dressed in immaculate expensive-looking business suits, were gathered around an oval-shaped polished wooden table. They broke from their conversation and looked up at the newcomers, their expressions displaying displeasure at being disturbed. The atmosphere was tense.

Avery Willis retreated, and the door closed behind them with a soft click.

"Mr. Chen, Ms. McFarlane, Mr. Diaz, thank you for seeing us at short notice," Adam said.

"DS Jackson and ah…" Mary McFarlane, seated on the far side of the table, began. She had the willowy figure of a fashion model, and her shoulder-length dark hair was styled into a long straight bob.

"Kat Munro." Kat filled the silence.

"Now, here, what's this murder nonsense? I thought Smyth topped himself?" Chen said, his public school voice sounding indignant. He shot his cuffs and leaned back in his chair. A pair of square black-framed glasses perched on his nose gave him an intellectual air.

Eduardo Diaz, mid-thirties, bald with a ruggedly handsome face, was studying them with a poorly disguised look of contempt. "'e did, Rog, that suggestion was just a ploy to get in here unannounced."

"Not entirely," Adam replied. "New evidence has come to light, suggesting Mr. Smyth may not have taken his own life."

"What evidence?" Diaz demanded as he shoved back his chair and stood. Kat watched him walk over to the window, intrigued. His East End accent was at odds with his otherwise glamorous image.

"We're not at liberty to disclose anything further at this point in the investigation," Adam replied.

"Is there anything that we can do to assist?" Mary McFarlane asked, smiling at Adam. Her eyes flicked over Kat from top to toe, and Kat felt herself bristle under the assessing gaze. McFarlane removed her blue-framed spectacles and placed them on top of a pile of papers on the table, looking at Adam expectantly.

Adam pulled a notebook from his pocket. "Could you all confirm your whereabouts on Monday evening between eight p.m. and midnight?"

"You're not suggesting…," Diaz said.

"I had dinner with Joey Martin, the actor and we went to the theatre. A large number of people saw us there," Chen replied, giving Diaz a pointed look.

McFarlane gave a saccharine smile. "And I was with the director of the London Wall Gallery finalizing details for the opening night gala we're hosting this week." Adam nodded and turned to Diaz. "And where were you?"

"I was working out at my gym on Cannon Street," Diaz said. "Really, is this necessary?"

"Until midnight?"

He nodded. "Their access system will confirm it."

Kat watched as Adam raised an eyebrow while he scribbled in his notebook. "We understand that someone from the firm entered Mr. Smyth's apartment shortly after his death and removed his laptop and other property."

McFarlane shrugged. "That would have been our head of security. It's the standard operating procedure to secure confidential information in an unfortunate situation such as this."

"We're going to need that laptop and anything that was taken," Adam said.

"I don't think so," Diaz said.

"Tampering with evidence at a crime scene is an offence," Adam said, his tone even and pleasant as though he were discussing the weather instead of a possible murder.

There was a moment's hesitation before Chen replied for them all. "Where would you like it sent?"

Adam looked to Kat, who pulled a business card from her bag and set it down on the table. "Address it for my attention."

"Now, was there anything else? We're in the middle of an important management meeting," Diaz said. He hadn't moved from his position leaning against the windowsill and continued to scowl at them. "Smyth has left us with a bit of a gap."

"Actually, there was one other thing. The night your security guard, Andreas Popov, was killed, records show that someone accessed the building through the first basement parking garage stairwell. Who parks on that level?" Adam asked.

"Partners and senior management," Chen replied. "It's normally locked by a security gate, with swipe access, but vandals broke it last week. You lot haven't found out who it was yet."

Kat opened her mouth to ask a question, but Chen held up his hand.

"And before you ask, there is no CCTV footage."

"So it's possible that whoever killed Mr. Popov entered or left the building through a stairwell that leads to that level," Adam countered.

The partners exchanged glances.

"We'll need to take a look," Adam said.

"The security desk in the lobby will show you," Chen said. "Now, if that's all, we need to get back to our meeting."

"That's all for now, but please continue to make yourselves available. We may need to speak with each of you again," Adam said, dropping his calling card on the table beside Kat's business card. "In the meantime, if you think of anything relevant, please don't hesitate to get in touch."

* * *

Adam and Kat handed in their security passes at the reception desk and retraced their steps across the foyer.

"I thought we were going to check out the basement parking," Kat said.

"We are, I just wanted to remind myself of something first," he said, standing just inside the revolving glass doors and looking up to the second floor of the atrium. He walked beneath the overhang and stopped, looking up again, before nodding to himself.

"Is that where Mr. Popov fell?" Kat asked.

"Yeah," Adam said and strode back across the lobby to the reception desk.

"I need access to the B1 parking garage," Adam said to the receptionist.

"Certainly, officer," she said, standing and leading them behind the bank of elevators to a door. She held a card hanging from a lanyard around her neck against an electronic reader, and the door popped open. "The gate to the street is damaged, and the engineers are coming today to repair it. The green exit button there will reopen this door when you're finished."

"Thank you."

Kat and Adam took the stairs down to the first basement level. The door at the bottom of the stairwell was ajar. They entered a parking garage with a low ceiling, filled with expensive late model cars. Adam glanced around, letting out a low whistle of admiration. He turned and walked to the far end, reading the nameplates on the wall behind each car. He walked back to where Kat waited as the overhead lights flickered and died, plunging the space into a dusk-like gloom. A wedge of light showed at the far end coming from the direction of the exit ramp.

"Really? They chose now to fail," Kat said, fumbling in her bag for her phone, but Adam was quicker and illuminated the flashlight app on his phone. He shone it towards her to help. A shadow moved behind him at speed.

"Look out, Adam," Kat exclaimed as Adam staggered forward, reeling from a blow to the back of his head. She reached out to catch him as he lurched towards her, but someone grabbed her arms from behind, and Adam fell. His phone clattered to the ground, the flashlight illuminating one side of the garage. Adam grunted as a heavy work boot slammed into his side.

Kat reacted on instinct and slammed the heel of her shoe back into the shin of her captor. He grunted in pain and released her. She swung around as the man lunged toward her, reaching for her arms again. Instead of running away, she stepped forward and grabbed his shoulders, pulling him towards her. She slammed her knee into his groin. Her attacker doubled over as the overhead lights flickered once again. The man howled in pain, raising his head in time for

Kat to smash the palm of her right hand onto the underside of his nose, forcing his head backwards. There was a loud crunch, and blood started pouring from it.

The man spluttered, holding his nose and backing away.

Kat turned her attention to the man laying into Adam. He was massive, wearing a beanie, black t-shirt and scruffy jeans.

"Hey," she shouted.

He turned to her with a sneer and pulled a knife from his belt.

Kat planted both feet and readied herself. The man rushed forward, jabbing the knife towards her as she raised her left arm to block his thrust. The knife hit her prosthetic hand with a thud. The man's eyes widened. Kat took advantage of his momentary surprise and twisted, kicking up and out with her right leg, landing a solid blow in his abdomen. He grunted at the impact and staggered back a step. Kat spun and followed through with her left hand, bringing the prosthesis down hard on the hand holding the knife, knocking it from the man's grip. It clattered as it hit the ground and skidded under a nearby car.

Kat bounced on her toes, readying herself for the next onslaught. Sure enough, the man roared as he charged at her. Kat waited until the last possible second to move. She stepped aside and lashed out with her leg, catching him on his thigh with her foot. His leg buckled and he went down on one knee before rolling back up onto his feet. Kat continued bouncing, waiting for his next move.

Adam pulled himself to his feet using the closest parked car for support. The shriek of the car's alarm rang out. Kat swung her head around towards the noise. The racket was enough for their two attackers to abandon the fight and instead begin running towards the exit ramp.

Kat started after them.

"No, Kat. Let them go," Adam shouted.

She stopped running and turned back towards him. He was holding his arm across his ribs with a grin on his face. He held his mobile in his hand.

"Hopefully, some of my colleagues will be waiting for them on the street."

"Are you okay?" she called above the din of the car alarm.

"Yeah," he said. "Where did you learn to do that?"

The alarm stopped mid-sentence so that he shouted the last few words.

"Learn what?" Kat shouted back, mimicking him.

"I don't know what I'd call it; it wasn't like any martial art that I've ever seen."

"When you grow up with two brothers, you learn to defend yourself any way you can," she said. "And thanks for your help, by the way."

"You had it under control, I would have just been in the way," Adam said.

"Lame." Kat laughed.

Adam pulled a plastic evidence bag from deep in one pocket and handed it to Kat.

"Can you reach under that car and collect the knife without touching it?"

Kat crouched down and reached for the knife which had come to rest against the back tire of a black Mercedes coupé. She bagged it without touching the handle. She returned the sealed bag to Adam, who was on his phone, giving a detailed description of the attackers. He acknowledged her with a nod. He ended the call. "We have to wait here," he said.

"Do you think those guys were expecting us?"

"Yeah, I'm not sure that was random," Adam said. "I suspect someone followed us from Smyth's apartment."

"But how did they know that we'd come down here?"

"I'm not sure, but I suppose they guessed I'd want to check on Smyth's movements on the night he died. Street CCTV footage has his car leaving by the ramp that leads down here."

Kat nodded and went to sit on the bottom step in the stairwell. She let out a breath and closed her eyes for a moment.

"Are you okay?"

She opened her eyes to find that Adam had followed her and was seated at her side.

"Yeah." She looked down at her trembling right hand.

"Adrenaline rush wearing off?" he asked.

Kat nodded. "I guess."

"Seriously, where did you learn self-defence like that?"

"I do a couple of kickboxing classes most weeks, among other things. After the accident, I decided that I needed to be able to defend myself," Kat said, waving her left hand in the air.

"That makes no sense. If it was an accident, defending yourself wouldn't have made any difference," Adam said, looking sideways at her.

Kat hesitated. "Well, ah… it made sense to me at the time."

"How…" Adam began. Footsteps thundered down the stairs behind them, and two uniformed police officers appeared.

Kat leapt to her feet, and Adam somewhat gingerly climbed to his, hissing as a shooting pain wrapped around his middle.

* * *

By the time a police car dropped Adam and Kat back at her office, it was mid-afternoon.

"I don't know about you, but I'm starving," Adam said, getting out of the car.

"Me too, but my priority is to freshen up," Kat said.

"Thanks, mate," Adam said to the driver before they crossed the street.

"The partners didn't seem all that concerned that someone attacked us on their premises," Kat said as they entered the building.

"I know, although they did seem surprised. According to the receptionist, they've been having problems with people breaking into cars on that level. She seemed to think that we must have disturbed thieves."

Kat signed Adam in at the security desk and picked up a temporary pass for him. They took the stairs to the first floor. Kat strode across the office to join her team at their pod of desks, the heels of her shoes tapping on the wooden floor. Adam followed, nodding a polite greeting to a couple of Kat's colleagues who looked up from their computer screens with undisguised interest as he passed.

"Shamira, Nate, this is Detective Adam Jackson," Kat said.

Nathan jumped up from his desk and shook hands with Adam. "G'day, mate."

Shamira followed suit. "My God, what happened to you two?" she screeched. "You look like you've been in a fight."

"That's because we have. Two guys jumped us in the basement garage at Capital Investment Partners," Kat explained.

Nathan looked shocked. "I hope you kicked their arses."

"Yeah," Adam and Kat answered together.

"Are you going to claim that?" Kat said, looking at him

open-mouthed.

"Between us, we sent them packing." Adam grinned.

"Right, just as well you set off that car alarm when you did, cos it wasn't like I had it under control or anything," Kat replied. "Y'know, I read somewhere that people deliberately misremember events when it's too embarrassing or to place themselves in the role of hero to liven up an otherwise boring life."

"Ouch." Adam feigned hurt.

Kat chuckled. "Now I need to freshen up. Excuse me for a moment."

She closed the bathroom door and leaned against it. She caught sight of herself in the mirror above the double sinks. She looked dishevelled. She pulled a brush from her bag, ran it through her messy hair, and retouched her makeup. She slipped her jacket off and changed the dressing on the graze above her elbow. She removed her hand and studied the dent between the index and middle finger. She turned it over and saw a long crack across the palm and sighed. She rubbed her stump. Her arm was a little tender after the fight.

When she arrived back at her team's pod, Adam had made himself comfortable at her desk and was chatting with Nathan and Shamira as though they were old friends.

"Kat, look what just arrived," Adam said, pointing to a box on her desk.

"Is that?"

"I assume it's Smyth's laptop and the other materials from his home office," Adam replied.

"That was fast. I would have thought that they'd have dragged their feet and taken an age. They seem keen to get us out of their hair. Let's take a look," Kat said, hunger forgotten.

Nathan jumped up and opened the box, prizing a thin matte-silver laptop from inside. He opened the lid and powered it up. They all watched as the screen flickered to life. The wallpaper displayed a man dressed from head to toe in ski gear grinning at the camera from the top of a ski slope, the snow-covered valley below him sparkling the sun.

"That would be our Mr. Smyth, I presume," Nathan said.

"Yup," Adam agreed. "Now, what's he got on here that was so sensitive that it required removing from his apartment?"

"Password?" Nathan asked, pulling out a chair and sitting down. A rectangular box had appeared in the centre of the screen requesting a password.

"Ah."

Kat rummaged around in the box and lifted out several files and books. She held out an envelope, addressed to 'Ms. Munro.' She opened it, sliding out a piece of paper with the words 'Password: CapitalXI'. "Seems they are going out of their way to be helpful." She held it out to Nathan, who typed it into the box on the screen.

The words 'Welcome Hooray Henry' appeared on the screen. Nathan smirked at the pejorative term. He began moving his fingers across the keyboard at speed, pulling up a tree of directories. Adam leaned on the back of his chair and watched.

"Try the CIP folder and work down," he instructed.

* * *

Nathan pushed the laptop away in frustration. "There's nothing of interest here. If I were to hazard a guess, it would be that it's been cleaned of confidential CIP data. I've one further program that I can run to ensure that nothing is hidden behind an inaccessible firewall or in the system recycling bin. Still, I don't expect that to reveal anything," he said.

"Explains why they were so keen to give us the laptop," said Kat.

"What else is in the box?" Adam asked.

"Several finance books and some folders of quarterly performance reports for their various investment funds. Nothing commercially sensitive that I can see," Kat replied.

"That's so frustrating, but not entirely unexpected. There's nothing in the delete folder on the laptop?" Adam asked, turning back to Nathan.

Nathan shook his head. "Nope, the trash has been emptied."

"Interesting," Adam said. "If they've deleted files from Smyth's laptop, then that is a criminal offence."

"Or maybe Smyth deleted them before he died?" Kat said.

Adam straightened up and groaned, holding a hand to his ribs. "Well, I'll head back to the incident room and let you get on with the review. Great to meet you all. I will see you again soon."

Kat walked with him to the reception area at the top of the stairs. "Are your ribs a bit sore? You might need to get them checked out."

"I've had worse. Nothing a good night's sleep won't fix." He reached out and took hold of her left hand, running his thumb over the dent between her fingers that the knife attack had caused. A hairline crack ran across the palm and disappeared beneath the cuff of her jacket. Kat flinched and started to pull her hand away, but Adam held on, studying it.

"Will you be able to get that fixed?" he asked.

Kat nodded, swallowing hard. She didn't usually allow anyone, apart from her doctors and close family, to touch her prosthesis.

"It's got great functionality, Kat. I have a mate who lost an arm in Afghanistan, and his artificial limb is nowhere near as functional as yours."

Kat swallowed again. "It depends where he got it from, mine's a new model, a prototype, using myoelectric technology."

Adam let her hand go and looked her in the eye, registering her discomfort. "Sorry, I don't mean to make you uncomfortable."

"It's okay, I just don't normally discuss it with strangers," she said.

Adam grinned. "I think we shot past that stage when I saved you from those attackers today."

Kat raised her eyebrows. "Really? Surely you're not so insecure that you can't admit that a woman had to defend you?"

"No, it's just a new experience for me," he said. "And those guys were not messing about; they were the real deal. It wasn't some spotty teen trying to snatch a bag. I was impressed."

Kat felt an unwanted blush creep up her neck and face.

"Can I buy you a drink after work to say thank you?"

Kat's smile disappeared. "No. That's not necessary."

Adam's phone rang. He answered as Kat backed away to join her colleagues.

"I think you won yourself a new admirer, girl," Shamira said as she approached her desk.

"Nah," Kat said.

Shamira looked across at Nathan, who pulled a face. "Yeah, it would take more than a few stupid kickboxing moves to impress a man like that," he said.

Kat opened her mouth to retort when she realised that they were teasing her. "Ha, ha, very funny."

"Kat," Adam called, striding back across the office. "That was the pathologist. The toxicology report on Henry Smyth has just come back. He had ingested enough heroin to kill an elephant, and there was a large amount of BZP, you know, the date rape drug, in his system. Why would you sedate yourself if you were trying to end it all? We're now looking at murder."

Chapter 5

"If I have to look at one more set of financial statements, I swear I will go cross-eyed. We really should get a boredom allowance for days like these," Nathan said. Kat and Shamira smirked.

"Seriously, there is nothing here. These guys appear to be running a great business," Nathan said.

"I have to agree," Kat replied. "Let's distil our findings; I have to report back later on today." She rubbed her aching arm.

"Is your arm sore after yesterday?" Shamira asked, noticing her friend's discomfort.

"Yeah, a little bruised. Although not as bad as I hope those thugs are feeling. I got a couple of great kicks in."

"You had quite a day. Did you damage your hand?"

"Yeah, unfortunately, this one needs repairing. I'll drop it off after work. I should probably have used my spare today, but it's not as comfortable as this one," Kat said, holding up her arm, turning her prosthesis over and flexing the fingers.

Kat was putting the final touches to her report for the meeting with Stephenson, DI Greenwood, and Adam, when Nathan pushed back from his desk with an emphatic, "Yes, you little beauty."

Kat looked over at him. "What?"

"There was something else on Smyth's laptop that CIP's techies didn't erase. I've run a program that replicates the deleted files in a certain way, and bingo."

"Is that even legal?" Shamira asked.

Nathan shrugged. "Yeah?"

"What have you found?" Kat asked, wheeling her chair over to his desk, using her feet to propel her across the floor.

"A client list by the looks of it, dated one month ago and some other files that I'll need to clean up," Nathan said.

"Show me after my meeting."

Nathan nodded. "I probably won't have them cleaned until tomorrow."

"Okay, let's keep it between us for now, it may contain nothing useful."

* * *

Kat joined Stephenson, DI Greenwood, and Adam in the large meeting room at Forensic Accounting Associates. Kat looked through the floor-to-ceiling windows and watched the Union Jack flag fluttering on top of a building across the river for a moment before sliding into a chair at the conference table. She tapped her iPad, sharing her report to the screen on the wall at the end of the conference table.

"I will email you a copy of the report so you can read the detail later. We have reviewed all of the publically available material for CIP, annual reports, press releases, Companies House material, social media, and short dossiers on the key personnel," she began.

DI Greenwood nodded. "Good."

"The business has been running for four years; it appears to be operating efficiently with low overheads, at least compared to other industry players. It's been profitable from day one. Their taxes are all filed and paid, no employment disputes on record, and it even has a good record of corporate charitable giving," Kat said.

"That's what our team concluded also," DI Greenwood said. "So, what are we missing?"

"It's almost too good to be true. Start-ups usually have an issue somewhere, whether with cash flow or disgruntled employees who thought they were getting share options, or itchy investors wanting an immediate return, but there's not even a hint of that," Kat said.

"Yet, the partners were evasive, sent you a cleaned laptop, and probably had those guys waiting in the basement for us," Adam said.

"Can you prove any of that?" DI Greenwood asked.

"No."

DI Greenwood stroked his chin. "Kat, can you take a deeper look at each of the partners? Start with Smyth, because we have access to his financial records, and I'll try to get you as much financial information as I can on the other three."

"Okay," Kat said.

"I've sent the crime scene team back to secure the apartment," Adam said. "But I'm not expecting them to find anything, as the Smyths had already started tidying."

"There's something else in play here," DI Greenwood mused. "Why would someone send thugs to see off a police officer?"

"Smyth's murder..." Adam began.

"Suspicious death," DI Greenwood interrupted.

"Very suspicious death," Adam continued. "Are we sure

that his demise is related to something at CIP? It could be something else entirely, jealous lover, money, family dispute?"

"Who benefits from his death?" Kat asked.

"We've yet to see a will, but I have people back in the incident room digging into all aspects of his life," Adam said.

"I agree that we need to look at this from all angles, but the fact that he was at CIP removing files and his laptop the same night that he and a security guard died, points to something at the firm," DI Greenwood said.

Stephenson had been quiet throughout the discussion and now spoke up. "Can we get access to their client records, internal and external audit reports?" he asked. "See if there are any anomalies there."

"Leave that with me," DI Greenwood said.

Chapter 6

Adam glanced at his watch; 12:45 p.m., the perfect time to blend in with the lunchtime crowd. When the traffic lights changed to red, he crossed Whitehall, turned the corner at the next block, and jogged up the front steps of a grey brick six-storey office building. It was no different from any other historic buildings on the street, all housing various government agencies, except that this one was home to a secret department within the Ministry of Defence. He showed his warrant card to the soldier operating the tiny reception area. A flicker of recognition crossed the man's face as he nodded and indicated that Adam could pass through the metal detector.

"Weapons?" he asked almost as an afterthought.

"No, just me," Adam replied, emptying his keys and wallet from his pockets into a plastic tray and walking through the scanning unit. The light on the top of the machine flashed green. Adam gathered his things and continued towards the wide curving staircase at the rear of the lobby. Taking the stairs two at a time, he arrived on the first floor and followed a wood-panelled corridor to the far end and knocked on a closed door.

"Come," a commanding voice called from inside.

Adam turned the knob and entered a small, well-proportioned corner office. Bay windows overlooked the two street frontages of the building. A large wooden desk dominated the room, and low bookshelves lined one wall.

"Jackson." The man in his mid-fifties behind the desk was dressed in the uniform of a colonel. His short-cropped hair was flecked with grey, and his eyes, behind wire-rimmed glasses, were intelligent and alert.

"Sir." Adam came to attention and saluted. Old habits died hard, and Colonel Wilson had been his commanding officer in Afghanistan seven years earlier.

Wilson extended his hand across the desk, and Adam walked forward and shook it.

"Thanks for coming," Wilson said, indicating with a wave of his hand for Adam to sit in one of two visitor chairs.

Adam sat down, glancing at the framed photo of an attractive smiling woman on the corner of the desk. "How is Mrs. Wilson?"

"Very well, I'll tell her that you were asking after her," Wilson said. He paused. "Thank you for coming so quickly. I have a lead on Jake."

Adam sat forward in his seat. "After all this time? How?"

"You will recall the guesthouse where McCall was staying when he disappeared?"

Adam nodded. "The landlady contacted the police after a week when he never returned."

"That's right, and when questioned, she had no idea what his movements were that weekend, as she was away," Wilson reminded him, although it was unnecessary. Adam knew every aspect of McCall's case backwards. His best mate had disappeared off the face of the Earth two years earlier.

"Don't tell me that she has miraculously remembered something?" Adam said, unable to keep the dubious tone out of his voice.

Wilson shook his head. "No, but her daughter has just returned from spending two years on a working holiday in Australia. She left the UK a few days before we realised that McCall was missing. She and her mother must have been discussing McCall, and the daughter remembers him asking about local attractions within walking distance, including a nearby manor house. The mother contacted me, thought it might be useful."

"Have you interviewed the daughter?" Adam asked.

"I spoke with her over the phone from Australia briefly at the time. Adam, I was hoping that you'd have time to drive out and see her. Take another look at the area while you're there. I've already checked into the manor house. It's owned by a London barrister, William Huntly-Tait, a well-respected member of the profession by all accounts. I'd like to know what else Jake was doing before he disappeared."

"I'll see what I can find out," Adam said.

"Be discreet. No unwanted attention," Wilson cautioned.

Adam nodded.

Wilson slid a piece of paper across the desk. "Here are the daughter's details."

Adam picked up the paper and read it. Amanda Harding and a phone number. He stood, folding the piece of paper and slipped it into the front pocket of his jeans.

"I'm attending a Valkyries' fundraising picnic at Bletchley Park this Saturday. Why don't you come, meet up with some of the old unit, and let me know what you find out?" Wilson suggested.

Adam nodded.

* * *

Adam rode the Underground to his rented flat after leaving Wilson's office, going inside only long enough to grab his car keys. He wrinkled his nose at the smell wafting from the overflowing rubbish bin as he scooped the keys up from the end of the kitchen bench, making a mental note to attend to that later. Casting a disparaging glance around the tiny, gloomy flat, he pulled the door shut behind him and jogged back down the stairwell to the street. He dug into his pocket for the piece of paper with Amanda Harding's number. He called her as he walked towards the narrow side street where he'd parked his car several days earlier, cursing the lack of affordable parking spaces in central London. She answered on the first ring.

"Mandy here."

"Mandy, DS Adam Jackson. Your mother spoke with Colonel Wilson this morning regarding the disappearance of one of her guests, Jake McCall."

"Yes, she said someone would most likely call me."

"I was hoping that I could come and see you. Are you free this afternoon?" Adam said.

"Sure. I'm staying at the guest house until I get a job. Do you have the address?"

"Yeah, I do. I'll see you in about an hour."

Adam located his car, a restored 1976 Ford Capri, several blocks away from the flat. He was soon driving down the A3 tapping the steering wheel in time to a rock anthems playlist, as his mind revisited the details surrounding the disappearance of his friend. In the last two years, Jake's bank accounts and phone hadn't been accessed, but neither had his body been found. It was as though he'd vanished into thin air. The police case had gone cold, and a thorough investigation by Wilson's office had produced no additional information.

Just over an hour later, he slowed the car as he entered Cobham High Street. Gloria Harding's guesthouse was on the edge of the village, where the rows of houses gave way to swathes of farmland. Adam pulled to a stop in front of a detached red-brick two-storey house. A shingle swinging in the light breeze announced the Cobham Cottage Guesthouse. Adam's shoes crunched on the gravel as he approached the front door and rang the doorbell. He heard footsteps before the door was swung open by a tanned young woman wearing sprayed-on jeans and a white t-shirt.

"G'day," she said. "You must be DS Jackson. I'm Mandy."

Adam showed her his warrant card, and she invited him inside, leading him through the hallway and into a sitting room crammed with floral patterned sofas and armchairs. Framed watercolours of single blooms covered the walls, and overflowing vases of flowers sat on side tables throughout the room. Adam looked around, trying, and failing to place Jake in this room.

"We call this the floral room," Mandy said, noting his appraisal. "It's a bit over the top, right?"

"It's very, ah… colourful," Adam said with a grin.

Mandy flopped down on one of the sofas and tucked her legs beneath her. "I'm not sure how much I can help you," she said,

Adam sat opposite her. "Perhaps just take me through what you remember of your last conversation with Jake."

"Sure, um, it was over breakfast. Mum had gone away for the weekend to visit my grandmother, and I was looking after things. It was early, perhaps seven a.m., and Jake was the only one in the dining room. He said he was looking into his family history."

Adam nodded.

"Was that true?" she asked, tilting her head to one side and studying him. "'Cos it's funny that the army and the police are looking into his disappearance, after all this time."

"He was in the army when he disappeared, and missing persons cases get reviewed by the police every so often," Adam said. "So, where was he planning to go that day?"

"I don't remember, sorry." Amanda frowned, looking thoughtful. "Although, perhaps he was planning to go to the local airfield because I overheard him on his phone making an appointment. Did he fly?"

Adam shook his head. "Do you mean Wisley Airport?"

"No, he mentioned something about Surrey Flats. Wisley's been closed for years," Mandy said.

"Do you remember anything else from your conversation with him that morning?"

"Only that he asked how long it would take to walk to South Hill Manor, which was odd, given what happened."

"What do you mean?"

"The son had a party there that night. I don't know the details as I was on a plane to Sydney the next day, but there was a car accident, and someone died. Mum said it was all hushed up at the time – a drunk driver, according to the local gossips."

* * *

Adam left the guesthouse and drove further out of the village. The GPS on his phone indicated that South Hill Manor was four miles outside the town, and the Surrey Flats Aerodrome was in the opposite direction. A visit there would have to wait. The River Mole meandered alongside the road for the first two miles. Adam spied several anglers perched along its banks before the river disappeared from view as the lane entered dense shaded woodland. The road emerged again at the top of the rise, looking down on the green rolling countryside.

Adam slowed the car when a large manor house came into view, nestled back from the road on the gentle slope of a hill. Behind its square Georgian façade, the roof rose steeply. Two wings extended from either side of the central part of the residence. The house, partly hidden behind a tall brick fence, was accessible through imposing black wrought iron gates. Adam pulled to a stop in a farm gateway, grabbed his phone, and snapped several photos of the property.

Voices drew his attention, and he swivelled in his seat to watch a trio of walkers climb over a stile and cross the road behind him. They continued along a public footpath, which ran along one side of the manor's perimeter wall.

Adam pulled his car further off the road and climbed out, locking it, before following the walkers. The footpath continued uphill alongside the tall brick wall for several hundred meters before disappearing into woodland covering the hillside. He took several more photos before returning to the front gates and peering through towards the house. A long gravel driveway extended straight from the gateway before curving around a circular green lawn to the front entrance. The rose garden running along the fence was well maintained as though no weed dared grow there. Adam was aware of security cameras tracking his every move. He found an intercom set into the brick wall beside the gate and pushed the button.

"Yes," a disembodied male voice answered straightaway.

"Is Mr. Huntly-Tait available?"

"I'm afraid he is in London. Can I help you?"

"No, I will contact him there."

"Can I say who called?"

Adam thought for a moment. "No," he said, turning on his heel and walking back towards the road.

Behind him, he heard rapid movement in the driveway's gravel and turned as two large Doberman dogs rushed at the gate snarling. Adam sauntered across the road back to his car. He climbed in and rolled his shoulders to shake off the feeling of being watched, before reversing out of the farm gateway and driving away.

Not for the first time when on surveillance did he wish that he didn't own such a distinctive car. He soon dismissed that ridiculous notion and drove on past lush fields of wheat and barley, following the directions on his GPS for a road that would link up with the A3 to take him back to London.

Hearing the whine of an airplane passing low overhead, he leaned forward to look out through the top of the windscreen. He spotted a small fixed-wing aircraft climbing as though it had just taken off. He looked across the fields to his right and saw a single hangar-like shed on a side road. Curious, he turned and drove along a narrow lane bordered by hedgerows and pulled to a stop beneath a sign which read 'Private Property. Trespassers will be Prosecuted.'

He got out of the car and looked across a field of grazing sheep to where a lone airplane stood beside the tarmac of a short runway next to a small corrugated iron hangar. The word 'fertiliser' stood out on the side of the bags stacked in front of the building. It seemed the airfield was used for aerial topdressing.

Adam started the car again and turned it around, continuing his journey back to London as he thought over what he'd learned. Something that Mandy Harding had said tugged at the back of his mind, and several miles further on, he pulled into a service stop and put a call through to the incident room on his mobile.

A male voice answered. "It's Julian, how can I help?"

"Hey, Julian, can you find me the details of a car accident two years ago around May twenty-fifth near Cobham in Surrey? There was a death."

"Sure, hang on."

Adam could hear the man typing on his computer keyboard.

"Okay, it looks like a single-car accident. They lost control on a country lane and rolled." He let out a soft whistle. "Fancy car; Porsche 911 Cabriolet. One death, one seriously injured, the driver escaped injury. They'd come from a party at South Hill Manor. No charges were brought."

Chapter 7

"That building never fails to impress me," Shamira said as they climbed from the taxi on the north side of the Thames. She stood with her hands on her hips, soaking in the view across the river where floodlights coloured the entire Tate Modern frontage in a blue hue for the exhibition's opening night. The imposing former Bankside Power Station on the South Bank of the Thames was given a new lease of life when the Tate Gallery trustees decided to develop the site as a space to house international modern and contemporary art. The architects and developers stripped the building of its giant turbines and electrical equipment but retained its steel and brick structure. White lights beamed from the narrow vertical windows facing the Thames, and the glass-enclosed top floor running the entire length of the building shone like a giant fluorescent bulb.

Behind them, St. Paul's Cathedral stood as it had for generations, iconic and reassuring, its white stone giving off an eerie glow in the twilight.

"So is that why you insisted we get dropped here and walk over the Millennium Bridge?" Nathan said, joining Shamira, admiring the spectacle while straightening his suit jacket.

"You Aussies catch on quick," she teased, nudging him with

her shoulder. Her beautiful red and gold dress glinted under the street lights.

"It's such an iconic London landmark now, although I guess it was throughout the twentieth century. I mean, that chimney must have dominated the skyline before the city skyscrapers took over," he continued.

Shamira nodded. "It was one of the first post-World War II structures that were part of London's rebuild after the Blitz. Although I have to say, I love the new extension. It's like someone dropped a giant deconstructed brick pyramid behind the building."

"If you two have finished your architectural love-fest, let's go. It's cold." Kat shivered in her little black dress, which had long sleeves but did little to keep out the night chill. They started walking down the cobbled pathway of Peter's Hill to the footbridge spanning the river. The edges of the bridge were lit with the same blue light as the Tate, in essence guiding the way.

"You have to admit this is one of the best views in London," Shamira said, pausing after they walked onto the Millennium Bridge. She hung on to the railing and sighed with contentment. Kat and Nathan followed her gaze. Across the river nestled next to the Tate Modern was the replica of Shakespeare's Globe Theatre, its round black and white Tudor structure utterly unique in modern-day London. Further down the river past Southwark and London Bridges, the top of the twin towers of Tower Bridge could be seen. To the right, the modern, sleek glass skyscraper known as The Shard dominated the skyline.

They continued walking, following a group of tourists and other opening night attendees, judging by their attire.

"Thanks for getting us these tickets, Nate," Shamira said. "I've never been to the opening night of an exhibition at the Tate Modern."

"No worries, mate. I know a guy who works for the PR company who runs these things, and he slipped them to me. Although I'm not sure that I understand contemporary art; give me a good watercolour any day." he said.

Kat smiled. "I know what you mean; it can be something of an acquired taste. I'm more interested that Capital Investment Partners are the major sponsors of this exhibition."

"I don't expect any of them will be there, especially after Henry Smyth's death," Shamira said.

"Don't be so sure," Kat replied. "The people that I met the other day weren't the grieving type. If they consider this good for business, they'll be here."

"Speaking of the other day, anything more on that threatening note you received?" Nate asked.

Kat shook her head.

"You need to be careful, mate, you've ruffled someone's feathers," he said.

"You should tell DS Jackson," Shamira said.

"No, no." Kat waved her hand, dismissing their concern. "It's nothing to do with him."

They reached the end of the bridge, followed the ramp down to the Thames Walk, strolled along the waterfront to the Tate Modern entrance and joined a stream of people making their way down the wide ramp into Turbine Hall.

The hall was impressive; long and narrow, with a high cathedral-like ceiling comprising glass panels. The walls retained their industrial concrete structure to remind visitors of the building's original purpose. Waiters balancing trays of prosecco stood in a line at the bottom of the entrance ramp. Kat, Nathan, and Shamira relieved them of a glass each and joined the crowd, who were making their way deeper into the hall. Above them, giant metallic installations hung suspended. They stopped to look.

"It's supposed to be a modern take on Van Gogh's 'Starry Night'," Shamira explained.

Kat and Nathan tipped their heads back to study the tangle of broken, disjointed gold-coloured steel above their heads. Dark blue lighting along the roof meant that the glass ceiling virtually disappeared, and it was impossible to see where the roof ended, and the night sky began.

"Hmm… I wonder what old Vincent would make of that. It looks like someone has spewed out shards of scrap metal," Nathan said, screwing his nose.

"It's actually very clever," Kat said.

Shamira looked at her in surprise. "Ooh, we might make a modern art fan out of you yet."

Kat smiled. "I wouldn't hold your breath." She scanned the hall, her gaze landing on a raised platform in the centre towards which the other guests were gravitating.

"Hey, look at this," Nate said, drawing their attention to a free-standing banner listing the names of the evening's minor sponsors. "Isn't that…"

"Huntly-Tait and Partners? Yes, that's Gabe's firm," Kat said as a shiver ran through her. "I hope they're not here."

The level of noise in the hall was at a low hum. Kat estimated that there would be at least five hundred people in the cavernous space.

"Hello." They spun around to see that Adam had joined them. Gone were the jeans and leather jacket, replaced by a tailored black suit, blue shirt, and thin black tie. Kat's mouth dropped open in surprise.

"I didn't expect to see you here," she said.

"What?" Adam cocked his head and looked at her. "Did you think I was a bit too common for modern art?"

Kat blushed. "No, I didn't mean that."

Nathan stuck out his hand to shake Adam's, saving Kat from further embarrassment. Shamira gave him a small wave. A waiter passed by and Kat took the opportunity to replace her empty flute with a full one.

"If I could have your attention, please?" A woman's voice echoed through the hall. The tinkling laughter and chatter among the crowd softened, and after a moment, the woman continued. "I'd like to thank you all for attending the opening of Stars, our exhibition featuring twenty of the UK's brightest, pun very much intended, up-and-coming young artists." There was a sprinkle of polite laughter and applause. "To officially open the exhibition, I'd like to give a very warm welcome to our principal sponsors from Capital Investment Partners, Roger Chen and Mary McFarlane."

Adam's eyes narrowed as the two partners stepped onto the podium and waved to acknowledge the crowd. Mary McFarlane's diminutive form was draped in a simple sheath of a sparkling silver fabric, and her hair pulled into an elaborate up-do. A diamond choker was wrapped around her neck. Roger Chen wore a simple but elegant black tuxedo.

"Thank you for joining us at the Tate Modern tonight. We're honoured to put Capital Investment Partners' name to such an important showcase of young British talent," Mary said, smiling. She paused for the ripple of applause. "We have long been patrons of the arts, and so it seemed fitting that we partner with the London Wall Gallery for what we hope will become a key event on the London arts calendar." She paused as another wave of applause sounded.

"Roger and I, and our partners at CIP, have long been supporters of young creatives and entrepreneurs. It is in that spirit tonight that we'd like to announce an annual prize to be awarded to an up-and-coming talent each year to enable them to continue to evolve and grow as an artist." She paused again as an excited gasp went through the crowd.

"As you may have heard in the news this week, we have suffered the tragic loss of one of our own. Henry Smyth was not only a bright, visionary financier, but he was also my friend." Mary's voice broke on the last word. Roger stepped forward and placed a hand on her shoulder and whispered something in her ear. She nodded and turned her head to look straight at Kat and Adam, her expression becoming hard. She dragged her eyes back to the centre of the crowd and smiled.

"In his memory, it has been decided to name this award The CIP Smyth Prize," she finished to resounding applause and moved away from the microphone. Chen stepped up.

"Wonder if they're going to do one in the security guard's name too," Adam muttered.

"She didn't look that pleased to see us," Kat murmured.

Adam laughed and looked up at Roger Chen, who was wrapping up his remarks.

"I'd like to declare the exhibition officially open. If you'd like to make your way up to Level 3, the artists are available to discuss their work. We sincerely hope you enjoy your evening. Thank you."

There was another round of applause, and the crowd began to disperse towards the escalators and lifts.

"If you'll excuse me, I'll just find the bathroom," Kat said.

"I'll come too," Shamira said, taking her arm.

Adam watched them depart and turned to Nathan.

"Kat is quite a dichotomy, isn't she? She looks so sophisticated tonight, yet you should have seen her fighting yesterday when we were jumped in the parking garage," Adam said.

"Yeah, she's pretty tough," Nathan agreed, adding with a grin. "I wouldn't want to get on her wrong side."

"How did she lose her hand, Nate?"

"Car accident. It was unbelievably traumatic for her, but it's amazing how quickly she recovered and got used to using an artificial one," Nathan said.

Adam nodded. "She doesn't like talking about it, though."

"No, she can be quite, um… prickly with people who ask too many questions."

"Noted."

Adam spotted Kat and Shamira, making their way back towards them.

"This is so cool, there's even a DJ in The Tanks," Shamira said, pointing below their feet. "We can have a boogie later."

Kat snorted. "Like that's going to happen."

"It's alright, Shamira, I'll dance with you if stick-in-the-mud here won't," Nathan said, taking Shamira's arm. "Let's go and look at some stars. You can explain the pieces to me."

"Hello, are you here in an official capacity or for pleasure?"

Adam turned at the voice. Mary McFarlane sashayed toward them, champagne flute in hand. The smile she'd given the audience during her address seemed to be a permanent fixture, although Kat noted that it didn't reach her eyes, which were cold and assessing.

"Ms. McFarlane," Adam replied.

"Mary, please," she all but purred.

Kat controlled the immediate instinct to roll her eyes.

"And, I'm sorry, I forget your name," she said as she turned to Kat, her eyes narrowed as though trying to remember.

"Kat Munro."

"Ah yes, did you find out any more about the spot of bother you ran into in our parking garage the other day?"

"I think it was the spot of bother that ran into trouble," Adam said. "They weren't expecting Kat."

"From all accounts," Mary replied, looking Kat up and down, her eyes resting for a moment on Kat's left hand. "It's like one of those riddles; when is a disability, not a disability?"

Kat flinched but ignored the comment. "It was nice of you to name the prize in Smyth's memory," she said.

"Yes, it was the least we could do. So tragic. You never know what's going on with someone. Anyway, I must mingle. Enjoy your evening." She turned away to join another group, exchanging air kisses as she greeted several people.

"Do you think she could be any more insincere?" Kat said, knocking back her glass. "I keep thinking of Henry Smyth's poor parents; I wonder if they're here."

Adam shook his head. "I doubt it."

"Mary is certainly a piece of work. 'When is a disability, not a disability?'" she mimicked Mary's sultry voice. "When you don't have to live with one, that's when," she added.

Adam studied her for a moment. "I'm sorry, Kat."

"Don't be," she said, the effects of two glasses of prosecco on an empty stomach hitting her. "Let's find the food, or I'm going to say something I really mean."

Chapter 8

Kat was nursing a hangover. She caught up to Nathan and Shamira as they exited the tube station near their office, and together they joined the throngs of morning commuters waiting to cross at the lights. One look confirmed that they, too, were dealing with a similar legacy from the night before.

"Glad I'm not the only one," she said.

Shamira pulled her sunglasses from her hair down over her eyes. "I would have thought all that dancing would have worked off the effects of the alcohol."

"Not when you keep topping it up," Nathan replied. "What say we get a fry up at that little greasy spoon around the corner?"

"Ew," Shamira said as she wrinkled her nose.

"Come on, it'll put hairs on ya chest," Nathan said, elbowing her.

"Great idea, except I'm late for a meeting," Kat replied as they crossed the road outside the station.

"So." Shamira turned her attention to Kat. "Where did you and our ruggedly handsome detective get to last night?"

"The bar on Level 6. We were people watching. Roger and Mary and their cohorts specifically," Kat replied.

"So why are you looking green? I thought cops weren't supposed to drink on duty or didn't he join you?" Nathan asked.

"I don't think he was officially on duty."

"So, what did you learn?"

"Not much beyond the fact that they are obnoxious and rich, but there's no crime in that," Kat replied. "Although you won't believe who was there – William Huntly-Tait."

"Gabe's father?"

Kat nodded.

"Did he see you?" Shamira asked.

"He didn't acknowledge me if he did," she said.

They arrived at the office, passed through the security turnstiles, and climbed the stairs to their floor. Adam and Charles Stephenson were already seated at one end of the conference table in the main meeting room, with the door open.

"When you're ready, join us, Kat, and bring Nathan. Oh, and can you order coffee?" Stephenson called.

Kat gave him the thumbs-up sign and continued on to her desk.

"I don't know why he can't order his own coffee," she grumbled, dumping her bag.

"I'll do it, you two just get in there," Shamira offered.

Adam was back to his usual attire of jeans and leather jacket. "Morning," he grinned as Kat and Nathan walked into the room. "Oh, I've seen you two look better."

Stephenson looked confused.

"I bumped into some of your team at the opening night of an exhibition at the Tate Modern last night," Adam explained.

Stephenson raised an eyebrow.

"CIP sponsored it, and Nathan managed to score three tickets," Kat explained.

"Ah," Stevenson said. "Anyway, now that you're here, DS Jackson is ready for our update on CIP's partners. I thought I'd sit in."

Kat nodded and sat down beside Adam as the receptionist entered carrying a tray with freshly brewed coffee.

"Here we are, these look like they are much needed," she said, patting Kat's shoulder with her free hand.

"Oh, yes." Kat took a grateful sip and opened the file on her iPad. She shared the content with the large screen on the wall at the end of the table. "Nate, jump in if I miss something," she said before beginning. "Capital Investment Partners or CIP is the brainchild of four thirty-something rock star investment bankers." A picture of the CIP building flicked up on the screen. "It was established four years ago and has gone from strength to strength. Recent reports show that they have £2.25 billion under management."

"That's from a zero base in four years?" Stephenson asked.

Kat nodded. "Yes, and their profits have grown exponentially." She tapped her screen for the next slide displaying an earnings graph.

"The founding partners are Roger Chen, Mary McFarlane, Henry Smyth, and Eduardo Diaz." As she spoke, a photo of each popped up on the screen.

"They all worked together at the International Bank of Commerce, IBC, before leaving to set up CIP. It's an industry full of acronyms, so stop me if you need me to explain," she said to Adam. He nodded.

"Roger Chen and Mary McFarlane are usually the public faces of the enterprise, Henry Smyth and Eduardo Diaz are considered the brains," Kat continued.

"I can't imagine Eduardo Diaz being a great PR man from our meeting with him the other day," Adam agreed.

Kat nodded. "Okay, so Roger Chen." She tapped her screen, and Roger's image enlarged over the others. "Roger was born in London to Chinese immigrant parents who own a takeaway in Lewisham. He's a scholarship kid who left Cambridge with a first in economics. He moved through the ranks quickly at IBC making VP within three years.

"Mary McFarlane is Irish." Mary's glamorous image filled their screens. "Educated at Trinity College in Dublin, Mary comes from a privileged background. She's a little older than the other three, and founded then sold several successful start-up businesses before settling on a career in finance. She is often in the society pages with a revolving door of actors and musicians on her arm.

"Henry Smyth was at Cambridge a year ahead of Roger Chen. He got a blue for rowing, worked hard, played hard, and had a reputation for being something of a playboy. His financials are clean. No secret payments or hidden accounts that we could find, his taxes are filed, and he was a regular generous donor to several charities. He was a very wealthy man with a large well-diversified investment portfolio, a house in the country, a ski chalet, and his London penthouse. He was astute and well-liked by all accounts."

Stephenson nodded. "I met him on a couple of occasions. He seemed like a nice chap."

"And finally, Eduardo Diaz. Eduardo was born Eddie Doors in Essex," Kat began as Henry's image was replaced by Eduardo's grinning face.

Adam threw his head back and laughed. "Brilliant."

"Eddie grew up on a fairly rough council estate and left school aged sixteen working various jobs. He eventually managed to talk his way into a job as a junior bond trader at The International Bank of Commerce. And by all accounts, he was fantastic; ruthless, nerves of steel and flamboyant. Somewhere along the way, as his fortune grew, he changed his name and reinvented himself as Eduardo. He owns an apartment around the corner from Harrods. He has a Porsche, a Ferrari, and a Lamborghini parked in his garage."

Nathan let out a low whistle. "Hope we get to audit those."

"So, your conclusions, Kat?" Stephenson asked, stroking his chin.

"They all live well beyond the means of your average Londoner. They regularly dine out at expensive restaurants, own multiple properties, expensive toys, and take luxurious holidays abroad if their social media accounts are any indication. But they have each made a fortune as traders and investment bankers, which, if invested well, would provide that lifestyle. So we can't use the usual red flag of living beyond their means. They each take a £1 million salary annually from CIP along with bonuses and dividends. The company and their personal taxes appear to be up to date. But, they're almost too clean, if you know what I mean."

Stephenson nodded. "You thought that about CIP yesterday, Kat. Perhaps they are just diligent business people. The risk in our business is that we end up being suspicious of everyone and go looking for issues where there are none."

Kat nodded. "That's true."

"This is useful background, but it doesn't get us any closer to who murdered Henry Smyth or why," Adam said. "Greenwood expects to have all of the other information on Smyth's financial situation for you later this morning. In the meantime, my team is looking into the other aspects of Henry Smyth's life. I should have access to his phone and email records by the time I get back to the office."

Chapter 9

When Kat rushed through the door of the restaurant at one p.m. the following day, her parents were already seated perusing menus. Phil Munro was a fit-looking man in his late sixties, and his wife Maggie, with her short-cropped light auburn hair and trim figure, looked younger than her years.

The restaurant was modern and airy, located on the top floor of the National Theatre with an outlook towards Westminster. The tables, set with crisp white cloths, sparkling glasses, and shiny silverware, were mostly full. The buzz of conversation interspersed with the clink of cutlery against china filled the room.

"Sorry I'm late," Kat said as the maître d' guided her to their table. "The traffic was horrible." She kissed them both on their cheeks. She registered the pile of shopping bags on one chair and grinned.

"I don't have to ask how your morning was, Mum," she teased.

Her father rolled his eyes but gave her mother an indulgent smile.

"Oh, just one or two bits for the new season," she replied. "I have to make the most of my trips up to London, they're not happening as much as they used to, are they, Phil?" She gave Kat's father a pointed glare.

"And looking at that haul, you wonder why, Maggie?" he said.

Kat smiled and sat down, accepting a menu and a glass of water from the waiter hovering near the table.

"So, what's been happening with you?" Maggie asked, leaning across the table and patting Kat's arm.

"No, I haven't been on any dates. No, I don't have anyone I'm interested in, and no, I won't be settling down anytime soon and providing you with grandchildren," Kat replied.

Maggie removed her hand with a click of her tongue. "Oh, I wasn't asking any of those questions."

"Sure, Mum," Kat replied, winking at her father, who busied himself looking at his menu.

The waiter arrived back at the table to take their orders, and Kat steered the conversation toward her parents, and let them fill her in on the gossip from their small village.

"I went to the opening of an exhibition at the Tate Modern a couple of nights ago. Nate got some free tickets," she said at a pause in the conversation. "It was called Stars and had some cool pieces."

Maggie rummaged in one of her shopping bags. "Is this it?" she asked, handing Kat a flyer that she'd picked up somewhere. Kat nodded.

"Is it sponsored by CIP?" Phil asked, taking it from her.

"Yeah. How do you know CIP, Dad?" Kat took a sip of water.

"I invest with them," he replied.

Kat choked on her water. 'Since when?" she spluttered and put her glass down.

"Oh, it's been a while now, a couple of years. One of the guys at the golf club put me onto them. He was bragging about the spectacular returns he saw on his investment portfolio. Hence, a few of us put some money in too, the best thing I ever did. The returns have been fantastic with low fees," Phil explained.

"What exactly are you invested in?" Kat asked. "The markets have had a rocky run for the last couple of years."

"A diversified international portfolio. These guys are brilliant because if one region or industry does badly, it's more than compensated for by another area or industry doing well," Phil said. "In fact, I just added some additional funds last week."

"Not everything, I hope, Dad," Kat said. "Don't go putting all your eggs in one basket. You can't diversify the risk of poor investment manager performance if you do that."

Phil shook his head and waved a hand at her. "These guys are solid. They have a stellar reputation in the City. It's fine. Here, I can show you my latest portfolio report." He dug into the inside pocket of his jacket, retrieving his phone and brought up an email containing the report and passed it to Kat.

Kat perused the one-page report. It was a very high-level summary but showed an annual return of 12.5%. Kat let out a low whistle. Phil smiled.

"If you'll excuse me, I'm off to the loo before lunch arrives," he said, pushing his chair back and unfolding his tall frame.

"Don't discourage him, dear. What do you think paid for this shopping spree?" Maggie said, patting Kat's arm again. She signalled for the sommelier and started discussing which wine to have with lunch. Kat tapped the screen of her father's phone and sent a copy of the report to her email address while her mother was distracted. She put the phone back down beside her father's place setting.

The waiter delivered their meals as Phil returned to the table, and the conversation turned to food and family.

"I hope you're still coming to the Valkyries' picnic on Saturday?" Maggie said between mouthfuls.

"Yes, of course. I wouldn't miss it. Will that brother of mine be there?" she asked.

A shadow of sadness crossed Phil's face. "Yes, they'll be there."

"What happened to your hand?" Maggie asked, looking across at Kat, concerned. "Not kickboxing again?" she added with a sniff of disapproval.

Kat lifted her damaged prosthesis and held it out to show her mother the crack across the palm. "Not exactly. I did have to use my kickboxing skills, though, or I would have had a knife in me."

"What?" Maggie dropped her cutlery with a crash, drawing attention from neighbouring tables.

"I was out on an investigation with a police officer that we're working with, and we got jumped in a parking garage by two guys," Kat explained.

"Didn't the officer protect you?" Maggie asked, her eyes wide.

Kat laughed. "I don't need protecting, Mum, don't be so old fashioned. I actually protected him because he took a heavy blow, which knocked him down."

Phil shook his head. "Oh, Kat," he sighed with resignation. "Did the police catch the men?"

Kat shook her head. "Not that I know of, they ran off before the uniforms arrived. But unfortunately, my hand took a knock. The robotics guys won't have it fixed it until Monday. It's a shame, as it's my best one so far. No chafing and excellent functionality."

She started eating again.

Maggie stared at Kat for a long moment. "I'm still so angry that you even need it. I will never forgive those people," she said.

Kat smiled at her. "You and me both, Mum, but let's not spoil lunch by going there."

* * *

Kat rushed back up the stairs to the office after a taxi dropped her off following lunch.

"Nate, do you still have CIP's client list from Smyth's computer? I can't believe I didn't notice this," she called before she even reached the desk.

"Notice what?" Nathan asked, tapping on his keyboard and finding the relevant file.

"My father has a portfolio with CIP."

Nathan looked up. "No, that can't be right. I would have noticed his name or has he invested in the name of a company or trust?"

Kat pulled out her phone and opened the email that she'd sent herself at lunch containing her father's report and showed him. "It's in his name."

"Send that to me, and I'll search on his portfolio number."

Kat pulled her chair around to Nathan's desk and watched as he searched Henry Smyth's client list using both her father's name and the client number from the report. But each search option came up blank.

"That makes no sense. Smyth can't have had their full database downloaded," Kat said.

"Maybe, although the total number of clients as reported in their annual filing to the Bank of England equals the number of clients on Smyth's database," Nathan replied.

"How strange," Kat said, her brow furrowed.

Chapter 10

The sun was beating down when Adam's train pulled in at Bletchley Park Station. He followed the crowd getting off the train and crossed the road.

A large sign welcomed visitors to Bletchley Park, Home of The Codebreakers. Adam waited in line at the entry gate. An older man wearing a World War II private's uniform was seated in the ticket booth. When Adam's turn came, he held up his phone, displaying the ticket Wilson had sent to him earlier.

"Ah, you're here for the picnic, sir. If you just follow the path to the left and around the lake, everything is set up on the lawn. You're very welcome to look through the visitor centre and any of the restored huts while you are here," the man said with a smile. "And there are guided tours leaving from in front of the mansion on the half-hour throughout the day."

"Thank you." Adam made his way through the gates and into the grounds of the now famous Bletchley Park. He strolled along the driveway until the chimneys and roofline of the mansion house, which housed the best-kept secret in Britain during and for many years after World War II, came into view. The almost 10,000 people who'd worked at Bletchley during the war had signed the Official Secrets Act, so Bletchley Park became a secret that many took to their graves, and its role in winning the war was almost forgotten. He recalled reading somewhere that a small group of enthusiasts bought the estate in the late 1970s, and turned it into a museum. Without them, this crucial piece of English history would have been lost to make way for yet another satellite sub-division of modern homes feeding the trains to Milton Keynes and London.

"Jackson."

Adam looked in the direction of the voice and saw four people approaching, one pushing a wheelchair.

"Hey," he called, a broad grin spreading across his face. A giant of a man with a dark buzz cut stepped forward and embraced him. Adam returned the embrace, slapping him on the back. "Don, it's been too long."

The man pushing the wheelchair extended his hand. "Jacko."

"Watto," Adam replied, shaking his hand before saluting the man in the chair, dressed in a navy polo shirt. The cuffs of his shorts flapped where his legs should have been.

"Sir."

"Jackson, good to see you again," Col. Wilson replied, returning the salute and maintaining the pretence that they hadn't been in contact for a while.

"Adam, me old mate. How's the Old Bill treating ya?" The fourth man in the group raised his hand and high-fived him.

"Tommy," Adam drew out the last syllable. "I can't complain. I'm still with CID, although my latest case has me working with a bunch of bean counters associated with the Financial Crimes Unit, which is a little different for me," he replied.

"What do you call an accountant without a calculator?" Watto said.

"I dunno."

"Lonely."

Adam shook his head and groaned. "I see the jokes don't get any better. But it's great to see you guys; it's been too long."

"Ben, Ivan, and Muddy should be here somewhere," Tommy said, looking over towards the mansion house.

"They've probably found the beer tent," Don said.

"Which is exactly where we should be going," Watto said, pushing Wilson's chair forward. Adam fell into step beside them.

"How's Nancy?" Don asked, looking at Adam.

"It's complicated. We separated six months ago."

Don nodded, keen understanding registering in his expression. "Where are you living?"

"A mate who is working in the US has loaned me his flat while things are getting sorted out."

"You two were always an interesting mix," Don said, bumping his shoulder. "She was way too glamorous for you."

Adam snorted and looked across at Col. Wilson. "How are you keeping, sir?"

"Very well, I have a desk job now, in Whitehall. I'd rather be in the field with the men, but as second options go, it's a good one," Wilson replied.

"More people like you are needed high up. Ones who've seen action, not just paper soldiers," Adam said.

Adam turned to the others. "Are you guys all still enlisted?"

"Yup, still serving Queen and Country," Don said. "Don't know what else I'd do."

They rounded a corner, and the stately home with its spacious forecourt and sloping park-like lawn came into view. The building's style could only be described as eclectic. It looked as though every time the owners had added a new extension, they'd adopted a different architectural style. A large number of people filled the lawn, some standing in groups, others seated on outdoor chairs or sprawled on picnic rugs. Several open-sided marquees decorated with lines of Union Jack bunting flapping in the gentle breeze were set up on the driveway, serving food and drink. A jazz band played on a raised dais in front of the mansion, and children ran around in between groups of people, giggling and laughing.

"Looks like a good turnout," Adam said.

"Yes, apparently they tried to get Prince Harry to drop by after the Invictus Games press that he's been doing this week, but he got on a plane back to North America instead," Tommy said.

"If I had Meghan Markle waiting at home for me, I'd be on the first plane out of here too," Watto said.

"What did I tell you?" Don said with a laugh as an arm waved at them from the drinks tent. "Muddy's propping up the beer tent."

Muddy, a broad-shouldered, fit-looking man in his late twenties, wove his way among the picnickers to where they were standing, balancing a cut-down cardboard box filled with plastic cups of beer.

"Just in time, boys," Muddy said, holding the box in front of them as they helped themselves to a cup. He nodded at Wilson. "Sir," he added, balancing the box on one arm and passing one to Wilson. Muddy continued walking and stopped after several paces and spun around. "Well, don't stand there like gormless idiots, this way. Not you, sir," he added when he realised he'd just called a superior officer an idiot.

"No, of course not, son." Wilson tried and failed to hide a

smile.

They followed him to a cluster of stools at the edge of the lawn. Three other men in their late twenties were seated and in deep in conversation. They jumped up and greeted the new arrivals.

"Captain." Adam turned as the youngest member of the group scrambled to his feet.

"I'm a civilian now, Ben, you can call me Adam," he said, extending his hand. Ben looked hesitant for a moment before breaking into a grin and returning Adam's handshake.

"It's so good to see you, cap – I mean Adam."

"You too, Ben, what have you been up to?"

"Just back from another deployment to Afghanistan," Ben said, moving to Adam's side.

"You went back?"

"Yeah, didn't think I was gonna be able to after, y'know."

"Yeah, I know," Adam said, giving him a pat on the back. "Did they give you plenty of support?"

Ben nodded. "The first few days were hard. I kept thinking that I saw the lads, but I knew that was impossible."

"I know, mate, it still haunts me," Adam said as a familiar laugh drew his attention. He frowned and looked around. To his surprise, across the lawn in the centre of a group gathered beneath a flowering cherry tree, stood Kat. She was wearing cutoff denim shorts with a black tank top and had thrown her head back laughing. Her hair spilled over her bare shoulders and tumbled down her back. He stood fixed to the spot and watched her for several moments. She was entirely at ease, her arms uncovered, and her prosthetic hand on full display.

"Wow, who's that?" Ben asked, following his gaze.

"Someone that I work with," Adam replied.

"I might have to join the police force if the WPCs look like that," he said.

"She's not with the police, she's an accountant," Adam replied.

"Well, she could do my *taxes* anytime," Ben said.

"Are you still talking finance?" Watto said. "Why did the accountant cross the road?" He paused. "So he could claim it on his travel expenses." Ben laughed and turned back to the group.

Adam started towards Kat, then stopped when a man in uniform approached her and slipped his arm around her shoulders. She squealed with delight and reached up to kiss him on the cheek as a small boy barrelled across the lawn before launching himself at her. Kat caught him with one arm and hoisted him up onto her hip with ease. Adam watched as he clung to her like a monkey and rained kisses all over her face, while she giggled.

"Aren't you going to say hello?" Don interrupted his scrutiny, nudging his shoulder.

"Maybe later, she's busy with her family," Adam said, turning away.

"Do you know her well?" Don asked. "I heard you say that you work together."

"No, I haven't known her long, but in the short time that I have, I've never seen her carefree and relaxed like that."

"The city is a tough place for people with a disability," Don said.

"You wouldn't know that she had one, the way she acts," Adam said.

"That sounds like Kat. Come on; I'm going to say hello to her brother," Don said.

"Brother?" Adam replied.

Don gave him a knowing smile. "Yeah, that's her brother. You don't know much about her, do you?"

Chapter 11

Kat sensed that she was being watched and felt the hackles rise on her neck. She hated people looking at her and forming an opinion because of her injury. On the one hand Kat knew that, surrounded by family, friends, and other service families with members far worse off than she was, she should be at ease. She'd deliberately worn a sleeveless top, perfect for the hot late summer's day, yet still felt self-conscious. Kat wondered if that would ever stop; that feeling of being judged, of being different, not quite whole. She adjusted the little boy on her right hip, holding on to him a little tighter. He rested his head on her shoulder and nestled in like a bear cub snuggling against its mother. She inhaled the soft scent of his hair and felt a rush of love for him. Kat looked up and watched with surprise as Adam Jackson walked across the lawn towards her. It was difficult not to notice how the fitted t-shirt he was wearing moulded around his biceps. She wondered how it would feel to have those arms wrapped around her. She batted the errant thought away.

"Adam, what are you doing here?" She blushed, hoping that he couldn't mind-read.

"Hello, Kat," he said, smiling at her. "I'm catching up with some of my old battalion."

"You were in the army? I should have guessed," she said, looking over his shoulder at the man following him. "Hello, Donny."

"Hello, kitten," Don said, stepping around Adam and leaning down to kiss Kat on the cheek. He ruffled George's hair and winked at Adam.

Don shook hands with Kat's brother before introducing him to Adam. "Major Munro, this is Detective Sergeant Adam Jackson. We served together in Afghanistan."

"Call me Carl. Good to meet you at last. Colonel Wilson speaks highly of you," Carl replied, shaking hands with Adam. "I see you know my sister?"

"Adam and I have been working together on a case," Kat explained.

"So, were you with her when she was attacked last week?" Carl asked.

"Yeah, we were jumped. Kat was amazing; she disarmed one of them."

"Kat, for God's sake, haven't I taught you to run, not stay and fight?" Carl said, turning to his sister and shaking his head.

She scowled at him. "When have I ever done what you said, and besides, I couldn't leave Adam there to take a beating."

Don and Carl looked at Adam, who shrugged. "It's true," he said. "Those two would have been sore the next day. She got several good kicks in."

"Are you still training with Marco? I thought that had soured," Carl said.

Kat nodded. "Like most men, he has his uses."

Carl shook his head in mock disgust as a woman with long honey blonde hair approached carrying an ice cream cone.

"Oh, George, look what Mummy's got for you," Kat said to the little boy in her arms.

A strange look passed across Adam's face, and Don laughed.

"Not hers," he muttered to Adam.

"I think you'd better put him down, or you'll end up wearing most of this," the woman said to Kat with a laugh.

Kat eased George to the ground and watched as his mother settled him on their picnic rug to eat his ice cream.

"Adam, this is my dear friend and sister-in-law, Sara," Kat said. "Adam is a mate of Donny's who's with the Met. He and I have been working together."

Sara straightened and looked Adam up and down. "Hello."

Kat watched him squirm under Sara's scrutiny.

"So, were you in Afghanistan too?" Kat asked, turning to Adam.

He nodded. "I did two tours."

"Oh, there you are," a shrill voice rang out.

"Brace yourselves, incoming," Carl deadpanned.

Adam swung around to see an older woman in a floral summer dress hurrying across the lawn towards them, staggering a little as her heels sank into the grass. She had one hand on her head, stopping a wide-brimmed straw hat from flying off.

"Darlings," she cried as she reached them.

"Mother," Carl replied, accepting a kiss.

"Hey, Mum, where's Dad?" Kat asked.

"Oh, he's here somewhere," Maggie replied, waving her hand around.

"Grandma, look," George called, lifting his dripping ice cream in her direction.

"Ooh, Georgie, you lucky boy. Hello, Sara dear," she said, kissing Sara's cheek.

"Hello, Mrs. Munro," Don said.

"Hello, Donny," she replied, patting his arm before her eyes came to rest on Adam.

"Maggie Munro," she said, reaching out to shake his hand.

"Adam Jackson," he replied.

"Mum, Adam is the police officer that I'm working with at the moment," Kat replied.

Maggie's eyes widened. "Oh," she said. "You're the one leading my little girl into danger."

"Mum," Kat said with a sigh.

"Not intentionally, Mrs. Munro, I assure you," Adam replied.

Maggie looked unconvinced but pulled her gaze away from Adam and addressed her daughter. "Oh, Kat, I meant to tell you that I was going to go to that exhibition that you went to at the Tate Modern," her mother said. "But when I looked at the program again, I saw that one of the sponsors was William Huntly-Tait's firm, so I couldn't bring myself to go."

"I know, I couldn't believe it when I saw that too," Kat agreed. "I'm certain that he's rotten, but I think I'm the only one."

"You're not still obsessing over him, are you?" Carl asked.

"What's this?" Don said.

"Nothing." Kat glared at her brother.

"Anyway, Kat, I talked to Mrs. Peters; they want you to speak in about five minutes," her mother said, looking Kat up and down. "Did you bring anything else to wear?"

"Like a pretty frock, Kat," Carl teased.

Kat glared at her brother for a moment before looking down at her tank top and denim cutoffs. "No. And besides, no one told me that I had to address the picnic."

"As the new co-chair of the fundraising committee, she

thinks it appropriate if you say a few words," Maggie said.

"Perhaps you two could swap outfits?" Carl suggested, his eyes dancing with mischief. The grin forming on his face disappeared as both women turned and glared at him. He held his hands up in defence. "Just a suggestion."

Kat waited until her mother had turned her back and flipped him the finger. He threw his head back and laughed.

"You don't half regress to a teenager when Mum's around," he said.

"Dad, save me from this lot," Kat called to the tall thin man strolling towards them, a straw trilby covering his bald head.

"Aw, kitten, are they being mean to you?" he teased.

Kat threw her arms in the air. "I give up," she said. "Why couldn't Prince Harry have been here? He'd do a much better job than me." She sighed. "Lead me to Mrs. Peters."

Adam watched her stalk away ahead of her mother, amused by the conversation he'd just witnessed.

"Which fundraising committee is Kat co-chair of?" Adam asked Sara.

"The Valkyries," she said. "They support the rehabilitation of women in the armed forces wounded in action. After losing their brother Joe and then her accident, she got involved. She realised how hard it is to keep going after something as devastating as losing a limb. You have to agree, she's a great role model for not letting disability get in the way of living a full life, even if she'd never admit it."

"I understand she lost her hand in a car accident," Adam said. "How long ago?

"Did she tell you that?"

Adam shook his head.

Sara smiled. "It's her story. She will tell you when she's

ready."

Adam nodded as a voice came over the loudspeaker, asking for everyone's attention. He turned and saw Kat step up to the microphone vacated by the singer of the jazz band. She didn't appear nervous as she looked out over the crowd of people who had turned their attention towards her, but he noticed her left hand slide behind her back for a moment before she caught herself and lifted it to the stand, releasing the microphone, which she held in front of her mouth.

"I'd like to welcome you all here today to this wonderful venue for our annual picnic. This is a chance to get together with family and friends, to remember those no longer with us." Her voice caught on the last couple of words, and Adam watched as Kat's father slipped his arm around Maggie, and Carl stood a little straighter.

"It's also a day to celebrate diversity and resilience. There are many here today who have been injured or lost limbs in the service of our country. We need to ensure that we provide excellent rehabilitation facilities so that they can continue contributing to society and live full, meaningful lives. We must continue to fight discrimination and ignorance. Just because we may be missing a limb, does not mean that we've lost our intelligence or humanity or purpose. Our lives may be a little more difficult. Still, humans are resilient, and I have seen strong military women, time and again, rebuild their lives after devastating and debilitating injuries. So let us celebrate that strength and courage. Enjoy the day. Collectors will be moving around with buckets, so if you can, please donate to help us continue supporting these wonderful warriors on their next adventures in life. Thank you."

Kat handed the microphone back to the jazz singer with a

shaky hand.

"Jeez, I'd vote for her," Don whispered to Adam.

"Yes, she's very impressive," Adam agreed.

"I heard you asking about her car accident," Don said.

"When did it happen?"

"A couple of years ago, I don't know all the details, just that her dropkick boyfriend at the time was driving drunk, but somehow got off," Don said. Adam held his eye, waiting. "She's pretty messed up about how it happened, if you ask me," Don continued. "I know that she doesn't like to talk about it."

Kat rejoined their group, and her mother embraced her.

"Well done, dear," she said. "I don't think anyone noticed your outfit or lack thereof." She tugged at the hem of Kat's shorts.

"Mum." Kat laughed.

"Now, where's Adam?"

"Here, Mrs. Munro."

"Are you free for dinner tonight? We're heading back to ours when this finishes," she said.

Adam glanced at Kat, who looked as though she'd happily kill her mother.

"Thank you, that's very kind of you, but I have to get back to London shortly," he said.

Kat let out a breath as Sara pulled Kat to one side.

"He's cute," she said in a quiet voice, looking towards Adam, who was saying his goodbyes to their group.

"If you say so," Kat replied. "God, why does Mum insist on being my personal Tinder?"

"Kat, she means well. Besides, did I mention that he's cute?"

"I work with him."

"So? He's perfect, ex-armed forces, handsome, funny, good

job."

"So nothing," Kat replied, reaching down for George's hand. "Come on, George. Would you like a go on the bouncy castle?"

George whooped, jumped up and slipped his hand in hers and began to pull her in the direction of the children's playground. Kat glanced over her shoulder and watched Sara engage Adam in conversation. She groaned, wishing her family would stop trying to match-make. After the way her last relationship had ended, she had no interest in starting another.

Adam watched Kat and the little boy walk towards the bouncy castle on the far lawn, excused himself and made his way back to his group of mates.

Col. Wilson saw him walking over and manoeuvred his wheelchair beside an empty park bench. Adam lowered himself onto it, accepting another beer from Watto.

"So, how did your excursion go the other day?" Wilson asked in a low voice.

"Amanda Harding remembers Jake asking directions to South Hill Manor. I drove out to it, and it's a big country house as you'd expect, surrounded by a tall brick wall with fairly hi-tech security."

"Interesting."

"What was Jake doing down in Surrey?"

"He was following a lead that took him to Cobham. As you know, I received a garbled message from him the day before he disappeared, but it made no sense."

Adam nodded. "Apparently he'd been out to a local aerodrome that day. I could go back down and check it out. I didn't have time the other day. What do you think?"

Wilson looked thoughtful. "Aerodrome? That wasn't in any

of his reports. We were due to meet the following week, but there was nothing about an aerodrome in his notes. Perhaps he found the arrival point, although it seems unlikely, as those places have to log flight plans with the aviation authorities."

"I also came across a disused airfield in the area. Well, perhaps not disused, there was a sign which said 'private property'. It was on farmland, just a runway surrounded by sheep, a small hangar, and an agricultural-type aircraft. That could be worth further investigation."

"Agreed."

"What are you two so serious about?" Don asked, dropping down onto the bench beside Adam.

"We were just discussing the fact that we can't believe that you haven't been court-martialed for insubordination yet," Adam said, leaning back.

Wilson laughed as Don feigned shock.

Chapter 12

"Just two today, Kat?" asked the elderly man behind the counter at the second-hand bookstore.

"Yeah, I haven't read all of the ones I bought last weekend," she said with a laugh.

"You must have quite a collection by now," he replied, pushing his glasses up his nose and smoothing a flyaway grey hair from his comb-over back into place.

She handed over a £10 note and slipped the books into her bag. "See you next time," she said.

She wove her way among the tables overflowing with stacks of books and stepped out into the sunshine. Hampstead High Street was bustling. A steady stream of cars crawled both ways, and people wandered along the footpaths at a leisurely pace enjoying the late summer weather while they could. Autumn was most definitely just around the corner, and there had been several cooler mornings of late.

Kat pulled her sunglasses out of her hair and over her eyes as she pondered what to do next. The coffee shop across the street beckoned, so she turned to walk towards the pedestrian crossing and bumped straight into a man coming from the opposite direction. He grunted.

"Sorry," she said, steadying him with her hands on his arms.

"My fault," he said, smiling, but holding an arm to his ribs.

She looked up into his face, "Adam," she said in surprise.

"Hi there," he said.

"Are you still sore?" she asked.

He nodded. "A little, especially when someone bulldozes into me."

"I'm sorry," she said. "What are you doing in Hampstead? Do you live around here?"

"No. It's such a lovely day that I thought I'd take a walk on the heath, clear my head. Did you enjoy the picnic yesterday?"

"Yeah, I did," she said.

Adam nodded, and a moment of awkward silence passed between them.

"Well, enjoy your walk. I guess I'll see you at work next week." Kat's voice trailed off as she made to leave.

"Would you like that drink that I keep trying to buy for you?" he asked, stopping her with a hand on her arm.

Kat bit her lip. "I was about to grab a coffee across the road."

"I was thinking of something a little stronger. The King William has a lovely sunny garden," he said, pointing to the pub on a corner further down the hill.

Kat's mind immediately said no, but she overruled it for once. One drink couldn't hurt, could it? "Sure, why not."

The pub was busy, but they managed to find a single table with two chairs in the corner of the garden bar and carried their drinks over to it. Kat dropped her bag beside the table.

"What have you been buying?" Adam asked.

"Books; it's kinda my Sunday thing, trawling through bookshops and markets. Having lunch somewhere new," she said.

"That sounds like a great way to spend a Sunday, especially

when the weather's like this."

"Yeah," she smiled and picked at the label on her bottle.

"How's your hand?" Adam asked.

"This is my spare one. I'm seeing the specialists tomorrow about getting the other one fixed. This one is not as good; it's an earlier model." She flexed the hand and held it out for him to see. "The big problem is that the nails are permanently painted red, so I have to keep the nails my right hand painted red too, which is hard to do myself. Fortunately, I was able to pop into a nail salon on Friday after work."

Adam looked bemused.

"First world problem, I know," she said, catching his expression.

"Actually, I was wondering if they charged you half price?" he said.

Kat stared at him for a moment before she burst out laughing. "You are the only person who has ever asked me that. In fact, you ask me about my hand more than anybody I know." She took a swig of her beer. "Most people avoid the subject."

"I used to be in the line of business that means I have more than my fair share of mates that have been... er... hurt," he said, holding her gaze. "And, it's part of you, and I find that I want to know more."

Kat took another swig and glanced at her hand before looking up at him again. Her heart thudded in her chest.

"I don't do relationships, Adam," she said.

"I don't recall offering," he replied, his tone even and unemotional.

"Good, just needed to be clear on that," she said. "Now tell me, how did you go from the army to the police?"

Adam looked across the table at her, sunglasses covering her eyes, the red highlights in her hair glinting in the sun as she sipped her drink. If he didn't know better, he would have thought how relaxed and at ease she was, when in fact he was beginning to realise that the opposite was true. She was always on alert.

"You are a master of redirection, Kat Munro. Why don't you ever talk about yourself?" Adam said.

Kat thought for a moment. "I recall reading somewhere that when Richard Burton and Elizabeth Taylor went out drinking, the last thing they wanted to talk about, with the people they encountered, was themselves. Instead, they were far more interested in learning about the people they met. Perhaps I'm a little like that."

"Jackson?" A man stopped at their table, swaying.

"O'Connor, how are you?" Adam jumped up and shook hands with the man.

"Kat, this is Frank O'Connor. We served together."

"Hello." Kat nodded to him, taking in Frank's dishevelled appearance and noticing the beer on his breath.

"How are you doing, man?" O'Connor asked. "Still having them nightmares?"

"Sometimes," Adam replied. "What are you doing now?"

"Bit of this, bit of that," O'Connor replied.

"Are you working?"

O'Connor's lip curled. "'tween jobs, mate." He caught someone's eye across the garden. "Gotta go."

"Sounds like there's a story there," Kat said.

"A very long and tortuous one," Adam said.

"Nightmares?"

"If you've seen some of the things that we have, it's impossible not to have them."

"Afghanistan?"

Adam nodded.

Kat swallowed. "We lost my eldest brother over there," she whispered. Her voice cracked, and she took a hasty sip of her drink. She wasn't sure what it was about Adam. Despite his assertion that she never talked about herself, she couldn't seem to stop sharing things with him that she didn't tell other people.

"God, I'm sorry," Adam said. "I didn't know."

"Landmine," she said. "Blew his Foxhound to pieces."

"How long ago?"

"Three years."

"Before your accident, then?" Adam asked.

Kat nodded. "A few months. I was heading off the rails, unsure how to cope with his death when the accident happened." She let out a long breath.

"Sounds like there's a story there?" Adam echoed her earlier remark.

Kat gave a half-smile. "Oh yeah."

They were silent for a few moments, each deep in their own thoughts and memories. Kat drained her bottle.

"Would you like another?" Adam said, standing.

Kat nodded.

"There's something that I haven't told you," she said when he returned with two bottles in his hand.

Adam quirked an eyebrow as he slid into his seat. "And there's something I haven't told you," he said.

"You first."

"One of the CIP partners has form," Adam said.

"Which one?"

"It seems that Eddie Doors has several arrests for drunk and disorderly, threatening behaviour and domestic violence," Adam said.

"Another tough boy with short man syndrome who can't hold his drink," Kat said, shaking her head. "I can't stand men who hit their partners, whatever the reason."

"Agreed, but Henry Smyth's death wasn't violent as such; I mean, it wasn't like he'd been in a fight."

"No, he didn't have a chance to be violent, 'cos someone drugged him," Kat replied.

"Or he drugged himself."

"I don't think we really believe that, do we?"

Adam took a swig from his bottle. "Trying to keep an open mind. Now, what did you have to tell me?"

"You met my father yesterday?"

"Briefly," Adam said.

"He's been investing with CIP for the past two years. Making spectacular returns," Kat said.

"Good for him."

"No, not good for him." Kat shook her head and leaned forward. "He's made an annual return of 12.5% on a diversified international equity portfolio when the market has been tanking. No one, and I mean no equity fund, has made double figures in the last two years."

Adam frowned. Kat rested her elbows on the table.

"And that's not all. Nate found a deleted file on Smyth's laptop, which purported to be the firm's client list, from about a month ago. However, Dad's name is not on it. We're waiting to get the official client list from DI Greenwood tomorrow to compare it with Smyth's. Still, the total number of clients, as noted in their recent annual report, is in the ballpark, so there's no reason that Dad's name wouldn't be there."

"That's odd," Adam agreed.

"I know," Kat said. "I'm excited that we've finally found an anomaly, but also scared because it involves my dad."

Chapter 13

Adam's mobile rang as he arrived at the incident room the next morning. The unadorned room allocated for the investigation into Henry Smyth's death contained four desks with computers, a cluster of uncomfortable plastic chairs against one wall, and a large whiteboard on wheels at one end of the room. The incident board contained photos of security guard Popov and Smyth, both alive and deceased, and images of the remaining CIP business partners. Notes, dates, and times were scrawled beneath each photo.

Adam nodded his greeting to the uniformed officers seated behind two computer screens as he answered the call.

"Detective Jackson, it's Alfred Smyth. You said to call if I had any more information on Henry's death."

"Yes, of course, good morning, Mr. Smyth."

"Your colleagues have released Henry's apartment to us, and when we started packing his belongings this morning, we came across his mobile phone. It appears to have fallen behind the bedside table, so I thought perhaps the crime scene people had overlooked it? Do you need it?"

"Yes, that does seem to be an oversight," Adam said.

"We will be at his apartment all day, packing up his things," Mr. Smyth said.

"I'll pop over this morning."

The next call Adam made was to Kat. He'd enjoyed having a drink with her the previous day and was surprised that she'd opened up to him as much as she had. She was smart, sassy, and attractive, all the things he liked in a woman, but he was going to have to be careful; it was too soon to get involved with anyone again. Yet he found himself with an excuse to call her and hear her voice.

"Adam?" She sounded surprised to hear from him.

"Kat, Greenwood is sending over everything that we've been able to gather on the assets of CIP's partners."

"Okay. I spoke with my mother last night and got the names of Dad's golf buddies who have also invested with CIP. Nate and I will check them against the client list that we have."

"Let me know how you go. I'm off to see Smyth's parents. They've come across a mobile phone that I'm going to collect."

Adam turned around and headed back out, hailing a taxi from in front of his building. He climbed in the back and checked his email on the drive to Smyth's apartment. He groaned out loud, reading a note from Nancy. *Remember, we are meeting tonight to go over the final details of the settlement.* He ran his fingers through his hair as his irritation spiked; even now, she was still trying to organise him and make sure he remembered appointments.

* * *

Henry Smyth's father was boxing up books when Mrs. Smyth let Adam into the apartment a little while later. He declined her offer of tea.

"Hello again," Adam said, shaking Mr. Smyth's hand. "Have

you got some help?" He turned to look at the wall of books. "You've got a big job there."

"The movers are coming later in the week, but I thought I'd make a start. I can't sit around and do nothing," he said. "Have you made any more progress?"

"We're looking into several leads," Adam said, feeling inadequate. He wanted to give this lovely couple some solace, and soon.

"Let me get you that phone," Mr. Smyth said.

Adam followed him through into the study. In comparison with his earlier visit, the room was tidy, and the desk clear. Several sealed cardboard cartons sat on the floor near the door. Mr. Smyth opened the desk drawer and withdrew a phone.

"Would you mind if I took this?"

"Not at all, I thought you would want to."

Adam produced an evidence bag from his pocket and held it open for Mr. Smyth to drop the phone.

"Thank you. We'll return this once we've analysed it," Adam said, filling out a receipt from the notebook in his pocket and passing it to the older man.

Mr. Smyth nodded.

"Now, I have a few minutes," Adam said, looking at his watch. "Can I pass you down the books from the top shelves?"

"Well, I wouldn't say no to an extra pair of hands."

Adam followed him back to the living room and began unloading books from the higher shelves as the lift chimed, announcing the arrival of a visitor. The doors swished open.

"Hello," a voice called.

Mrs. Smyth hurried towards the lift.

"Eddie," she said. "How lovely of you to drop by."

Adam turned to see Eduardo Diaz standing at the doors with a large bouquet in his arms. He kissed Mrs. Smyth on both cheeks before handing the flowers to her.

"I don't know what to say," he said, running his hand across his bald head.

"I know, dear, we're still in shock too," Mrs. Smyth said, patting his arm. "Will you stay for a cup of tea?"

"Yes, please."

"Right then, I'll put these into some water and put the kettle on." Mrs. Smyth bustled from the room into the kitchen.

Diaz stepped further into the apartment but stopped when he spotted Adam handing books to Mr. Smyth.

"Eh, you're that detective," he said, his eyes narrowing.

"Yeah, good to see you again, Mr. Diaz," Adam said.

"I hear you were jumped by car thieves in our parking garage the other day, and that chick stopped you taking a beating," Diaz smirked.

Adam gave a wry smile. "Yeah, 'car thieves'. What can I say, she's got hidden talents. So you have a lift pass for Henry's apartment?"

"Yeah, Henry gave it to me ages ago. I guess I won't be needin' it anymore," he said, pulling it from his pocket and setting it down on a side table. "So, what brings you here?"

"As I said the other day, two suspicious deaths in as many days needs careful review," Adam replied.

"Yeah," Diaz said. "I can't believe that Henry would have killed that security guard. He wasn't that kind of guy." He sighed before continuing. "But then again, I can't believe that Henry would have killed himself."

"He didn't, Eddie," Mr. Smyth said.

"What?" Diaz asked, looking at Adam. "You were serious

the other day?"

"There is strong evidence to suggest that someone murdered Henry."

Diaz dropped down onto the closest chair and ran his hand over his face. "That would make more sense, but why?"

"That's what I'm trying to work out," Adam said.

"We were supposed to go out that night," Diaz said. "But Henry called me cancelling at the last minute, said there was something he needed to do."

"How was he in the weeks leading up to this death?"

"Distracted, come to think of it, but I didn't think anything of it at the time. Now I wish I had. I wasn't a very good mate."

"How long had you known each other?" Adam asked as he continued to remove books from the shelves and stack them on the dining table where Mr. Smyth was loading them into boxes.

"The day we both started at IBC. We hit it off straight away. Two guys from wildly different backgrounds, but two peas in a pod, really," Diaz said with a smile. "We worked hard, but we both loved a party."

"So, did Henry have any enemies that you can think of?"

Diaz looked thoughtful for a moment before shaking his head. "No one springs to mind. Everyone loved Henry."

"Well, someone clearly didn't," Mr. Smyth said.

When Mrs. Smyth returned with the tea, Adam took his leave. He hailed a taxi on the street outside the building. As he sat in the cab on the return journey to the incident room, Adam turned Henry Smyth's mobile phone, sealed in its evidence bag, over and over in his hand. He stared hard at it for several seconds before reaching for his own phone and making a call.

"I have a small job for you."

He listened before replying. "6:30 tonight. See you then."

He slipped Henry's phone out of the evidence bag and slid it into his jacket's inside pocket.

Chapter 14

Charles Stephenson stopped by Kat's desk as she and Nathan searched the client list from Smyth's laptop for the names of her father's golfing friends.

"Making any progress?" he asked.

Kat looked up and shook her head. "Something doesn't feel right, but we can't find any evidence to allow us to dig deeper. There's a slight anomaly with client numbers, so we may not be comparing a complete list. It's very frustrating."

"In that case, until Greenwood obtains further information for us, let's put it to one side; a new case has come across my desk. Suspicion of embezzlement and it appears that the evidence is strong, but we need to put together an airtight case for the trial starting next month. I want your team working on that from tomorrow," he said.

Kat nodded, hiding her disappointment.

"Can I have your interim report on CIP by the end of the day?"

"Sure," Kat said.

"Damn," Nathan said as Stephenson walked back to his office.

"Let's save everything. I don't think we've seen the end of this one," Kat replied.

"Do you think you should tell Stephenson about your father?" Shamira asked. "You know what he's like about disclosing any personal involvement."

Kat shook her head. "No point if we're closing it down. I'm just going to take one more pass over everything that we have and finish drafting the report."

A short while later, an email arrived in Kat's inbox.

She clicked on the attachment.

"Nate, I'm forwarding you the client lists that DI Greenwood has managed to obtain," she called to him. "Can you run a comparison to Henry Smyth's list, and I'll run my eye down and see if I can find Dad and his friends' portfolios."

Half an hour later, Nathan pushed back his chair and looked across at Kat and Shamira. "They're not there," he said.

"None of them?" Shamira asked.

"Also, I've just noticed that Dad's portfolio number is quite different from any of their other client numbers," Kat said.

"Something doesn't stack up," Nate agreed. "The number of clients on the reports DI Greenwood just sent tie exactly to the lists on Smyth's laptop."

"So, where are Dad and his friends' portfolios?" Kat mused. She picked up the printout she'd made of her father's report. "It can't be in another company, because this quite clearly says CIP diversified global fund, which is the same name as one of CIP's core offerings, and the contact details are the same."

She grabbed her mobile and keyed in the customer service number from the bottom of the report.

"Capital Investment Partners, how can I help you?" a friendly voice answered.

"Yes, I have a query on my portfolio?"

"Just one moment."

Kat connected through to another person.

"Investor services, how can I help you?"

"I'd like to check which fund my investment is currently in?"

"Certainly, but first, I'll have to get some details to verify your identity."

"Okay."

"Portfolio number?"

"F4-50019532."

"And your name?"

"Munro."

"Your address?"

Kat relayed her parents' address.

"Yes, here we are, Mrs. Munro."

The sound of keyboard strokes echoed down the phone line for a moment before the man spoke again. "I'm sorry, but the portfolio is just in the name of Mr. Munro, so we can't give any details to you. Is he there?"

"No, but I will get him to call. Thanks."

Kat hung up and looked across at her colleagues.

"I need to talk to Stephenson," she said.

Chapter 15

Adam pushed open the door of the old pub in Rotherhithe at 6:30 p.m. It was gloomy and somewhat dingy, but most of the tables and stools at the bar were full. Lights flashed from a row of gambling machines along one wall, and the dull thud of pool balls connecting echoed off the high ceiling.

Adam scanned the room, his eyes alighting on the man that he was meeting, sitting at a table by the window nursing a pint of beer. He acknowledged Adam with a flick of his head. He was younger, a pale, gaunt face emerging from beneath a mop of wild hair. Tattoos crawled around his neck.

"What can I get ya, love?" the barmaid enquired.

"Becks, thanks," Adam replied. He paid and wandered over to the table by the window and sat down.

"Adam."

"Dave."

"What do you have for me?"

Adam slid Smyth's mobile from his pocket and placed it on the table. "I need to get into this."

Dave sat back and pulled a face at Adam. "Child's play, I thought you might be bringing me something difficult to hack?"

Adam laughed. "There are degrees of difficulty. For you, this might be simple; I don't know where to start without being locked out."

Dave took a large swig of beer, burped, cracked his knuckles, and picked up the phone. "First, I need to know a little about whose phone this is such as name, date of birth, date of his wedding, children, pets, business name, etc."

He reached into a bag and pulled out a laptop and cable and attached the phone to the computer. His fingers flew across the keyboard for a moment before he looked across at Adam, waiting for his response.

"Henry James Smyth, 13 February 1983, no children, no significant other, no pets. Worked for Capital Investment Partners, lived in Southwark," Adam said.

"Dead, I take it?"

Adam nodded.

"What else can you tell me about him? Interests, hobbies?" Dave asked.

"Making money and partying," Adam said.

"Hmm… let's try some combinations of all those things. Did you know that 93% of people use either a pet's name or important date as their password?"

"No, I didn't."

They sat in silence for a couple of minutes while Dave's computer program ran. Adam knew from experience that Dave didn't appreciate small talk while he worked. A soft ping indicated when the program finished.

Dave pulled a face. "Okay, so he is not in the 93% then. Can you tell me anything else about this guy? Otherwise, I'll have to take it back over the road to my office and set the random password generator going; he may have used one of those."

Adam sat back, spinning his beer bottle around in his hands and thought for a moment. The image of Kat coming out of the bookstore in Hampstead's sunshine the previous afternoon sprang to mind. She had looked so unguarded and content, that he almost wished that he hadn't orchestrated bumping into her.

"Books," he said, sitting up straight. "He was into books." He closed his eyes, trying to bring up the bookshelves in Smyth's apartment. He wished Kat were there; she would know what was on them. All he could remember were the coloured spines. He reached for his phone and called her, but it went straight to voicemail.

"He was a collector, I think. Classics perhaps?" he said.

Dave started typing.

"Hey, try Kipling, *The Jungle Book*." The thought came to Adam in a rush.

Dave didn't pause his typing, and several seconds later, there was an audible click, and the screen of Smyth's phone lit up. Dave unplugged the phone from his laptop, slammed the lid shut and slipped it back into his bag. Adam slid a fold of £20 notes across the table and picked up the phone.

"Mowgli123," Dave said with a grin, pocketing the cash. He sculled the remainder of his pint and stood. Adam did the same and shook his hand.

"Thanks."

Together they left the pub. Dave waited for a gap in the traffic to cross the road back to his office, housed above a kebab shop in the centre of a shabby row of shops. He raised a hand in a farewell wave as he stepped into the street. Smyth's phone chimed in Adam's pocket. Adam frowned and fished it out, looking at the screen.

Jackson. You'd be best to stop, or you'll be next.

An explosion ripped through the night, the force throwing him back against the wall of the pub. He covered his head with his hands as debris rained down on him. There was silence for a few seconds before a car alarm began screaming, and people started running. In the distance, he could hear sirens.

"Are you okay, mate?" a man said, crouching down in front of him. His voice sounded distant, as though he was speaking from far away.

Adam nodded and allowed the man to help him to his feet.

"Where's Dave?" he asked and realised by the man's reaction that he was shouting.

The man shrugged. He bent down and picked something up and handed it to Adam. "Looks like you won't be using this again."

Adam glanced down at the shattered remnants of Smyth's phone before looking across the street. A small fire had taken hold at the front of the shops below Dave's office. The twisted wreckage of a car littered the road, and several people were trying to divert traffic.

Adam pushed off the wall and took a step into the street. "Dave," he shouted.

When there was no response, he began jogging across the road towards the fire. "Dave," he called again. Two men lay on the footpath in front of the shop. He rushed forward as one of them groaned. Both men were strangers to him.

"Are you hurt? Can you move?" he asked.

The man nodded and tried to sit up. Adam supported him until he was sitting with his feet in the gutter. He had blood pouring from a wound in his head. "Help my father," he said. "We were just outside having a smoke."

Adam moved towards the older man. Through his ripped shirt, Adam could see a large piece of glass embedded in the man's shoulder. Adam put his fingers to the man's neck. There was a pulse, but it was faint. He looked around and saw an ambulance coming down the street towards them with its siren blaring and lights flashing. He stood up and waved his arms above his head to attract their attention. He winced as he did so, his already injured ribs screaming in protest.

Within seconds the paramedics were at his side. "We'll take it from here."

Adam wandered away from the injured men and checked the surrounding area for Dave, but there was no sign of him. He crossed back over to the pub, where the publican and barmaids were standing, looking at their shattered windows.

Adam pulled his own phone from his pocket and called Dave. He answered after one ring.

"I'm okay. I just got the hell out of there. I'm not sure who's after me this time."

"That was intended to send me a message, not you."

"How do you know?"

"There was a text on Smyth's phone seconds before the explosion, warning me off from my investigation," Adam replied.

"Sounds like good advice. Later." Dave disconnected.

Chapter 16

Kat stepped from the shower and wrapped a fluffy white towel around herself. She grabbed a second towel and carefully dried her stump, checking for any abrasions. Finding none, she reached into her gym bag for her hand and reattached it. She'd left her damaged one with the lab at lunchtime. She dressed quickly and stood in front of the mirror to fix her hair and makeup.

"See you on Thursday, Kat," a slim, athletic woman called as she walked out of the changing room, a small backpack slung over her shoulder.

"Bye," Kat said.

Five minutes later, Kat packed her bag and headed out into the gym's busy foyer. She stopped to refill her drink bottle from the water cooler by the reception desk and watched people arriving for their evening workouts, along with those who were finished and going home. She glanced outside before the doors closed behind them. The sun was beginning to set.

"Ready, ma chérie?"

Kat turned at the sound of the voice. Marco, her kickboxing instructor, sauntered towards her. He was muscular, with a swarthy complexion and dark eyes. His jet black hair was pulled back into a ponytail. He slipped his arm around her waist, resting his hand on her right hip and guided her towards the automatic door. The door swished open, and they stepped into the night.

"Kat."

She turned to see Adam leaning against the wall beside the gym's entrance. His clothes were dusty, his hair messy, and one cheek was covered in small cuts and scratches.

"Adam, what happened to you?" she asked, reaching out instinctively to him.

Marco's hand tightened on her waist.

"Long story." Adam's eyes narrowed as they focused on her companion.

Kat disengaged from Marco, who released his arm and instead snagged her left hand, interlinking his fingers with hers. He looked Adam up and down before holding his gaze.

"Adam, ah… this is Marco, my kickboxing instructor. Marco, Adam and I work together."

The two men nodded to one another.

"Kat, there have been some developments tonight that I need to go over with you," Adam said.

"What? Now?"

He nodded.

She looked at Marco. "Sorry, I'll have to take a rain check."

Marco lifted her prosthetic hand to his lips. "Of course, ma chérie, but come over when you've finished."

"It could be late."

"Never too late for you." Marco dropped her hand and sauntered away without another word.

Kat shuffled and looked down at her feet. "So, what do you need to go over with me?"

Adam studied her for a moment. "I'll tell you in the car. This way." He led her towards a vintage gold two-door Ford Capri parked at the curb, and opened the passenger door.

"Nice car, Adam. It suits you," she said as he climbed into the driver's seat. "Do you fancy yourself as Bodie or Doyle?"

"I would have thought you too young to have watched *The Professionals*?" Adam said.

Kat shrugged. "Re-runs, I guess."

"So, your kickboxing instructor is also your boyfriend?" Adam asked.

Kat shook her head. "No, as I told you yesterday, I don't do relationships."

Adam quirked an eyebrow.

"Don't you dare judge me," Kat said, turning to glare at him. "Marco is a good guy. He does a lot of great work with amputees and burns victims. That's how I met him and ended up going to his gym. There's a lot of anger and grief in the rehabilitation process, and Marco works with people to get it out in a positive way."

Adam started the car's engine and swallowed the comment that sprang into his mind concerning Marco. "I'm not judging you, Kat. Marco is a fortunate man to have your respect and affection." He eased the car out into the traffic. "I'll drop you home, where am I going?"

"Thank you," Kat said, chastened by his response. "Head towards Green Park. Now, what did you want to tell me?"

"This goes no further at this stage, okay?" Adam said.

"Sure."

"I met a contact tonight, in a pub across the road from his office in Rotherhithe. I needed some help to unlock Henry Smyth's phone," he explained. "We were successful, but as we were leaving the pub, I received a text message on that phone telling me to stop, or I would be next."

"Next, what?"

"Seconds after receiving the message and saying goodbye to my contact, there was a small explosion near the pub."

"God, that's why you have those grazes on your cheek. Was anyone hurt?"

"Two men from a nearby shop."

"That's awful," she said. "And your contact?"

"He's fine."

"Did you come straight from there?" Kat took a deep, shaky breath.

"Yeah."

They pulled away from the lights and drove along the Embankment, both silent for a moment.

"Adam, you have to stop the car now. Let me out," Kat said, pulling at the door handle.

"Whoa, hang on, Kat." Adam manoeuvred into the next lane and pulled over into a bus stop. Kat leapt from the car as soon as he stopped and stood in the bus shelter. She bent over, with her hands resting on her knees, gulping in one lungful of air after another.

Adam jumped out and ran to her. Tears streamed down her face, and he reached out, but she pushed him away. "You smell of smoke." She pressed the heel of her right hand into her eyes and swiped at the tears. "Give me a minute," she said, walking several paces away from him.

Adam stood still and watched her. After a few moments, she turned and retraced her steps. She stopped in front of him and looked up into his face, her expression one of embarrassment.

"I'm sorry. I didn't mean to freak out. Being in a car and

smelling smoke is not a good combination for me."

Adam ran his hand through his hair. "No, I'm sorry, I didn't know."

Kat looked away. "Just take me home, please."

They drove in silence to Kat's flat with the windows down and the fresh night air blowing through the car. Kat leaned against the passenger doorframe with her head turned away from Adam and stared out at the oncoming traffic.

Kat's flat was on the second level of a four-storey Victorian building on the edge of a square with a private garden in Mayfair.

"This is really nice, Kat," Adam said as they stepped into the entrance hall. Kat threw her keys on a narrow table inside the door. She dropped her gym bag underneath the table and walked across the wooden floor into the living room. Adam pulled off his leather jacket and hung it on an empty hook and followed Kat. The living room was light and spacious with a soft cream sofa along one wall and another at right angles to it facing tall French doors leading to a private balcony. To the left was the kitchen, separated from the living room by a long bench with two stools tucked in under it.

"Thanks, I like it," she said. "Would you like tea or something stronger?"

"Tea would be good, thanks."

Kat padded into the kitchen as a smoky grey Persian cat sauntered into the room. She stopped in front of Adam and appraised him for a few moments before curling around his legs. Adam bent down and scratched behind her ears, setting off a purr that resembled a small motor.

"You've done it now, she will never leave you alone," Kat said.

Adam looked around the room. The wall behind the sofa displayed black and white photos in simple black frames. He walked over to study them and was surprised to recognise several desert scenes from his time in Afghanistan. His view of the country was so coloured by war and death that he was shocked to notice that there was such a stark beauty to it.

"Who's the photographer?" he asked.

"My brother."

"Carl?"

"No, Joseph. He was a keen photographer. These were on his camera when they shipped his belongings home. Framing and displaying them seemed like a way to be close to him and not lose him. Seems a bit stupid now, because he really is gone," Kat said, coming up behind him and handing him a steaming mug of tea.

"Not at all, we all deal with grief and loss differently. Your way seems as good as any, and they're great photos." He smiled at her. "Is it okay if I wash my hands, I came straight to you from the explosion?"

"Of course, the bathroom is through there. There are fresh towels under the sink. Help yourself." She pointed to a doorway at the back of the room and took back the mug of tea, setting it down on the breakfast bar. Adam passed a box room that Kat used as an office as he walked down the hall. A tall cupboard stood in one corner opposite a desk and chair, and a Roman blind covered a small window. He washed his hands and face before standing for a moment staring at his reflection in the mirror. He looked rough. Tired and beaten. He rolled his shoulders and left the room.

Kat was seated on a stool at the bench. Adam noticed that she'd closed the door to her little office. He slid onto the other stool and took a sip from his mug.

"Kat, do you have reactions like that often?" he asked.

She shook her head and looked down into her cup. "No, not anymore. I'm sorry you had to see that."

"Don't be. I've seen plenty of guys with PTSD, that's what it looked like…" he trailed off.

"I know."

"What happened, Kat?"

"I don't want to talk about it."

"Well, if you do…"

"I know where to find you," she said, her eyes downcast.

"I was down in Cobham the other day," Adam said after a moment's silence.

Kat's head snapped up, and she stared at him.

"Have you been there?" he continued.

"Yeah, and I don't care if I never step foot in the place again."

Adam raised his eyebrows. "Why's that?" He glanced at her hand.

Kat breathed deeply before leaning towards him. "Have you been looking into me? Please don't. You need to keep out of my business," she said in a low voice.

Adam didn't react or move back. Instead, he held her gaze until she looked away.

"Now, tell me what exactly was your contact doing for you tonight?" she asked, leaning back, making it clear that the subject of her past was closed.

Adam regarded her before answering. She really had mastered the art of deflection. He decided to let her deflect, for now.

"He's a technical expert," he said. "He was helping me to unlock Smyth's phone."

Kat looked at him. "Technical expert? Or hacker?"

"I think he prefers 'technical expert'."

Kat gave a weak smile. "Is that even legal?"

"It's on the edge. Let's just say any evidence found isn't admissible in court."

"So what did you find on Henry's phone?" she asked.

"Unfortunately, I didn't get to look. We unlocked it, but it's now in pieces thanks to the explosion, which tore it out of my hand."

"So, no way to trace the message?"

"I've handed it on to CSU to try, but even if they do, it's likely to be from a burner," Adam said as his phone rang. He pulled it from his pocket, looked at the screen and uttered an expletive.

"Sorry, I gotta take this." He stood and wandered to the far side of the living room.

Kat jumped up and busied herself by unloading the dishwasher.

"Look, I'm sorry. Something came up." Kat heard Adam say.

The person on the other end appeared to be shouting.

"Why don't you call tomorrow when you've calmed down, and we'll reschedule." Adam listened for a moment. Kat heard him controlling his breathing. "What's more important? Tell you what, check the news reports about a bomb blast in Rotherhithe tonight and tell me what's important. I was in the middle of that." His voice rose at the end, anger spilling over as he lost a little of his ironclad control.

"I'm fine. Please don't pretend that you care." He stabbed the end button on his phone.

Kat looked across the room and caught his eyes, which were blazing with anger.

"Don't ask, it's complicated," he ground out.

She nodded.

"There's one other thing. Greenwood has arranged for a car to pass by your flat tonight, because if whoever set that explosive knows that I'm investigating Smyth's death, then they possibly know that you are involved too. So it would be good if you remained here tonight," Adam said.

Kat hesitated for a moment before nodding. "Okay."

Adam drained his cup and stood up. "Try to get some sleep; I suspect we could have a busy day tomorrow."

Chapter 17

"Kat, when you have a moment," Charles Stephenson called from his corner den, as Kat walked across the Forensic Accounting Associates floor the next morning, dark rings under her eyes. "You too, Nathan."

Kat wove her way among the pods of desks, many still unoccupied, to tuck her bag under her desk, and followed Nathan into Stephenson's office. She gazed through the floor-to-ceiling windows to watch a small riverboat chugging along the Thames in the sunshine before sinking down into a visitor's chair in front of the large mahogany desk.

"Close the door," Stephenson instructed.

Nathan pushed the door shut and joined Kat facing Stephenson's desk.

"There's been progress on the CIP investigation. I've just had a call from DI Greenwood. He's expecting to have a search warrant issued this morning, allowing us access to CIPs servers on their premises, based on providing false data to the regulators. He wants you there ready to go at eleven because you'll only have a short time before they get their lawyers to issue an injunction."

"What changed?" Nathan said.

"The judge thought that the missing client records were

enough."

"Seems a little tenuous," Kat said.

"Perhaps, but Greenwood argued a good case and found a judge willing to listen. With the news full of firms flouting the anti-money-laundering filing rules, the authorities are keen to make an example of someone."

Kat nodded. "I'll take Nate and Shamira with me."

"Agreed. Gather what you think you'll need. DI Greenwood is in court this morning, so DS Jackson will meet you outside CIP and give further instructions. I have one meeting that I can't get out of, and then I'll join you," Charles said. "Use the opportunity to look for anything unusual."

"I hope we're right about the missing portfolios," Kat muttered to Nathan as they returned to their desks.

"We are," he said. "I've run it from all angles."

* * *

They squeezed into the back of a taxi heading for London Wall.

"The first things we go for are the full client lists and fund reports," Kat said. "We may not have access for very long, as I'd expect they'll get their lawyers involved fairly quickly and shut us down."

"Do we know what client management system they use?" Shamira asked.

"I believe it is a bespoke, in-house system," Nathan replied. "But we're about to find that out."

Kat spotted Adam's car parked in a side street near the CIP building as they drove past.

"Can you swing back around and drop us in that side street

back there?" Kat asked the driver.

The driver obliged, and Adam climbed from his car to greet them as they unloaded from the taxi.

"We just need to wait for the go-ahead," Adam explained, as another vehicle pulled up and a uniformed police officer leapt out and handed him an envelope. He scanned the contents. "Okay," he said. "We are a go."

They strode around to the front entrance of the building, where four uniformed officers joined them. Adam marched straight to the security desk showing the receptionist his warrant card. He indicated to one of the officers that he was to remain at the counter.

The glass elevator was waiting on the ground floor and carried everyone to the eighth floor. When the doors opened, they were met by the same efficient office manager as on their earlier visit.

"Can I help you?" she asked, scowling at them and giving the uniformed officers a wary look.

"Avery, right?" Adam asked. She nodded. "Avery, we have a search warrant allowing us access to the firm's servers," Adam said, thrusting the envelope at her. "Can you set my team up on your network, please?"

"I will have to run this by the partners," Avery said, sliding the pages from the envelope and scanning them.

"You can take me to them, and I'll explain," Adam offered.

"Wait here." Avery turned on her heel and hurried down the corridor to an office at the end. She knocked, entered, and closed the door behind her. Several seconds later, the door burst open, and Eduardo Diaz stormed down the corridor towards them, Avery running to keep up with him.

"How dare you? What is the meaning of this?" Diaz shouted,

waving the document in Adam's face.

"Some discrepancies have come to light concerning your Common Reporting Standard filings with Her Majesty's Revenue and Customs," Adam replied.

Diaz's eyes narrowed, and he stood with his hands on his hips. "Avery, get the solicitors on the phone," he said, without taking his eyes off Adam. Adam, in turn, held his ground and didn't flinch.

Diaz pointed to an empty meeting room. "In there."

Nathan and the team filed into the room.

"Gather everything you need," Adam instructed them.

Kat loitered behind Adam to hear what else Diaz had to say.

"Exactly what discrepancies do you think there are with our filings?" Diaz asked through clenched teeth.

"We believe there are several missing client records," Adam said.

Kat watched as Diaz's face and stance relaxed. He took a step back and smiled. "I'm sure that's just a missing file, something that wasn't attached to the return."

Adam pulled a face. "Perhaps. We need access to your client database so that we can check your client numbers against your return. I don't have to remind you that filing a false return with HMRC is a criminal offence."

"Avery, get the Compliance team down here. Now," Diaz ordered.

But it appeared that someone had already made that call, as a tall, slim woman in a sharp black suit stepped from the elevator.

"Tamara, filing discrepancy, sort it," Diaz said. He turned and stalked back to his office.

"So that's Eddie Doors," Nathan muttered to Shamira.

Shamira nodded. "Sparkling personality," she murmured.

"I'm Tamara Marshall, Head of Compliance for CIP. What do you need to see?"

Adam once again explained the filing discrepancy, and Tamara made a phone call bringing one of her team and his laptop into the meeting room.

"Luka should be able to bring up the last returns," Tamara said. Luka's hands were shaking as he logged on to the system. He pushed his glasses back up his nose and glanced around at those assembled.

Nathan slipped into the seat beside him and opened his laptop. "Hi, I'm Nate."

Luka gave him a grateful smile and offered a limp handshake.

"Luka, can you log me on to your network? I will be able to get this done quicker if I can look at your client list at the same time."

Luka glanced at Tamara, who was standing to one side with her arms folded. She nodded. Luka leaned across and typed a long string of code into the browser on Nathan's computer. A 'Welcome to CIP' message displayed on the screen. Nathan navigated the home page and found the link for CIP's Investment Portfolios. He clicked on it, and a login box popped up on the screen.

"Does your warrant allow you to look at that?" Tamara asked. "That's highly sensitive."

Adam ignored her and passed a piece of paper to Nathan, who glanced at it and typed Henry Smyth's email address and the password that Adam's hacker had obtained, into the login box. An incorrect password box appeared. Nathan tried again, using lower case letters, and a new screen displayed four icons, each with a name underneath.

Tamara Marshall took a step towards the door, but Adam nodded to one of the police officers to block her exit.

"This shouldn't take long," he said.

"I don't think your warrant allows you to access our fund information," she said with a note of defiance in her voice. "Or hold me hostage. Unless you intend to arrest me."

"There is no need for the drama, and I think you'll find that it does," Adam replied, and turned back to Nathan. "Kat, explain these to me."

Kat leaned over Nathan's shoulder and read the names of the four funds. "CIP Growth Fund, CIP Balanced Fund, and the CIP Conservative Fund. Those three are CIP's key public offerings. I don't know what that one is," she said, pointing to an icon of a fleur-de-lis. "Fund 4."

"Open it," Adam said.

Nathan clicked the icon, and the trading system opened on his screen. He followed the links for funds under management, which displayed a total of £500,500,250. He let out a low whistle.

"Now, let's look at the client list."

Nathan navigated to the client tab. An alphabetical list of names filled the screen.

"Search on the ones we couldn't find," Adam instructed in a low voice.

Nathan glanced at Kat and typed her father's name into the search box. Philip Munro's name popped up on the screen. Nathan tried the names of Munro's friends who had also invested in CIP, and they were all there. He turned to Adam.

"Can I download this to compare with the other list we have?" he asked.

"No," Tamara said before Adam had a chance to answer.

Adam raised his eyebrows at her. "Court order, remember."

She sighed and folded her arms across her chest.

"Search for those names in the other three funds," Kat said.

They all watched as Nathan continued typing on his keyboard.

"Not in any of them," he said after several minutes of running searches.

There was a tap on the meeting room's glass door, and Avery Willis beckoned to Tamara, who held her hand up indicating that she would have to wait.

"Luka, have you got the latest CRS return?" Tamara asked.

Luka nodded.

"Good, print it, and then you can all go," Tamara said.

"Huh?" Nathan said, leaning forward and peering at his screen as though he couldn't quite believe what he was seeing.

"What?" Kat asked.

Nathan looked up at Tamara. "Do you invest Fund 4 mainly in cash?"

Tamara shook her head. "This is the first I've heard of Fund 4; it must be a demo or test fund, you'd need to talk to Roger."

"Not a test fund if that's the only place that missing names are showing up," Kat murmured.

"Hey, look at this," Nathan said. "Of the five hundred million in the fund, one hundred million is in equities, two hundred million is in bond funds, and only twenty million in cash. By my calculations, that's a gap of one hundred and eighty million. How can that be?"

Adam frowned and glanced at Tamara, who looked perplexed. "That makes no sense; you must be reading the report wrong. Let me look." She squeezed between Adam and

Kat and turned Nathan's laptop towards her. After several minutes she stepped back. "I don't know what to say. Fund 4 must be a test fund."

"Can we follow an individual client's portfolio over the past year?" Kat asked.

"Sure," Tamara replied. Luka jumped up and offered his chair to Tamara, who sat down and started typing on his laptop, producing a report showing the Fund 4 client list.

"That one," Adam pointed, selecting a name at random. "Mr. M. Worthington."

Tamara brought Mr. Worthington's portfolio up on the screen.

"So he first invested two years ago with £200,000. You can see that he is invested in a mixture of shares, bonds and cash. His growth is added each month, here." Tamara tapped the screen. "And eight months later, he added another £250,000. That's his closing value today."

"So today, his portfolio is worth £566,000?" Kat asked, reading off the screen.

Tamara nodded. "Looks that way."

"But how is that even possible? That's like a 12% return each year, and the last two years have been tough across all markets. No one is seeing returns of that magnitude," Kat said.

"The team here contains some of the smartest money managers in Europe," Tamara said. "And there will have been several derivative products working in the background to hedge the currency and credit exposures."

"What are the returns like in your other funds over that time period?" Adam asked.

"Of course, you can't compare across our funds, because

they are all made up of a wide variety of different investments," Tamara said.

"Humour me," Adam said. "Let's look at the CIP Growth Fund."

Tamara turned back to the screen and ran a summary performance report for the CIP Growth Fund. The return each year for the last three years was a modest five to six percent.

"That's more what I'd expect to see," Kat said. "Can we compare total funds under management to the sum of each component for this fund?"

Tamara ran another report and brought it up on the screen. The total was equal to the sum of the component investments.

"Now that's also what I'd expect to see," Kat said. "Tamara, can you run that report for each of the other funds?"

Tamara nodded and ran the reports. The Balanced and the Conservative Funds produced the same result, but when she reproduced the report for Fund 4, the gap of one hundred and eighty million was still there.

Adam looked at Kat and frowned. "What are we missing?"

Tamara, thinking the question directed at her, sat back in her chair. "I don't know, but I have to agree, this is odd. As I said, it must be a demo fund for testing out new strategies. Even so, it should add up. I'll have tech support look into it; something can't be calculated correctly in the background."

"It's not a test fund; it's live. We know of several individuals who have investment portfolios with CIP, whose names only appear on the Fund 4 client list," Kat said.

"Can I check one of them?" Tamara asked.

Kat glanced at Adam, who nodded.

"Try Philip Munro, portfolio number F4-06030119," Kat

said.

"Our portfolio numbers don't start with F4," Tamara said.

"This particular portfolio does. Can you try it?"

Tamara nodded and typed in the number. Philip Munro's portfolio filled the screen. Kat handed her phone, open to a copy of her father's report, to Tamara.

Tamara studied the two screens for a moment. "Did you get this from Philip Munro?" she asked.

"Yes."

"He must be in one of the other funds," Tamara said. "Let me show you."

Adam nodded.

They watched as Tamara opened up each of CIP's other funds and searched on Philip Munro's name. There were no results.

Tamara's hands flew to her mouth. "How is this possible?"

"What happens if, say, Mr. Munro wants to withdraw his funds?" Adam asked.

"He puts a call into his broker, who places the sale orders, and once they have settled, the funds are deposited into his nominated bank account," Tamara said.

Adam nodded. "What happens if everyone invested in Fund 4 decides they want their money back today? Even if you sell all of the shares and bonds, there won't be enough cash to pay everyone out."

Kat gasped and shook her head as her eyes rose to meet Adam's.

"Don't tell me this is one giant Ponzi scheme?"

Chapter 18

The door to the meeting room was flung open, and Roger Chen strode in with a broad smile that didn't quite reach his eyes.

"Hello, I hear we've missed something on one of our filings," he said.

"Yes, the client compliance information for Fund 4 seems to have been missed for starters," Kat said.

The smile fell from Chen's face. "Fund 4? How do you know about that?"

"What is Fund 4, exactly?" Adam asked.

"It's our private equity venture capital fund. Mainly high net worth investors who are looking for a little more risk," Chen said.

"That's the first I've heard of it," Tamara said.

"Surely, you wouldn't put retirees in a fund such as that?" Kat asked.

Chen's mobile rang. He pulled it from his pocket and glanced at the screen. The colour drained from his face, and beads of sweat broke out on his brow. "You'll have to excuse me for a moment, I need to take this call," he said, backing out of the room and hurrying towards his office.

"Tamara, can you get Diaz to come and explain Fund 4 to

us?" Adam asked.

"Sure," she said, pushing back from the desk and following Chen down the corridor towards the executive offices.

Adam put a call through to DI Greenwood. "I think you need to get over to CIP; we've found something odd. The missing clients appear to be invested in a fund that very few people know much about, which is looking increasingly like a Ponzi scheme."

He held his phone away from his ear as a loud curse came down the line.

Tamara walked back into the room. "I'm sorry, but it looks as though Diaz has left for lunch."

Adam glanced at his watch. "Better get Mr. Chen back, then."

They watched through the glass walls of the meeting room as Tamara knocked on Chen's closed office door. There must have been no reply because she rapped her knuckles against the wood a second time. After several knocks, she tried the handle, but the door was locked.

She rushed towards the office manager's cubicle near the elevator. "Avery, can I have the key to Chen's office? Quickly," Tamara said.

Adam hurried from the meeting room to join her. "What's wrong?"

"He's not answering, but I saw him go in there. He has heart problems..." she trailed off.

Avery produced a set of keys with some reluctance and led them back down the corridor to Chen's office. Kat followed and watched as Avery knocked on the door and called out Roger's name. There was still no reply.

Kat felt a shiver of discomfort.

"Turn the key," Adam instructed. "But let me open the door. Step back, please."

Avery did as instructed and moved aside for Adam. He turned the handle and eased the door open.

"Mr. Chen, are you okay?" he called. There was still no reply.

Adam stood to one side of the door frame and pushed the door open with his foot. "Roger?" He peered into the office. It was empty. He moved inside, checking behind the door and under the desk.

"He can't have left, or we'd have seen him," Tamara said, following Adam into the room.

"What is through these two doors?" Adam asked.

"Roger's bathroom and private elevator," Avery replied from the doorway.

"What?"

Adam opened the bathroom door to find the room empty. He turned his attention to the other door. He swung it open to reveal a closed pair of steel elevator doors. The illuminated red digit above the door indicated that the elevator was travelling past level G to B1.

"B1," Adam asked, poking at the call button with his index finger.

"It's the senior manager's parking garage."

"I know." Adam stuck his head back out into the corridor and called to one of the uniformed officers. "Get your mate in reception to run down the stairs to B1 to see if they can stop Roger leaving. What does he drive?"

"Silver Mercedes," Avery replied.

"Kat, you're with me. Nathan, wait here with Tamara until DI Greenwood and his team arrive and take them through what you've found." Adam issued instructions as he ran towards the main set of elevators. The glass doors were open. Adam and Kat descended to the ground floor, where they exited at a run.

"Why are we not going to the basement?" Kat called, jogging to keep up with him as he burst through the main doors and out onto the street.

"Because the exit to the garage is down the side street here," he replied as they rounded the corner into the narrow lane where Adam had left his car. A silver Mercedes bounced up a ramp and crossed the footpath in front of them at speed.

"Come on," Adam said, unlocking his car, throwing himself in the driver's seat and sliding his mobile into a phone holder attached to the dashboard. Kat had only just closed her door as he accelerated away, the tires swishing on the wet road. A light drizzle had started to fall while they were in the building. Adam took the corner at speed. Up ahead, they could see the silver Mercedes half a block in front.

Adam tapped the screen of his phone before he spoke. "Following a late model silver Mercedes, rego begins RXC 4, west along London Wall, require immediate support. The driver is Roger Chen."

A few seconds later they heard a muffled voice announce, "All units near London Wall, an unmarked officer in pursuit of a silver Mercedes registration beginning Romeo X-ray Charlie number 4 requires immediate assistance." Adam tapped end on the call.

Kat pulled the seatbelt across her body, clicking it into place, and held on to the door as Adam took a sharp left onto Princes Street. Dark clouds filled the sky overhead, and the rain began to fall again in soft sheets.

"Where's he going?" Kat asked.

"I think he's going to cross the river," Adam said. "Hold tight, Kat."

Kat took a deep breath, her heart racing, and concentrated on the road in front of them. They heard the honking of horns and screech of tires at the intersection ahead of them where the ancient thoroughfare of Cornhill met Cheapside. They slowed as they passed the imposing Bank of England building. The Mercedes cleared the intersection, but Adam had to weave his way through the traffic.

Adam glanced sideways at her. "You okay?"

She nodded.

Adam tapped his phone and spoke again. "In pursuit on King William Street; heading towards London Bridge."

Kat could hear several sirens coming closer as they raced past the entrance to Bank Underground station. The narrow road widened as they crossed the end of Cannon Street and drove by a building site with massive cranes lifting long pieces of steel into place. The Monument column topped with a flame of remembrance for the Great Fire of London stood proud to their left.

"We're catching him," Adam said. "Look."

The Mercedes had slowed several cars ahead. Adam leaned on his horn, and the vehicles pulled to the side. Coming towards them from the other side of the bridge were three police cars with their lights flashing and sirens ringing out. All of a sudden, the Mercedes accelerated and mounted the footpath, scattering pedestrians who turned and ran for their lives. The car hit the low concrete wall at the edge of the bridge. The driver's door opened, and a dishevelled Roger Chen leapt out. He climbed onto the railing and held his arms out as if he were about to fly.

Adam cursed and braked hard. He jumped from the car before it had come to a complete stop.

"Roger, no," he shouted.

Roger turned to look at him. "They will kill me too," he said and stepped off the railing and tumbled into the murky Thames below. He hit the water on his back and sank from view.

Adam tore off his jacket, throwing it at Kat, and ran for the steps at the end of the bridge. He raced down the stairs, kicked off his shoes and dived into the river, swimming towards the point where Roger had entered the water.

A police car screeched to a stop behind Kat and two officers joined her on the bridge, looking down into the water. There was no sign of either Roger Chen or Adam in the dark swirling river.

"Who's the jumper?" one of the officers asked.

"An investment fund manager – DS Jackson has gone in after him," Kat said.

The officer nodded. "I've radioed; the police launch is coming."

"They won't get here soon enough," Kat said, looking back at the water as Adam surfaced and turned in a circle, treading the water. Across the river, the shining glass structure of The Shard rose to a dramatic pointed peak dominating the surroundings. There was no sign of Roger Chen, only a mass of ripples breaking the water's surface. Adam dived again, until finally, as Kat was beginning to worry, he reemerged. He swam back towards the river bank. She ran along the footpath and down the steps to meet him.

An officer helped Adam over the low wall beside a boat-tethering pylon. He collapsed on the river path, shivering and panting. A second officer arrived with a silver hypothermia blanket and wrapped it around Adam's shoulders.

Kat crouched down beside him. "You did all you could," she said, resting her hand on his arm.

"I couldn't see anything below the surface. I didn't even know if I was looking in the right place," Adam said, shaking his head. "Why did he have to go and do that? We could have protected him."

* * *

Adam had changed into a dry police tracksuit, and after lengthy discussions with the river police, followed by a long telephone conversation with DI Greenwood, he and Kat were free to go. A police launch continued scouring the river around the bridge and put divers down, but there was no sign of Roger Chen's body.

"My flat is just across the river from here," Adam said. "I need to get out of these attractive borrowed clothes. Do you want to come, and I'll update you on what Greenwood said."

Kat nodded. "Okay. I hope you've got something hot to drink. I'm frozen."

"I think I can manage that. Come on."

Adam's flat was in an apartment building off Pickford's Lane.

"It's not actually my flat," he said as they climbed the stairs. "I'm house-sitting for a while."

Adam unlocked a door on the third floor.

"Excuse the mess. I don't often have company," he said, scooping newspapers into a pile and moving them from one of two armchairs to the coffee table. "Have a seat while I get changed." He disappeared through a doorway on the far side of the room. Kat heard the sound of running water as Adam turned on the shower.

The flat was tiny and dark. Kat walked over to the small window in the lounge and looked out. The view was of the brick wall of the apartment block opposite. She could just make out a sliver of the Thames through a gap in the buildings. The real estate advertisements would probably advertise this flat with a river view, she thought. Turning her back, she wandered into the little kitchen. A window above the sink looked down into a courtyard. The rain had begun to fall in earnest. Kat filled the kettle with water and switched it on. She opened up the cupboards above the bench until she found two mugs and popped a tea bag in each from a canister on the counter.

"That's better," Adam said, walking back into the room dressed in clean jeans and a white t-shirt. His hair was damp and combed back off his forehead. "Here, let me make that. How do you have it?"

"Black," Kat replied, acutely aware of his proximity in the small space.

"I can't believe he did that. Chen, I mean," Adam said, pouring the boiling water into the cups and jiggling the tea bags up and down with a spoon, before tossing them in the sink and handing Kat a cup. Their fingertips touched, and Kat jerked her hand away.

"I know. That was a fairly extreme response when he didn't even know what we'd found," Kat replied.

"Oh, I think he knew what we would eventually find," Adam said. "But I don't think it was us he was concerned about; he was terrified of someone else. You saw the look on his face. He figured he was dead already."

"Then why not let us help him?"

"I dunno."

Adam took a sip and sighed. "Tea was a good idea; that water was cold."

"You were very brave to go in after him. The Thames is a dangerous stretch of water," Kat said.

"I was stupid. I couldn't believe that Chen had been pushed to that point so quickly, and I didn't stop to think," Adam said.

"That's honest."

Adam shrugged as his phone rang. Kat leaned against the bench and listened as Adam spoke with DI Greenwood again. Ending the call, he put the phone back in his pocket.

"They've secured the CIP office for tonight. Nathan is still there with our team trawling through the data. You and I are to go straight there in the morning."

"What about Mary McFarlane and Eduardo Diaz?"

"Greenwood is trying to locate them."

"It'll be interesting to hear what they have to say."

Adam nodded in agreement. They were silent for a few moments sipping their drinks.

"Kat."

"Adam."

They spoke over one another.

Kat blushed. "You go."

"I was going to ask if you were okay after last night. I didn't get a chance to ask today," Adam said. "Have you talked with anyone about your accident?"

Kat took a deep breath and exhaled slowly. "I'm so sorry that you had to see that. My life is complicated, Adam. I'm good at my job, and that's all that should matter to you." She put her cup on the bench.

Adam studied her. "We all have complications, Kat."

"We're not doing this," Kat said. "I'm fine, really."

"Except, when you're not," he said.

Kat pushed off the bench and took a step towards the door. "We're not having this conversation. I should go."

Adam straightened to let her past. She made the mistake of looking into his face. Beyond his steely gaze, she could see care and concern.

"Do you always run away when someone tries to help you?" he asked.

Kat cleared her throat. "I don't need any help." She lifted her chin defiantly and was met with his lips on hers in a brief tender kiss.

"Okay, then." Adam gazed at her for a moment before cupping her face with his hands and kissing her again. Kat moved closer to him and slipped one hand behind his head, resting the other on his chest. They kissed for a long moment before Kat pulled back.

"No," she said, pushing away from him and bolting towards the door. She pulled it open and glanced back. Adam was leaning against the bench, his expression blank.

Kat slammed the door behind her and raced down the stairs to the street. The word 'no' pounded through her head with every step.

Chapter 19

Adam didn't look up when Kat arrived at the CIP conference room on the eighth floor the next morning. He was standing next to Nathan, Charles Stephenson, and DI Greenwood, reviewing a series of printouts spread across the boardroom table.

"Hey, Kat," Nathan said. He looked tired but elated.

"Good morning. How's it going?" she replied.

"Okay. It's going to take days to unravel this, but you were right, it has all the hallmarks of a Ponzi scheme," Nathan replied.

"What's a Ponzi scheme?" a young uniformed officer asked, looking up from the paper files that he was recording on an evidence log.

All heads turned in his direction, and he blushed scarlet. "Sorry, I'm new to this."

Kat smiled at him as she dropped her bag on a chair and removed her raincoat. "It's a good question. Frauds such as this are named after an American called Charles Ponzi. He ran an investment scheme in the United States early in the twentieth century, where he paid spectacular profits to early investors using the funds invested by later investors. The later investors, attracted by the returns that the previous investors were getting, flocked to the scheme. It's all okay, so long as people keep investing. But if they all want their money back at the same time, it collapses. Hence the name Ponzi scheme, although you also hear them called pyramid schemes.

"The problem is that they are difficult to spot until things start to go wrong. In the early stages, everyone is happy, since they are getting good returns. It is only when the scheme struggles to bring in new investors that the cracks start to show."

"A house of cards, then?" the young man said.

"Exactly, there have been a number over the years. More recently, during the global financial crisis, a highly successful American financier called Bernie Madoff had a similar fraud exposed."

The young officer looked blank.

"Before your time, perhaps," Kat said.

"So, did you manage to get hold of the other two partners?" she asked the others.

DI Greenwood nodded. "Yes, they're with their lawyers now. We're meeting with them at eleven a.m. They're claiming to be as surprised as we were about the discovery. Apparently, according to them, this is something that Smyth and Chen dreamed up."

"Really? I find it hard to believe that the other partners wouldn't know," Kat said.

"Me too, but we will find out more when we meet them."

"Has Chen's body turned up?"

DI Greenwood shook his head.

Stephenson stepped away from the table and took Kat's arm, moving her to one side of the room.

"I know that your father has investments mixed up in this,"

he said.

Kat nodded.

"I hope you haven't said anything to him?" Stephenson looked at her over his glasses. "This has to be of the highest confidentiality until we can confirm our suspicions."

Kat shook her head. "No, of course not, I understand the implications, better than most. Although I admit, I am concerned for him."

Stephenson stroked his chin. "Are you going to be able to remain impartial working on this?"

"Yes, I think I have a strong incentive to help get to the bottom of this."

Stephenson studied her. "Okay, but if you feel compromised, you must let me know."

* * *

It was a long day, trawling through documents, computer networks, and bank accounts. Still, a pattern began to emerge that proved their suspicions. The team had lunch delivered to the boardroom and kept working, being careful to document everything.

After a lengthy discussion with the remaining CIP partners and their legal team, DI Greenwood and Stephenson returned to the meeting room mid-afternoon.

"McFarlane and Diaz maintain their shock at the discovery of this scheme. It does appear that Chen held most of the client liaison responsibilities in the business. This perhaps goes some way to support their assertions that they did not know that some new clients were onboarded into a Ponzi scheme," DI Greenwood said. "They're offering whatever assistance we need."

"I don't think I need to reiterate the absolute requirement that this is kept out of the public domain until we can establish the facts of what went on here. For the moment, the police presence is down to the untimely deaths of two of the firm's principals." DI Greenwood looked around the assembled team. "Is that clear?"

Murmurs of 'yes, sir,' echoed around the room.

"Right. I believe that we've quarantined the Fund 4 part of CIPs network from the rest of their systems, so we can continue our investigations without disrupting the firm's legitimate business." Greenwood looked to one of the Financial Crimes Unit technical analysts, who nodded his agreement.

"We've also isolated the bank account that Fund 4 is using," the analyst added.

"Has it been frozen?" Kat asked.

"No, we've taken the call to leave it alone for a day or two and monitor any activity," Greenwood said. "As the two partners purportedly running the scheme are dead, I expect there will be no activity."

"I think that's wise," Kat agreed. "The source of several large deposits going back over the last three years is unclear. They appear to be from clients investing in the scheme. Still, there's no corresponding investment portfolio matching either the amounts or the dates. We'll need to dig deeper."

"Let me know as soon as you find anything," Greenwood said. "I'm going to check in with Adam. His team is now looking into Chen's death too."

"We'll move the files and documents relating to Fund 4 to the Forensic Accounting Associates office at the end of today, and we'll continue to build the case from there," Stevenson said.

***

The King's Arms had been serving patrons for two hundred years, according to the legend above the door. They found an empty wooden table by the front window and sat down. Nathan returned from the bar with a pint of beer and two bottles of cider. He had three laminated menus tucked under his arm.

"Cheers, Nate," Shamira said, taking a long swallow from her bottle. Nate tapped his pint glass against the side of Kat's bottle.

"They've got blackboard specials too," he said. "I don't know about you, but I'm starving."

"You're always starving," Shamira said, laughing.

"What can I say? I'm a growing lad," Nate replied.

"I don't know where you put it all. If I ate like you, I'd have to go to the gym every single day," Kat said.

"Speaking of gyms, I hear Adam met Marco the other night. You didn't tell us that," Nate said.

"Nothing to tell," she replied.

"Really? So what was so important that Adam had to rush to see you after hours?" Shamira gave her a sly look.

Kat leaned forward. The other two followed suit, their expressions expectant. "I thought we weren't talking shop tonight," she said.

Shamira's sly look morphed into an exasperated one. "When your love life gets tied up with work, it's hard not to."

"When did we start talking about my love life? I don't have a love life, remember?"

"Oh come on. We've seen the way you two dance around one another. You hardly looked at each other today. Something's happened," Nate said.

"Nothing's happened, so please let's change the subject," Kat pleaded. "You're beginning to sound like my mother, who is forever trying to set me up with eligible dates."

"She's right about one thing; you really should date more," Shamira said. "Not all guys are like Gabe."

"Honestly, most are only interested until they see my hand, or they want to tell their mates that they've slept with a freak," she said, her voice laced with bitterness.

"Oh, I didn't realise that this was a pity party. Look at me, I'm so unlovable with my missing hand," Nate said.

Kat raised her eyes and glared at him.

"He does have a point. You're smart, funny, and gorgeous," Shamira said. "You just don't give any guy a chance to get close to you."

"Yeah, well, the last time I did, it didn't go so well for me," Kat replied, waving her prosthetic hand.

"That was more than two years ago. It's time to move on, sweetie," Shamira said.

"I have." Kat was indignant. "I've accomplished so much. I can do almost anything again. I'm working in my chosen field, I have a great flat and awesome friends, well, when they're not being arses."

"Friends who don't care about your missing hand," Nate said. "Everyone has their issues, look at me, I'm twenty-eight, gay and I still haven't told my dad. You think you've got problems?"

Kat felt the corners of her mouth twitch. "Okay, point taken."

"So no more of that poor me, okay?" Nate reached across the sticky bar table and squeezed her prosthetic hand.

Kat nodded and squeezed back. "It's fine, really. Besides, I have my fit Italian gym instructor to scratch any itch without the usual annoying complications," she said with a laugh.

"Mmm…" Shamira sounded unconvinced.

"Now, enough about me. What about you, Nate? How are things going with that guy from the Bank of England?" Kat asked.

Nathan waved his hand in the air. "Moved on from him. Too boring, only interested in working."

"So you're single again?"

"Yup."

Shamira raised her bottle. "A toast then, to the joys of being single." They tapped their glasses.

Kat watched as Shamira's bottle paused halfway to her mouth, and her eyes widened, looking over Kat's shoulder.

"What?" she asked, starting to turn, following her friend's gaze.

"Don't look now, but our resident detective has just walked in with a stunning blonde in tow," Shamira said.

Kat swivelled in her seat. Her eyes met Adam's as he scanned the room. Nate was right, they had avoided each other all day, and it was a jolt to see his unguarded gaze directed at her. He held her eyes for several seconds before steering his companion to the opposite end of the pub. Kat's eyes followed them. Adam's friend was tall and willowy, dressed in a tight summer dress and white stilettos. She had an expensive-looking handbag draped over her arm.

Kat turned back to find her friends watching her with undisguised interest.

"And what exactly was that look?" Nate asked

"And why didn't he come over and say hello?" Shamira said.

"Who knows? The next round is on me. Are you ready to order dinner?" Kat asked, pushing her chair back and standing.

* * *

Kat received an email from DI Greenwood mid-morning containing the written statements from the legal team that Mary McFarlane and Eduardo Diaz had retained. She clicked open the attachment and gasped as she recognised the letterhead.

"What is it, Kat?" Shamira leaned across.

"Look who's representing the remaining CIP partners," she whispered.

"Isn't that Gabe's father's firm?" Shamira squinted, trying to read the logo. "Huntly-Tait and Partners."

Kat nodded.

"Why are you whispering?" Shamira asked.

"Because something strange is going on at CIP, and now Gabe's father is involved."

"Just because his firm is involved, it doesn't mean that he is." Shamira's voice was gentle.

"I know, but…"

Shamira looked concerned. "He might be a cold-hearted man, but he gets huge respect in the City. It makes sense that they'd want a top law firm on board."

Kat sighed. "I know. I just wish I could remember what happened before we drove away from the house that night. I think he was there, and I was scared and couldn't wait to leave, but I can't remember why."

"But it wasn't necessarily him you were afraid of," Shamira said. "You were never scared of him before that night."

"I know, but I just have this feeling about him. He couldn't wait to pay me off after the accident and get me out of Gabe's life. And I know it wasn't that way before that night. I suspect that threatening note I got the other day was from him, although I can't prove it." Kat looked back at the screen, staring at the firm's name.

"Why would he send you a threatening note? What have you been doing?"

"Nothing really, just keeping an eye on him."

Shamira gave her a gentle smile. "Kat, you have to let it go. You might have to accept that you may never know what happened that night."

Chapter 20

Kat closed the door and leaned against it. In her rush, she'd forgotten her workout gear that morning, so she'd come home to get it on her way to the gym. She dropped her keys on the hall table and carried a single bag of groceries into the kitchen.

Setting the bag down on the kitchen counter, Kat spun around. Something was off, and where was Zelda? She slipped her feet out of her heels and tiptoed towards the bedroom.

Her room looked the same as she'd left it that morning. The bed was made, and the previous day's clothes were either put away or in the washing hamper. She walked into her wardrobe and studied the hangers and drawers. Nothing was obviously out of place, yet something was amiss. She opened the top drawer and gasped. Her neatly arranged underwear was a mess. In the next drawer, Kat usually rolled her gym gear and arranged it in neat rows by colour. Now her black leggings weren't together, and her blue and green workout tops were scrunched up and pushed to the back. They had been disturbed. The bottom drawer was the same, her pyjamas no longer folded together but instead hastily shoved in. She shivered, feeling a trickle of sweat run down her back. She rushed to her bedside cabinet, pulling open the drawer.

The accessories for her prosthesis; anti-chafing cream, socks, and gloves were jumbled. Someone had been in the apartment and had rummaged through her stuff.

Kat whirled around as she sensed movement behind her. Zelda crept out from the back corner of the wardrobe and looked up at her, giving a plaintive meow.

"Oh, Zelda." Kat scooped her up and nuzzled her. Zelda snuggled into Kat's neck and started purring. "Poor baby, were you frightened? Who was here?"

A creaking sound followed by a soft click sounded from somewhere in the flat. Kat froze for an instant before placing Zelda onto the bed and tiptoeing to the door. She wrapped her fingers around the handle of her brother's old cricket bat, leaning against the wall beside the door ready for an instance such as this. She eased herself through the doorway and into the hall, pausing to listen. Silence. She crept towards her study. The door was ajar. Adjusting her grip on the bat, she flung the door wide open, so that it hit the doorstop. Apart from the furnishings, the room was empty. She continued along the hallway to where it widened into the living area.

Kat's breathing was shallow, and her heart raced as her eyes scanned the room. Empty also. She peered over the counter into the kitchen; nowhere for anyone to hide. Spinning around, she moved into the entrance hall. The front door was dead-bolted.

Relaxing her grip on the bat, she returned to the living room. She must have been hearing things. Whoever had been there was gone now. Zelda padded along the hallway and stopped at her feet, looking up expectantly before trotting over to the French doors and pushing through the cat flap. She was halfway through when the door sprang open, tipping her unceremoniously onto the balcony. She righted herself and looked indignant.

Kat stared, not comprehending what she was seeing. She kept the door to her little balcony locked at all times when she wasn't home and often when she was. She walked to the door and pushed it open further. The pane of glass beside the door handle lay in jagged broken pieces on the floor at her feet. The hole was enough for a hand to reach through and turn the key. Kat stepped over the broken glass and onto the balcony. She hurried to the edge and looked over. In the street below, two orange-vested workmen were loading a retractable ladder onto the roof of a van with a telecommunications company logo on the side. Kat watched as they climbed in and drove away. The van turned the corner and was away before she thought to take note of the registration plate.

Kat turned and rushed back inside, leaving the door open. She checked her study. Her laptop was sitting in its usual position, but the screen was illuminated, rather than powered down, which was how she usually left it. She turned to the cupboard and rattled the handle. It was still locked. She retrieved the key from the second drawer of the desk and unlocked it, holding her breath as she opened the doors. A shelf of ring binders containing her personal financial information didn't appear to have been disturbed, and the panel on the inside of the door looked untouched. She lifted off the false plywood cover and leaned it against the wall, revealing a pinboard underneath covered in photos, newspaper clippings, and yellow post-it notes. It didn't appear to have been discovered. She breathed a sigh of relief, replaced the door inset, and closed the cupboard.

She jumped as Zelda curled around her legs. She scooped

her up and returned to the kitchen. Before she could second guess herself, she grabbed her phone and searched up Adam's number. He answered on the third ring, speaking above traffic noise and sounding out of breath, as though he was out running.

"Kat."

"Detective Jackson, I'd like to report a break-in."

"Where? At yours? Are you okay?"

"Yeah."

"Don't touch anything; I'll be there shortly."

* * *

There was a loud knock at the door. Kat peered through the peephole before unlocking the door and letting Adam into her flat. His hair was damp, as though he'd recently showered.

"Your neighbour let me in the main door," he said, studying the front door locks. "These don't look like they were forced." He followed Kat through into the living room. "What was taken?"

"That's the thing. I don't think it was a burglary. Nothing's missing, but my belongings have been disturbed," Kat said.

Adam looked around. "Have you tidied up? I thought I said not to touch anything."

Kat shook her head. "I haven't. They didn't leave a mess, but things are not as I left them. I think maybe I interrupted them."

Adam studied her for a moment. "Show me."

Kat hesitated. "Don't judge me, okay? I'm fairly, ah, organised."

Adam raised his eyebrows. "Okay."

155

"My bookshelf," she said, pointing behind him. "Colour-coded by spine until I got home today. Now look."

Adam perused the neat and tidy four-shelf bookcase containing a mixture of fiction, business, and history titles. The rainbow pattern Kat usually arranged the book spines into was now just a patchwork of colour. He crouched down and picked up a leaf from the floor. Zelda trotted towards him and rubbed against his legs. Adam gave her a scratch behind the ears and stood.

"I did notice your rainbow bookshelf the other night," he said. "What else?"

"This way." She led him to her bedroom and into the walk-in wardrobe. "The hangers are in a different position, and the drawers rifled through."

"May I?" She nodded. Adam opened each drawer in turn and turned to her with a question in his eyes.

"I have a certain way of folding my clothes, and that's not it," she said. "And they've been through my bedside cabinets, where I keep my prosthesis gear." She let out a big sigh and wrapped her arms across her body. "I feel violated."

"And they didn't take anything?"

"Not that I can see."

"What about your office?"

"They've been through there too. My laptop is on, and I leave it powered down. I think perhaps that's where someone was hiding when I arrived home, so they didn't get to go through anything."

"You think they were still here?"

Kat shrugged. "I thought I heard something, but I'm not sure."

Adam followed Kat through the bedroom, back into the

living room and over to the French doors leading to the balcony.

"That's how they got in," Kat said. "And out, I believe."

"What?" Adam asked.

"They broke the glass and got the key," she said, indicating towards the broken pane of glass. "Two workmen were loading a ladder onto a van when I realised what had happened and looked over the edge. They drove away before I thought to get the reg."

Adam pulled his phone from his pocket.

"DS Adam Jackson, I'd like to report a break-in."

Kat listened as he gave her address and details to the dispatcher.

"Is there any point? They'll never find them, and it doesn't look like they've taken anything," Kat said once he'd ended the call.

"There will be an officer around first thing tomorrow to get the details. Who do you think would want to break in, go through your things so carefully…"

"Not all that carefully," Kat interrupted.

"Carefully, if they didn't understand your systems," Adam said. "Burglars don't normally take the time to hide their tracks. They want to get in and out as quickly as possible. Everything has been replaced, and nothing was taken. In these situations, the place is usually ransacked. Have you checked the kitchen?"

Kat shook her head as she walked over the bench and opened the overhead cupboards. "Yeah, things have been moved."

"Who else has keys?"

"Just my parents. I changed the locks when I bought the flat and put on the second deadbolt. They are supposed to be difficult to pick."

"You own this flat?" Adam said, surprised. He didn't think a twenty-something accountant's salary would afford a Mayfair apartment.

Kat nodded correctly interpreting his look of surprise. "It's surprising what a hand will buy you. Now, I don't know about you, but I could do with a drink." She reached up into the cupboard above the refrigerator and lifted down a bottle of gin. She waved it at Adam, who nodded.

"Does the building have security cameras?" he asked.

Kat paused mixing their drinks and nodded. "Yeah, actually it does. I'll call the manager." She added ice and tonic to his drink, handing it to him before walking into the small office. She returned a minute later.

"He will have the camera footage ready for the police when they come tomorrow, although it just covers the front entrance," she said.

"What would someone be looking for, Kat?" Adam asked, passing her drink.

Kat didn't meet his eye. "I dunno." She dropped down onto the sofa and pulled her legs beneath her.

"You sure?" Adam sat opposite her in the armchair. Zelda leapt up onto his lap and turned a full circle before settling down, neatly tucking her paws beneath her and gazing across at Kat. "Do you bring work home?"

Kat shook her head. "No, never. Anything confidential has to remain at the office."

"What else have you been working on?"

"I just finished two reviews which are heading to court, and I'm about to look into a suspected embezzlement, but nothing controversial."

"Mmm…" Adam frowned.

"This was a brazen break-in," Kat said. "Two stories up in broad daylight. Someone must have seen something. I'm going to call on my neighbours."

"I'll fix this up," Adam said.

"Don't we have to leave it for the police?"

Adam looked at her. "What am I?"

"Oh yeah, how could I forget?" She shot him a grin as he pulled out his mobile and snapped a few photos.

When Kat returned fifteen minutes later, Adam had picked up the broken glass and taped a piece of cardboard, from an empty cereal box he'd found in her recycling bin, over the hole. He was sitting back down on the sofa finishing his drink.

"Thank you. You didn't have to do all that," Kat said.

"It's no problem. What did your neighbours say?"

"The old lady across from me didn't hear a thing. But the guy who lives below had a sick day today. He said that a telecom's van was parked outside late afternoon, with technicians on ladders on the outside of the building."

"That's how they got onto your balcony then," Adam said.

Kat nodded.

"This wasn't random, Kat. Are you sure that you can't think of anything that you have that someone wants?" Adam watched her expression close down.

"No."

"Do you want me to stay here tonight in case they come back?"

"No."

"Can you call someone? Shamira?"

"I'll be fine. Whoever it was could have confronted me earlier, but they didn't, so I don't think they'll come back."

Adam frowned and looked thoughtful.

Chapter 21

Adam jogged down the front steps of Kat's building and across the road to his car. But instead of getting in, he kept walking to the end of the block. He took a turn around the square, checking in every parked car. They were all unoccupied. He lifted his gaze to the buildings in the neighbouring streets and shook his head. She could be under surveillance from any window, and he'd have no idea. He kicked at a stone and swore under his breath.

Stopping at a 7-Eleven, he purchased a bottle of water, several bananas, and a large packet of crisps. He returned to his car, slid in the front passenger side and lowered the seat's angle. He reached into the back and grabbed a blanket. He was in for a long night, might as well be comfortable.

Once settled, he checked his watch. Ten p.m. Not too late to update his colleague.

DI Greenwood sounded tired when he answered.

"Kat Munro disturbed an intruder at her flat this evening. He was partway through searching for something when she arrived home. It looks professional, they had telco technicians working on her building, and it appears he got in through the balcony doors," Adam said.

"Is she okay?"

"She's putting on a brave face, but she's shaken."

"What did they take?"

"Well, that's just it. Nothing. The intruder went through everything and put it back nicely, just not to her standards."

"What were they looking for?"

"I don't know, but I think she does, and she's not letting on."

"What do you mean?"

"Just that she was very cagey."

"Mmm… to do with CIP?"

"I don't know. Her father is involved, so perhaps."

"Where are you now, Adam?" Greenwood asked, suppressing a yawn.

"In my car, outside her flat."

"I guess you'll ignore me if I tell you to go home?"

Adam laughed then became serious. "I want to be here if someone returns tonight, and I'm also interested in seeing what she does next."

"Fair enough. I'll also have a unit swing by throughout the night," Greenwood said.

"Thanks."

* * *

Kat climbed the wide carpeted staircase, the heels of her shoes sinking into the deep pile on the landing. She glanced up at the formal portrait of a man dressed in what she guessed was eighteenth-century clothing and shivered. His stern gaze seemed to follow her. She hurried to the bathroom, bobbing in time to the music pounding through the ceiling from the rooms below. Even in the bathroom, the music was audible. Kat rushed to relieve herself and wash her hands. If she wasn't quick, Gabe would most likely leave without her, and she felt like a break from the party.

When she pushed open the door back into the hallway, she heard angry, raised voices coming from a room on the far side of the staircase. Curious, she crept along past the top of the stairs. One voice rose above the others, followed by a loud slap and a groan. Kat froze, knowing that she should go downstairs and through the front door to where Gabe would be waiting with the car, but instead, something propelled her towards the voices.

She'd never been in this part of the house. It was the domain of Gabe's father and housed his office and library. The door to the office was ajar, and a shaft of light cut across the hallway.

"I've told you, I don't know what you're talking about," a muffled voice said.

"And I don't believe you."

Kat gasped. She knew that voice. She crept towards the opening and peeked inside. A man, his face bruised and bloodied with one eye almost swollen shut, sat tied to a chair. Several fingers on each hand looked to be at odd angles. Two men Kat had never seen before stood either side of him. One had a gun pointed at the ground. Kat slapped a hand across her mouth to stop herself crying out, as Gabe's father strode into view.

"This is your last chance. Who sent you? Who are you working for?"

"No one. I'm not who you think I am."

"Then what were you doing trespassing on my property?"

There was a crackling sound as the men all stepped back, and Kat realised that the chair was sitting in the middle of a large piece of heavy polythene.

"It's a public footpath," the man said. "I was out for a ramble."

"In the middle of the night?"

Kat stepped backwards until she reached the landing. She kicked off her shoes and scooped them up in a single motion before she bolted down the staircase and across the marble foyer.

"Hey, you there. Stop." The voice came from above.

Kat pulled open the heavy front door and kept moving.

"Run," she screamed. "Run."

She could hear footsteps pounding rhythmically behind her—bang, bang.

Kat bolted upright. The room was dark, bedsheets twisted. Her breathing was coming in uneven gulps, and her heart was racing.

The banging continued, followed by someone calling her name. She looked at the bedside clock; 4:30 a.m. The knocking sounded again. Kat leapt out of bed and grabbed the cricket bat she had left beside the wall the night before and rushed through her apartment, turning on the lights as she went.

"Kat, it's me. Let me in." Adam called from the other side of the door.

Kat peered through the peephole before unlocking the deadbolts and opening the door.

"Are you okay? You were shouting," he said, stepping inside and closing the door behind him.

"What are you doing here?" she asked.

"Why were you screaming?"

Kat shook her head. "I had a nightmare, that's all. You can go. I don't need your help."

Adam took the cricket bat out of her hand and leaned it

against the wall. Kat looked wild. Her hair was messy and her pyjamas twisted around her as though she'd been tossing and turning. The desire to comfort her overwhelmed him, and he reached for her, but Kat took a step backwards.

"Were you camped out on the landing?" she demanded.

Adam held his hands up. "No, I was across the road in my car. I was just taking a walk around the block when I heard you scream."

Kat rested her forehead in her hand. "You heard me from down on the street?"

Adam nodded, and Kat closed her eyes for an instant and groaned.

"What was your nightmare about?" he asked.

Kat didn't meet his eye. "I don't remember," she mumbled.

"Liar."

Kat's eyes flashed. "Okay then, I do remember, but I don't want to talk about it."

Adam ran his hands through his hair in frustration. "You know, you really should talk to someone. It doesn't have to be me."

Chapter 22

Kat locked the door behind Adam and leaned against it. She didn't know what it was about him that made her want to unburden herself. She'd almost caved and told him everything, the dreams, her fragmented memories of that night, and her guilt over the deal she'd done.

She wandered back to her bedroom and crawled into bed. Zelda followed and curled up beside her. Kat stroked her as she lay down and stared at the ceiling. After all this time, she'd remembered something new. Before tonight, she knew she'd been running from the house, running to get away from something or someone. For long enough, she'd thought it was a mixed-up emotion related to losing her hand or from facing the fact that Felicity was dead. Her dealings after the accident with William Huntly-Tait, Gabe's father, had been a shock. He'd gone from being a polite, middle-aged father figure to a hard-nosed lawyer out to get the best deal for his client, in this case, his son, no matter the cost. And in her traumatised mind, she figured that she'd made him the enemy.

She recalled Gabe visiting her in hospital after the accident and the pained expression on his face. He'd cried and said sorry over and over until his father arrived and dragged him away. That was the last time she'd seen him alone. His father had controlled their interactions from then on, and he'd been forceful and a little frightening. His main goal was to get Kat to agree not to press charges and get out of his son's life.

It wasn't until much later, after months of rehab, that the nightmares and the overwhelming sense that she'd been running from something horrible that night had taken hold. The numerous counselling sessions had almost convinced her that it was just her mind trying to make sense of it all. She'd started gathering information on Gabe's father and adding it to a board in her home office to help organise her thoughts, and even she had to admit it had become something of an obsession.

Now, however, she wondered if there had been something after all. The dream had been so vivid; William Huntly-Tait shouting, the plastic on the floor, and the man tied to the chair. Surely she hadn't made that up? She closed her eyes and tried to recall the man's face from the dream, but it was gone.

* * *

Kat woke with a start, rolled over, and looked at her clock. It was 9:30 a.m. The police were due soon to take her statement regarding the break-in. At least she'd managed to get another couple of hours of sleep. She'd texted Stephenson the previous night to let him know that she'd be late getting to work. Forcing her feet over the side of the bed, she headed to the bathroom for a hot shower.

Half an hour later, as she sat at the kitchen counter eating breakfast and mentally planning her day, her phone chimed with notification of a missed call. She rinsed her bowl, put it in the dishwasher and retrieved the phone from the bedside table. The screen showed a missed call from an unknown number. Sitting down on the edge of her bed, Kat dialled her voicemail and listened.

"Kat, it's Gabe. Can you call me urgently on this number? Please, it's important."

Kat looked at the screen in disbelief before replaying the message. She put her phone down and finished getting ready for work. Only then did her curiosity get the better of her, and she returned the call.

"Kat," Gabe answered on the first ring.

"What do you want?" Kat said.

"How are you?"

"Still missing my hand."

There was a brief pause on the line.

"Kat, I'm calling to warn you."

"Warn me?"

"Listen, I've just overheard a conversation with a, er… security consultant that we sometimes use. Your name was mentioned."

Kat felt the blood drain from her face, and she sat down on the edge of her bed.

"What?"

"Yeah, he was given details on you, where you live, what you drive, and where you work. The thing is my father has a file on you. He had all that information to hand. What are you involved in, Kat?"

"I don't know." Kat's mind was racing.

"And it's not just you." Gabe's voice had dropped to a low whisper.

"Who else, not Nate or Shamira?"

"No, someone called Adam Jackson. Who's he?"

Kat gasped. "What does this security consultant normally do?" she asked.

There was a long pause on the line. "Various things, but he's good at persuading people to keep quiet. I know that you're working on the CIP investigation. McFarlane and Diaz have retained Huntly-Tait and Partners. I think they want you to stop whatever line of investigation you are undertaking."

"Gabe, you have to find another firm to work for."

"It's not that simple. Look, I gotta go, someone's coming. You need to get out of London for a few days, and I'll see what I can find out. Be careful, Kat."

Kat stared at the phone for several moments. She knew she should call Adam, but after the way she'd spoken to him during the night, she was hesitant. She wouldn't blame him if he didn't answer, but he was the only one who could make sense of this. Exhaling, she called him.

He answered on the first ring.

"Adam, I've just had a call warning me that a security consultant has my details and yours with instructions to stop our investigation, I'm guessing into CIP." Her words tumbled out.

"Slow down, Kat. Who called?"

Kat hesitated. "I can't say."

"Can't say or won't say?"

"Both."

She heard Adam sigh. "But you trust them?"

"Yeah, yeah, I do. He suggested that I get out of town for a few days."

"Good idea, pack a bag, and I'll be there in fifteen minutes."

Chapter 23

Adam started the lights and siren on his car. He watched the cars in front of him pull over, out of his path. He was already on his way to Kat's, having grabbed four hours of sleep and woken with a resolve to force her to tell him whatever it was that she was hiding.

Fifteen minutes later, he pulled into a loading zone near her building and threw his police parking permit on the dashboard before racing across the road and up the stairs to her flat.

Kat looked a little rattled when she let him in. A small overnight bag sat by the front door.

"Coffee?" she asked.

"Yeah, that'd be good."

He followed her into the kitchen and leaned against the bench while she fixed the drinks. Adam watched as she filled the kettle and got down the cups with one hand. The stump of her left arm was clad in a soft cotton sock. He'd never seen her without her prosthesis attached. He wondered whether she'd forgotten to attach it or whether she was getting more comfortable around him despite her words to the contrary.

"Kat, who called you?"

She tensed.

"You need to tell me. I can't help otherwise."

Kat sighed. "Gabe, an ex-boyfriend."

"How does he know that someone is after you?"

Kat handed him a cup and walked over to the sofa and sank onto it.

"Gabe is a lawyer. His firm has just been engaged by MacFarlane and Diaz to represent them. He just overheard my details given to a security consultant they use to do various things, including persuading people to keep quiet. The two things have to be linked."

Adam smirked. "Are you sure he hasn't been watching too many movies?"

Kat looked less than impressed. "You don't believe me."

"I believe you. I just don't believe him. Is this his way of getting you back? How long ago did you go out with him?" Adam took a sip of his coffee.

"He doesn't want me back, believe me," she said. "A Huntly-Tait only wants perfection, not someone with a deformity."

Adam did a double-take. "Your ex-boyfriend is a Huntly-Tait?"

"Yeah, do you know that law firm?"

"I know that name."

"There's something else," Kat said when he didn't elaborate further.

Adam gave her a wary look. "What?"

"Gabe didn't just overhear my name. They mentioned yours too."

A broad grin spread across Adam's face.

"Why are you grinning? I've just told you that your life could be in danger." Kat was incredulous.

Adam waved his hand, dismissing her concern. "My life has

been in danger many times. I'm grinning because it means that we've touched a nerve."

He took a long sip of his coffee, a frown furrowing his brow.

"Have the police been to take your statement about the break-in?"

"Yeah, an officer came while you were on your way here. Seriously, she was only here for ten minutes, took my statement, and had a quick look at the balcony door. She left me with the distinct impression that since I'm missing nothing, the intruder was in the wind, and that would be the last I would hear of the matter."

Adam shrugged. "Sad, but probably true. At least it's all on record. Okay, I need to make a couple of calls, then let's get you out of town for the weekend. I suggest booking yourself into a bed and breakfast somewhere near a train station. Somewhere you've been before so that you know the area," Adam said.

Kat thought for a moment and then nodded. "Yeah, I know just the place."

"Great, book it for the weekend. We should have this sorted out by Monday."

"Okay. What are you going to do?"

"I'm going to verify the credibility of this threat."

"You don't believe me."

"I believe you. I'm just not sure I believe your source. I also don't want to start overreacting if this threat is just hot air. This is not about trust; it's about assessing the threat and working out the correct response. However, the fact that Huntly-Tait is involved is most intriguing."

* * *

Adam pulled into a short stay parking space two blocks from Euston station and threw his police parking permit on the dash. He climbed from the car and retrieved Kat's overnight bag from the back seat, slinging the long strap across his body.

"I'm good from here," Kat said, joining him on the footpath and holding her hand out for the bag.

Adam shook his head. "Come on. I'll show you a shortcut to King's Cross."

Kat stood her ground. "What are you not telling me?"

Adam sighed. "I'll tell you while we walk, we need to hurry."

He led her around a corner and almost immediately around another onto Phoenix Road. "Did you know that this is called the Wellbeing Walk?" he said. Kat shook her head. "You're exposed to 50% less pollution if you walk this way between Euston and King's Cross than if you walked along the main road. It's a council initiative."

"Thanks for the urban planning lesson, but what are you not telling me?" Kat said, hurrying to keep up with Adam.

"Did you notice the white van across from your flat this morning?"

"No." Kat felt the first threads of fear begin winding their way around her stomach.

"It pulled out after us and has been following ever since. I lost it in the back streets just before Euston, but I'm not sure how much time I've bought us. We need to make sure that no one follows you into King's Cross. Hopefully, they are looking for you at Euston."

They raced along the footpath, Adam checking behind them several times. Other people also walked, some pulling wheeled suitcases, and they had to move out into the street to get around them. Phoenix Road became Brill Place, and as they crossed over, Adam noticed a white van about a block away cruising slowly.

"Quick, in here," he said, turning into a doorway. The doors opened automatically, and they found themselves in the large reception foyer of a modern office building.

Adam strode to the reception desk and showed his warrant card as he spoke to the receptionist.

"Is there another exit?"

The receptionist stood and pointed. "Yes, take the stairs to the first floor and follow the mezzanine to the very end and take the stairs down. You come out just opposite the station."

"Thank you."

He and Kat took the stairs two at a time and walked at speed along a mezzanine with offices on one side and open on the other to an atrium containing a café and clusters of seating on the ground floor. At the far end, they jogged down the second set of stairs. They strode across the floor to the plate glass windows at the front of the building. Adam peered out with caution. A loud ping announced the arrival of a lift on one edge of the lobby. Kat watched as the doors opened, and around twenty people piled out and walked towards the exit, chatting and laughing.

"Let's join them," Adam said.

When the lift's occupants passed through the doors to exit the building, Kat and Adam eased into the middle of the group. They crossed the road and entered St. Pancras Station, keeping to the centre of the group. A long line of people with luggage wound its way among the barriers outside the Eurostar terminal. Kat and Adam continued past until they reached the shopping mall, where they plunged into the crowds and were swept along until they reached the entrance to King's Cross station.

"Do you have a hat or scarf in your bag?"

Kat shook her head.

"Pop into that shop there and buy a cheap hat and put your hair under it," Adam said, stopping outside an accessories store.

"I thought we'd lost them," Kat said.

"Perhaps, but a light disguise won't hurt."

"You're worrying me."

"I don't mean to. I'm just being cautious."

Kat slipped into the shop. At the same time, Adam positioned himself beside a pillar with a clear view of people coming up out of the tube or entering the station from the direction that they'd just come.

When she joined him a few minutes later, Kat's dark auburn hair was tucked out of sight beneath a black beret, tilted at a jaunty angle. She had a leather choker around her neck and wore a black t-shirt with a plunging neckline tucked into her jeans instead of the white one she'd had on earlier.

"How do I look?" she asked.

Adam swallowed hard, taking in her freshly made-up face; eyes ringed with heavy kohl and dark red lips.

"Great," he said. "I mean, good disguise, very emo. Well done."

Kat grinned. "Am I okay to go from here?"

"Yeah, it looks all clear. I'll keep my distance behind you until you're on the platform, to make sure no one else is following you."

"Okay, and thanks, Adam."

"You're welcome. We'll sort this out," he said, lifting the strap of her bag over his head and handing it to her. "Call me if you have any concerns, but I'll speak to you later."

Kat strode away, joining a steady stream of people entering the station. Adam forced his eyes from her retreating figure and focused on those also heading towards the trains.

He watched a man rising from a table at a café further along the concourse. He moved into the flow of people in the direction that Kat had gone. Adam went to follow when a woman ran towards the man and leapt into his arms, kissing him.

Adam let out a breath; false alarm.

He watched the crowds for another minute or so, before being satisfied that no one had followed Kat into the ticket hall. He wandered closer and stood to one side, pretending to fiddle with his phone, while he continued to watch not only Kat at the ticket machine but also those around her.

Chapter 24

Waiting for her turn at the ticket machine, Kat had a change of heart. The bed and breakfast she'd planned to go to was in the next village to her parents, so she'd thought that perhaps on Sunday she could meet them for lunch. But suddenly, she wasn't sure that she could face her mother grilling her on her lack of a significant other or setting her up with yet another boring son of her Country Women's Institute friends. And for some strange reason, a weekend in the country, completely alone, no longer appealed. Usually, Kat enjoyed her own company, but she was feeling restless. The whole business with CIP and the deaths of two of its partners had disturbed her. Or maybe it was someone who was unsettling her rather than something. She glanced around, seeking Adam out in the crowd, but couldn't see him. Dismissing the idea as ludicrous, she pulled her phone from her pocket and searched for her sister-in-law Sara's number.

Sara answered on the fourth ring and sounded breathless, as though she'd run to the phone. "Hello."

"Sara, it's Kat, do you have plans for the weekend?"

"Not unless you count endless visits to the playground, building Lego and making Play-Doh?" Sara replied with a laugh.

"Fancy some company?"

"Hell yeah. The weekends are always so quiet when Carl's away."

"Fantastic, I'm on my way. See you in an hour or so."

"Awesome, see you soon."

* * *

The journey to St Albans took just forty-five minutes. Kat sat back and stared out of the window as the railway sidings, stations, and suburbs of London gave way to the green fields of the English countryside.

Sara and Carl lived in a small semi-detached house three blocks from the station. Sara was smiling when she opened the door to Kat's knock.

"Auntie Kat," George yelled, pushing past his mother and wrapping his chubby arms around her legs.

"Hey, munchkin," Kat said, smiling and running her hand over his hair.

George stepped back and studied her. "Why are you dressed funny? Are you in a play? We're doing a play at school. I'm a cat."

Over his head, Sara shook her head at Kat. She bounced her fingertips and thumb together, indicating that he never stopped talking.

Sara reached for Kat's bag, and George grabbed her hand and pulled her inside.

Sara dropped the bag at the bottom of the stairs leading to the bedrooms. They continued down the hallway and into the kitchen.

"It's such a lovely day, I thought we'd have lunch in the back garden," Sara said.

"Sounds perfect," Kat said. "Can I help?"

"Why don't you and George head out the back, and I'll join you shortly," Sara said, pulling the oven door open and removing a quiche. "I have to say I love your new look."

"Long story, but it's not here to stay."

Kat pulled off her hat, shaking her hair free, and sat in a chair at the table on the terrace overlooking a small, well-maintained garden bordered with colourful patches of wildflowers, swaying gently in the breeze. George climbed onto her lap and launched into a story about the Lego creation he was building. At one stage, he leapt off her knee and raced inside, returning brandishing a lightsaber. Kat laughed as he swung it dramatically, almost knocking over the pitcher of water and glasses that Sara had placed on the outdoor table. Kat reached out and gently moved him away from the table. He gave her a mischievous grin, which melted her heart when he realised his mistake. Kat looked up as Sara joined them on the terrace carrying a tray with the quiche and a salad.

"Run and wash your hands, George," she instructed.

"Actually, I'll wash mine too. Trains," Kat grimaced. "Come on, Georgie."

Lunch was a leisurely affair, after which the sisters-in-law chatted easily. At the same time, George alternated between racing around the garden battling imaginary enemies and playing in his sandpit.

"So, how's Adam?" Sara asked, looking sideways at Kat.

Kat laughed and looked at the time on her phone. "Well, that took all of an hour."

Sara laughed. "As I said at the picnic, what's not to like? And he couldn't take his eyes off you."

"Rubbish," Kat said, dismissing the idea with a wave of her hand.

"Then why are you blushing? I know you, Katherine Munro, don't tell me it hasn't crossed your mind."

When Kat didn't reply, Sara sat forward and stared at her, a smile forming on her face. "Something has happened with him. Tell me."

Kat sighed. "He's been around a bit, that's all."

Sara arched an eyebrow. "That's not all. Spill, girl."

"We kissed, just once."

"See, that wasn't hard. How was it?"

Kat's blush deepened as she recalled the kiss at Adam's flat. "It was a mistake, I work with him, and he's seeing someone, a gorgeous blonde."

"From what I understand, you're just working on this one case with him, and how do you know he's seeing someone?"

"I saw them having a drink."

"It could have been his sister? Hang on, did you say blonde? Donny said that Adam's ex is a blonde, could have been her."

"Donny said? Trust you two to be gossiping," Kat said, shaking her head.

Sara laughed. "Well, Donny agreed that you two would be perfect together, and he wouldn't have suggested that if he knew Adam was in a relationship."

"The day I start taking relationship advice from Donny Webster, is the day I know that I'm destined to be a spinster," Kat replied, laughing.

After clearing away the lunch dishes, they walked into the town, stopping at a playground for George to play on the swings and slides before picking up a few supplies for dinner.

"I never realise how much I enjoy getting away from London until I do. It's so quiet and peaceful here," Kat said as they strolled back to the house.

"Sometimes too quiet and peaceful," Sara said.

"You know you can always come and stay with me for a few days. You know that Mum would happily look after George," Kat said.

"Thanks, I might just take you up on that." Sara reached for Kat's hand. "How's the hand development going? Carl was so pleased that you got involved as a beta tester in his mate's research programme."

"It's going really well. The robotics guys are amazing. They've created a much improved artificial limb prototype. The tech they use is cutting edge. The prosthesis they've developed is lighter, more advanced, and more lifelike than anything on the market," Kat explained. "And I've been able to help them refine the design from a practical day-to-day perspective."

"That's great," Sara said.

"Yeah, it was just what I needed, something positive to focus on, after everything."

The rest of the afternoon passed quickly as the two friends sat in the garden chatting, watching George play. When Sara moved inside to start dinner, Kat took George's hand and led him upstairs for his bath. She sat on the floor beside the tub while he splashed among the bubbles, making engine noises with his various bath toys.

"I wished you lived at our house, Auntie Kat," he said after a while.

"I have my own house, George. Remember when you and Mummy came to visit me?"

He nodded, looking thoughtful.

"Do you want me to help you to wash your hair?" Kat asked.

The little boy nodded and dunked his head under the water, emerging dripping. Kat wiped the drips from his eyes and squeezed a small amount of shampoo onto his soft hair before massaging it into a lather.

"Will you be here tomorrow?" George asked, lying down on his back so that Kat could rinse the shampoo out.

Kat nodded. "For some of the day."

"Good."

"Perhaps when you're a little older, Mummy might let you come and stay a night at my house."

George squealed with delight, and Kat laughed.

Sara had George's tea ready when they climbed back down the stairs after his bath, George all clean and shiny in his pyjamas.

"Mummy, Kat says that I can stay at her house."

"When you're a little older and only if Mummy agrees," Kat said, smiling at Sara.

Half an hour and numerous stories later, Kat joined Sara on the terrace.

Sara handed her a glass of red wine. "There, I think you've earned this."

"He's sound asleep, gorgeous boy," Kat said.

"Thank you," Sara replied. "How many stories did you have to read?"

Kat laughed. "I lost count."

"Are you still seeing Marco?" Sara asked.

"Define 'seeing'?" Kat laughed.

Sara frowned.

"Yes, he's still my kickboxing instructor, but no, I haven't seen him for several weeks. It's nothing major, I've just been busy. I was supposed to go back to his the other night when Adam met me at the gym with an urgent update on the case we've been working on."

"Really? He just couldn't wait until the next day?" Sara teased.

"It wasn't like that," Kat protested.

"Whatever you say."

After a dinner of chicken and salad, followed by a creamy chocolate mousse, they moved inside to the lounge and selected a movie to watch.

When the movie credits rolled, Kat stood and stretched.

"I don't know about you, but I'm ready to sleep," she said.

Sara pointed the remote at the TV and switched it off. "Me too," she said, picking up their empty wine glasses to take into the kitchen as Kat's mobile chimed with an incoming text. She pulled it from her pocket and saw that the message was from Adam.

Too late to call?

She smiled and tapped the phone icon next to his name.

"Kat, how are you?" he answered.

"Good, about to go to bed," she said, following Sara from the room and switching off the light.

"I just thought I'd check in. The security where you're staying is tight, so you can relax and sleep without worrying."

"That's great, thank you," Kat replied. "But I'm not there."

"What do you mean, you're not there?"

Kat paused at the bottom of the stairs as Sara switched off the hall light and joined her. A shadow passed across the back garden.

"I'm at Sara's."

"What? You can't change location without telling anyone."
"I didn't think, sorry."
There was a loud knock on the back door, startling her.
"What was that?" Adam asked.
Kat grabbed Sara's arm as she turned towards the door.
"Don't answer it," she hissed.
Sara looked puzzled.
"Kat Munro," a voice called from outside.
"Kat, what's going on?" Adam said.
"They've found me," she whispered.
The tinkling of breaking glass obliterated Adam's reply.

Chapter 25

Terrified, the two women watched as a gloved hand reached through the pane of broken glass on the back door, unhooked the heavy chain, and started to turn the deadbolt from the inside. Kat rushed forward and grabbed the intruder's middle finger bending it backwards. There was a muffled curse, and the hand retracted, but not before pulling Kat's onto the jagged glass slicing across the back of her hand.

"Ow." She jumped back. "Sara, call the police."

Sara already had the telephone in her hand but shook her head.

"The line's dead." She replaced the handset into its cradle.

There was a loud bang, and the remainder of the glass in the door shattered but didn't break.

"Here, help me," Kat said, pulling a hall table across in front of the door. Sara dropped the telephone and got behind the desk and pushed. They wedged it against the door. They heard the intruder insert something into the keyhole, and the pins clicking as he picked the lock.

"What about the front door?" Kat asked. "I'll grab George, and we'll get out that way."

The lock on the back door sprang open, and the legs of the hall table scraped as it was pushed against the wall, blocking the door from opening any further.

"There's no time, and I'm not leaving without him," Sara said.

The two women rushed into the lounge and crouched behind the sofa, and Kat tried calling Adam back on her mobile, but the call wouldn't connect. She tried the police next, but no luck.

"The signal is jammed," she whispered, wiping the blood from her hand across her jeans.

"He's a tenacious burglar, most would have been scared off by now," Sara said.

Kat gulped. "There are some things I haven't told you about the case I'm working on," she whispered. "I think he's here for me. I'm so sorry, Sara. He must have followed me here."

A thud sounded from the kitchen. The two women looked at one another, terrified.

"I left the kitchen window open; he's come in that way."

"Kat Munro, I need you to come with me," the intruder called.

Sara shook her head at Kat.

"I just want you. No harm will come to your sister-in-law and nephew."

Sara's eyes widened.

A floorboard creaked in the hall. He was on the move, creeping closer to their hiding spot. The two women edged along the back of the sofa towards the door connecting the lounge with the dining room and kitchen.

"You climb out the kitchen window and go for help," Kat whispered. "I'll keep him distracted."

"What about George?" Sara asked. "I'm not leaving him."

"I won't let this guy get up the stairs, I promise."

They crept across the floor from the sofa to the door, slipping through as a flashlight beam swept the room.

"Kat, we can do this the easy way or the hard way," the man said.

Kat peered around the doorway and watched the man edge into the lounge and check behind the sofa. Behind her, she heard Sara climb on the bench. The man froze, cocking his head to one side, before moving across the lounge without a sound towards Kat's hiding place.

Kat took a deep, steadying breath, and as the man crossed the threshold into the dining area, she struck out with a sharp kick to his knee and a punch to the side of his head. He grabbed for her as he stumbled, but she spun out of his reach and raced through the kitchen. She paused by the open pantry and grabbed a couple of cans off the shelf. She lobbed them across the room at the man, who had regained his balance and was advancing towards her. Her aim was good, but he merely batted them aside with his forearms.

In the light shining in through the kitchen window, she could see that he was dressed entirely in tight black clothing. A balaclava covered his head and face, with holes for his eyes and mouth. He was tall, but not bulky and was carrying a flashlight in his left hand.

She picked up an open bag of flour from the shelf and threw it as he came closer. It burst in a puff of white powder as the man hit it away, covering him in a white film. He cursed.

"What do you want?" she said, backing out of the room and rushing back through to the lounge. She positioned herself in the centre of the room, bouncing on her toes.

"Mummy?" George called from upstairs.

The loose floorboard in the hallway creaked as the man

paused by the stairs.

"Wonder who will get to him first?" he taunted.

"No," Kat shouted and rushed through the doorway back into the hall.

The intruder was waiting for her at the bottom of the staircase.

"Mummy," George called again, this time with more urgency.

"Coming, George, just stay in your room, okay?" Kat called, not taking her eyes off the trespasser.

Without giving the man time to prepare, she launched herself at him with a swift kick to the knee, followed by a one-two jab towards his face. A look of annoyance passed across his eyes, but he parried her away with ease. Bouncing on her toes, she took a step backwards towards the lounge, luring him away from the stairs. As she hoped, he moved with her. She stopped and kicked out again, but this time he was ready and stuck her with his fist while she was off balance. The blow to her shoulder threw her into the wall, but she recovered, taking another step back and ignoring the searing pain shooting down her arm. She flexed her prosthesis.

"So what's with the balaclava? Are you that ugly?" she said.

The man tilted his head to the side and came at her again. Kat stepped back into the lounge and blocked his punches, first with her right arm, and then left. His fist hit her artificial hand, and his eyes widened in surprise. She took advantage of his momentary distraction to land a solid kick on his thigh. He staggered before regaining his balance.

"Oh, didn't they tell you that you were sent to beat up a disabled person?"

"I just need you to come with me. Some people would like

to talk to you."

"Yeah, that's not going to happen."

She bounced on her toes and took a deep breath, willing Marco's words of advice into her head. *Breathe, keep moving, and jab.*

Kat kicked out again and punched with her right hand, but she was too slow, and the man landed a glancing blow to the side of her face. She staggered and went down on one knee, knocking over a side table. A lamp and several framed photos toppled to the floor, the glass shattering in the frames. Kat twisted away as the man's boot came towards her face and scrambled to her feet. She was tiring.

The man sneered, and Kat realised that she couldn't stall him much longer. She sensed movement in the hallway behind the man.

"George, I said stay in your room," she said.

The man laughed, thinking that she was trying to distract him and came towards her in a rush. Kat reached out and grabbed the finger that she'd broken when he'd stuck his hand through the door and twisted it.

"Arrgh," he grunted and pulled away from her.

Over his shoulder, Kat saw Sara step into the room with a large vase raised above her head. Seconds later, she brought it down across the back of the man's head. The porcelain cracked and broke as the man slumped to the floor.

"Mummy." George rushed into the room, crying. He wrapped his arms around Sara's legs and looked wide-eyed from Kat to the man lying prone at her feet and back to his mother, as tears poured down his cheeks.

"Quick, let's tie him up," Kat said. "Where are the police?"

"On their way." Sara scooped George up into her arms and

rushed to the kitchen.

Kat studied the prone figure. She crept forward and pulled the balaclava off his head. Kat could only see the side of his face, but she didn't recognise the man she estimated must have been in his late thirties. Sara hurried back into the room, carrying a bundle of twine.

"It's all I could find," she began as Kat screamed.

The man's eyes flew open, and he clamped a hand around her ankle. She fell, landing hard on her backside, kicking out as she went down, trying to release her ankle from his grip. Her left foot connected with his jaw and his hold relaxed. She pulled herself free and scrambled to her feet, grabbing the poker from beside the empty fireplace.

"Stay down," she warned him.

"Police," a woman's voice called from outside.

"Thank goodness," Sara said, rushing to the front door to let them in.

Chapter 26

Adam drove Kat back to her flat, as day broke. Kat rubbed at her arm, wincing as she touched a tender spot.

"Are you sure you don't need medical attention?" Adam asked, glancing sideways at her.

"Nah, I'm just a bit bruised."

They drove in silence for a moment, each deep in thought.

"How did you lose your hand?" Adam asked, breaking the silence.

"I told you it was a car accident."

"A car accident, after a party outside Cobham, that left your best friend dead."

"You've been looking into me." Kat snapped her head around to glare at him. "I asked you not to."

"A friend of mine went missing near Cobham around the night of your accident. Your car crash only came up recently in my investigation."

Kat's expression changed. "What?"

"I wasn't looking into your background, honestly. I respect your privacy, but I also don't believe in coincidences."

"I don't know anything about your friend. I was a little busy that weekend, firstly trying not to bleed to death and secondly trying to stop them taking my hand."

"Kat, I'm so sorry."

"I don't want your pity," she spat.

"Believe me, pity is the last thing on my mind. I'm in awe of you. You are so capable and inspiring. I saw the way people responded to you at the Valkyries picnic and how you must have fought off that intruder tonight." Adam's voice was soft as he spoke.

Kat shrugged. "These have been the hardest two years of my life. I went through some very dark days initially, and I'm still just taking one day at a time. I don't want to be anyone's inspiration because I certainly don't have it all sorted."

"Well, you put on a good act."

"Yet somehow you, who I've only known for a short time, see through that act and know more about me than most. You know that I still have nightmares and that certain things trigger me. I haven't shared that with anyone."

"You realise they are perfectly logical reactions to a traumatic event."

"Thanks, Dr. Jackson. I'll keep that in mind next time I lose it in public."

"Kat…" Adam began as they pulled up outside her flat.

Kat had the door open before he had even stopped the car. "Now, I need to try to get some more sleep, and you should go home. You look like shit." She swung her legs out onto the footpath.

"Gee, thanks," Adam said, pulling a face at her. He reached over and put his hand on her arm. "But first, one last question."

Kat sighed, spinning back around to look at him, blinking slowly. "What?"

"Why was no one charged over your injury or your friend's

death?"

"It's complicated."

"I'll try to keep up," Adam replied. "Your boyfriend was driving, right?"

Kat stared at him for a long moment before nodding.

"And not even a careless driving charge?" Adam asked.

"Or an accidental death charge, a reckless driving charge, a leaving the scene of an accident charge, a drunk-driving charge or a generally being an arsehole charge," Kat added, bitterness lacing her words.

Adam didn't react but waited for her to continue.

"Look, I don't know what you want me to say. If you have a wealthy enough father who happens to be a lawyer, and complainants who will settle for cash, you can get off anything. I guess Gabe lucked out."

Adam nodded. "So Gabe Huntly-Tait was the driver of the car on the night of your accident," he said.

"Yeah." Kat took a deep breath. "I thought that he was the one. Gabe was charming, witty, and intelligent. But I discovered there was something that he loved more than me; himself. He left us there, me bleeding out, and Felicity dying."

Adam inhaled and closed his eyes, the rawness of her pain hitting him hard. How she kept that hidden each day, he didn't know.

Kat gave a slightly hysterical laugh. "And what do you think was the cost of buying my silence, so that Gabe wouldn't get prosecuted for drunk driving and ruin his promising career? You're looking at it." She gazed up at her flat. "But, I'm beginning to wonder if it wasn't that simple."

"Why did you get into the car with him? You're a smart woman; you must have known he'd been drinking?"

Kat looked across at him for a long moment, and Adam could sense that she was waging an internal battle. He kept quiet and let her come to a decision.

"I was running away from something I'd seen at the house that night," she said eventually. Adam felt his pulse quicken. "Until very recently, I didn't know what; it was just a feeling. My therapist had convinced me that the sense of fleeing was my brain's way of coping with the trauma of losing my hand and Felicity's death. It's all tied up with survivor's guilt or something. Felicity lost her life, whereas I'm still here, and I only lost my hand."

"Losing your hand is a big deal, Kat, you're allowed to grieve for that."

She swallowed and took another deep breath. "But I've remembered more about that night over the last few weeks. I now think that I was running away from something horrible, and I believe that we were deliberately driven off the road. I remember Gabe being dragged away from the car yelling, and Felicity and I were just left there as the car caught fire."

"What do you mean?"

"The car that ran us off the road stopped and pulled Gabe from the driver's seat and drove away."

"Bloody hell, Kat, you need to report this."

"Who would believe me after all this time, especially with various therapists agreeing that my mind was playing tricks?" Kat said with a heavy sigh.

"Can you tell me what you saw at the house that night?" Adam said.

Kat closed her eyes. "I can only recall bits and pieces, but I think Gabe's father was interrogating, for want of a better word, someone in his office at the house. He was shouting at a man tied to a chair. There were other men in the room, and one had a gun. The chair was on a plastic sheet," Kat's voice caught, and her eyes flew open. She looked up at Adam with tears in her eyes. "I think they were going to kill him," she said in a whisper.

Adam cursed and fought to control his emotions.

"Is that why you were in Cobham the other day?" she asked after taking a moment to compose herself.

Adam nodded. "My mate Jake was working undercover, and he went missing the same weekend as your accident."

Kat gasped and shook her head. "Do you think it was Jake that I saw? I'm sorry I can't even picture the guy."

Adam rubbed a hand over the back of his neck. "All this time, I figured he was dead, but I had hoped otherwise."

"I'm sorry, he still could be alive. I'm not a terribly reliable witness. I can only remember some of that night."

"Is that what your recent nightmares have been about?"

Kat nodded but didn't move to leave the car.

They were silent for a few moments.

"Kat, I need to make a phone call. Are you okay if I relay this?"

She nodded.

Adam dug his phone from his pocket.

"Sir, I have some new information. Kat Munro has recalled more details of her car accident in Cobham the same weekend Jake went missing. She is hazy on the details, but she believes that she was fleeing the Huntly-Tait residence after witnessing a man being interrogated and possibly shot."

Adam listened for several moments.

"Yes, sir. I'm with her now. However, we have a slight complication in that two of the CIP partners have engaged

Huntly-Tait's firm to represent them. We believe that the firm has hired someone to follow Kat and possibly me. She was attacked at her sister-in-law's home last night."

Adam listened again.

"Okay, sir, will do."

He ended the call. "I need to bring Greenwood up to speed."

Kat looked puzzled. "Wasn't that him?"

Adam shook his head.

"Okaaay," Kat said, not comprehending. "I don't understand, but try to keep Gabe's name out of it."

"I don't think you owe Gabe anything, do you?"

"True. But before you call Greenwood, there's something that you should see." Kat climbed out of the car.

Adam leaned over and rummaged in the glove box for his police identification and threw it on the dashboard. He got out, followed Kat across the footpath, and into her building.

Adam caught up as they climbed the stairs to her flat. She unlocked the door and led him through the lounge and into her small office. She reached into the desk drawer and pulled out the key to the cupboard. She unlocked it and folded both doors back before removing a false plywood cover from the inside of the left-hand door and setting it on the floor. Beneath the cover was a pinboard covered in newspaper clippings and yellow post-it notes. At its centre was a photo of William Huntly-Tait.

"What's this?" Adam asked, stepping forward and studying the board. He turned to look at her. "Is this what they were looking for the other night?"

"I think so," Kat replied in a quiet voice.

"So, you have been investigating him?" Adam poked his finger at the photo of Huntly-Tait.

"Yeah, deep down I knew that something wasn't right about that night, and I thought this might help me remember."

"Who else have you told about this?"

Kat shook her head. "No one. My brother Carl saw it once and told me that I was obsessing and needed to move on, and he's probably right, so I haven't shown anyone else."

Adam frowned. "Then how did they know to come looking for it?"

"I don't know. I have several Google Alerts running on him and his firm. Maybe I flagged something by checking his website too often."

"Okay if I take a photo of this?" Adam asked.

"Knock yourself out."

Kat covered the pinboard again and locked the cupboard, but not before Adam had snapped several photos of it.

Kat dropped down onto the sofa in the living room while Adam called DI Greenwood. The cat flap in the balcony door squeaked, and Zelda padded into the room. Kat jumped up and scooped her up, cuddling her. She walked to the kitchen and put her down before filling her bowl with dried cat food.

She looked up as Adam stood in the doorway.

"This just got more complicated," he said.

"What's happened?"

"The intruder from Sara's house is denying being hired by Huntly-Tait and Partners or CIP or even knowing who they are," Adam said.

"But he knew my name," Kat said.

"According to his statement, he's just your garden variety burglar, who happened to get caught."

"Rubbish," said Kat. "Ask Gabe."

Adam paused. "Well, that's the other thing. We can't locate

him."

"What? Shall I call him?"

Adam shook his head. "Not at this stage."

"What's the latest with McFarlane and Diaz?" Kat asked.

Adam gave a contemptuous shrug. "They're still claiming to be shocked by the discovery of Fund 4 and are busy laying the blame at the feet of Henry Smyth and Roger Chen."

Kat shook her head in disbelief.

"Do you fancy a drive? I have a couple of airfields in Surrey that I need to check out," Adam said.

"Airfields?"

"Yeah."

Kat thought for a moment. She had no other plans for the day, and after the events of the previous night, she found that she didn't want to be on her own, not that she'd admit that to anyone, especially Adam.

"Sure," she said, trying to sound nonchalant. "Can I shower and get changed first?"

"Of course."

Kat started down the hallway towards her bedroom and paused. "Actually, you'd probably like a shower too?"

"Are you asking me to join you, Kat?"

"No, Adam, I'm not. I was merely thinking that you'd been running around after me half the night and that perhaps you'd like one. You can go after me."

"Pity." Adam pulled a face.

"We're not doing this, remember?"

"So you keep telling me."

"Well, listen to me then," she replied.

"Although," Adam continued, ignoring her comment, "remind me, wasn't it you who launched herself into my arms when I arrived at your sister-in-law's?"

"I was just relieved to see a friendly face."

"Right," Adam smirked.

"And while we're talking about last night, I can't believe that you called my mother," she said. "You know I'll never hear the end of that."

"I figured that was the quickest way to get Sara's address after your phone cut out. But, now that you mention it, she sounded delighted to hear from me," he added in a teasing tone.

"Huh," Kat huffed before closing her bedroom door with a bang.

Adam chuckled as he undid his boots and slipped them off. He settled himself lengthwise on Kat's sofa to catch a few minutes' sleep. If the army had taught him one thing, it was to grab precious moments of rest whenever the opportunity arose.

When Kat came back into the lounge twenty minutes later after her shower, Adam was snoring softly. She smiled despite her earlier annoyance with him as she tiptoed into the kitchen, opening the refrigerator and retrieving eggs, cheese, and tomatoes. Kat didn't know about Adam, but she was ravenous after the events of the night. Letting him sleep a little longer, and waking him with breakfast would be a peace offering of sorts. She knew she was being tetchy with him, but he was ingratiating himself into her life and, despite her reservations, she seemed to be letting him. She looked across at the figure slumbering on her sofa. Monday couldn't come soon enough. She needed to get back to work and focus her attention on something else.

She whisked the eggs and started preparing their omelettes.

She reached into the cupboard for two plates and lifted them out. They fell from her grasp and landed on the floor with a crash, breaking into pieces.

Kat sighed and looked down at her left hand. The fight with the intruder had left a chip across the back of her fingers which was playing havoc with the electronics.

"Are you okay?"

Adam had jumped from the sofa at the noise and was at her side in seconds.

"Yeah, sorry to wake you," she said. She flexed her fingers. "This hand is damaged now too. It's not responding to my brain signals properly."

Adam crouched down and picked up the large pieces of broken china, while Kat took the eggs off the heat.

"Plates are in there," she indicated with a nod of her head. "Might be safer if you get them."

Adam retrieved two more plates and passed them across to her. "Broom?" he asked.

"In that cupboard."

* * *

"So, let me guess, the airfields that we're going to visit are near Cobham. And you're bringing me on the off chance that going there triggers another memory for me," Kat said as they joined the A3 leaving London.

"Can't I just enjoy your company while I'm following up on a routine lead?"

Kat laughed and shook her head. "No, there's nothing that you do that's routine."

Adam glanced across and gave her a gentle smile. "We won't

even go into Cobham. I'm a little hurt that you'd think I would do something so callous to jog your memory."

A frown creased the skin between Kat's eyes. "Why, then?"

"You forget that you still have a price on your head. Just because you stopped one guy, doesn't mean there won't be more. I'd rather have you where I can see you and know that you're safe until we get to the bottom of this."

"Okay." Kat sat back and considered this while trying to ignore the odd feeling of warmth that flowed through her. It was a long time since she'd allowed anyone outside of her immediate circle to get this close, and she wasn't sure how she felt about that.

They drove on a little further before Kat spoke again. "I have to admit that I'm a little scared now." She snuck a glance at Adam. His attention was focused on the road, but she saw his jaw clench at her comment.

"I didn't mean to scare you. I'm probably just being overcautious."

"Can you tell me why we're visiting airfields?"

Adam thought for a moment before replying. "I found out very recently that the day before Jake disappeared, he visited airfields around Cobham. There are two within easy driving distance, but only one is operational. I want to check them out to see if I can work out whether he discovered anything."

"And what would he have been looking for?" Kat asked.

Adam was silent for a long moment.

"This is where my job at the Met merges with my work for the British Army," Adam said, looking sideways at her.

"Your work for... hang on. I thought you were retired?"

"Yes and no. I'm retired from active duty, but I have retained certain duties which dovetail nicely with my role as a police officer."

"Ah," Kat said, not fully understanding.

When Adam didn't elaborate, she asked him outright. "And you can't tell me any more than that?"

"No, sorry."

"What if I guessed?" she said, giving him a sly grin.

"Well, I can't stop you from guessing."

"Alright, then. Why would the British Army be interested in small airfields outside London?" Kat frowned as she pondered her question. "Supplies, no, something covert, perhaps, people?" She looked across at him. "Transporting senior officers somewhere off the books."

Adam shook his head.

"Way off?" Kat asked.

"Yup."

"Maybe the army is trying to catch criminals who are smuggling? But that would be customs or border police, wouldn't it?"

Adam shrugged.

"Okay then, if it's not the British Army per se, then perhaps it's someone rogue within the ranks?" She saw a muscle flex in Adam's jaw, and his expression become serious. "People smuggling or weapons or drugs?"

Adam didn't respond.

"Ha, I'm right, aren't I?" Kat slapped her thigh, but her smile slipped when she registered Adam's grim expression.

"The thing is, Kat, I really hope you're wrong."

Chapter 27

Adam turned the Ford Capri down a long access road towards the airfield. On one side of the driveway, sheep grazed, and on the other, half a dozen small aircraft were parked on the grass.

They left the car in a small parking area outside a single level wooden building with the words 'Surrey Flats Aerodrome' painted in black lettering on the side. They got out of the car as a small single-engine aircraft swooped over them to land in a smooth motion on the runway. It taxied to the end, turned and bumped across the grass before coming to a stop beside the building. The whir of the engine cut off, and the propellers slowed their rotations. The aircraft's right-hand door opened, and a middle-aged woman wearing jeans and a brown bomber jacket stepped out onto the wing. She jumped to the ground, pushing her sunglasses from her eyes into her hair.

A man emerged from the building and greeted her. She hugged him and smiled, looking elated. Together they pushed chocks in front of the wheels of the plane.

Adam and Kat walked around to where the couple was standing.

"Good morning," Adam called.

They turned at his voice, and the woman smiled. "Hello, can we help you?"

"I hope so," Adam said. "I've inherited a small aircraft from my father and I'm trying to work out where I could keep it."

"Well, that depends on several things; how big it is, how often you'll use it, where you live. Where's the plane now?"

"It's at a small airfield in Yorkshire," Adam said. He looked behind the woman to the ten aircraft lined up on the grass. "It's no bigger than any of those."

"You don't know much about aircraft, do you?" the man said.

Adam gave a self-deprecating laugh. "Is it that obvious? Dad was the fly-boy, not me. I've been up a few times with him, but..." He trailed off.

"Well, I'm sure we can help," the woman said. "Follow me. Would you like a coffee?"

"That would be great," Kat spoke up.

The woman glanced at her and did a double-take when she noticed the bruising on Kat's face. "What happened to you?"

"I came off a motorbike. There's nothing broken thankfully." Kat smiled and touched her cheek. "I'm just a bit sore."

"I can imagine," the woman said. "I'm Annabelle, and this is Harold."

"Mark and Abbie," Adam replied before Kat could respond, giving false names as he stepped forward and shook their hands.

Kat and Adam followed them into the aerodrome building with Kat mouthing "Abbie?" at him.

The building itself was simple. There was an area at the front of the large open plan room containing square wooden tables and chairs. On the side wall, a small kitchenette with a coffee machine, microwave, and vending machine completed the café area. There were two offices along the back wall, and a small shop opposite the café sold what looked like aviation supplies, small parts, and clothing. The walls displayed framed photos of various types of light aircraft. Two of the tables were occupied by middle-aged men in overalls, sipping from mugs and talking. They all looked up and nodded their greetings to Annabelle, their eyes passing over the newcomers with fleeting interest, before returning to their conversations.

"Have a seat," Annabelle said, walking over to the kitchen area. "Coffee with milk?"

"Yes, thanks," Adam said. He and Kat sat at a table near the door. Kat noticed he turned his chair to have a view of the whole room, as well as through the windows.

"So what brings you to Cobham?" Harold asked.

"Abbie has always loved the area, and we're thinking of getting a weekend place around here," Adam replied.

"And you'll fly your father's plane down."

"Well, I won't," Adam said with a laugh.

"What sort of aircraft is it?"

"It's a Cirrus SR22," Adam replied, stumbling a little over the name. Harold nodded at the mention of the aircraft.

"Here we go." Annabelle returned, balancing a tray with four frothy coffees.

"Thank you," Kat said, accepting a cup and getting into her role. "Do you offer flying lessons?"

"We certainly do," Annabelle said. "I'll get you some information on that before you leave."

Adam smiled across at Kat. "That would be useful. No point having a plane and not knowing how to fly it. Although an acquaintance of mine who can't fly has a small aircraft, she suggested that we come here. She hires a pilot whenever she wants to go across to her place in Normandy."

"Oh, who's that?" Annabelle asked.

"Mary," Adam replied. "McFarlane, I think her surname is."

Kat hid her surprise and watched a fleeting shadow pass across Harold's face, but it was gone before she could identify the emotion.

"Oh yes, Mary." Annabelle spun around in her chair and looked outside. "Her plane is not here now, so she must be away for the weekend again."

"Al picked it up on Thursday," Harold said.

Adam turned his attention to Harold. "Can I get the number of the pilot she uses? Did you say his name is Al? I'm going to need someone to fly Dad's plane down from Yorkshire."

"Of course, he's always looking for a little extra work," Harold said, pushing his chair back and standing. "Now, if you'll excuse me, there is some paperwork with my name on it that needs my attention."

"And we should be going too," Adam said, draining his coffee.

"Let me just get you Al's number and the details of our flying lessons," Annabelle said, following Harold across the room to an office.

"So, Mark," Kat grinned at him.

"So, Abbie."

They stood and made a point of looking interested in the photos hanging on the walls. A framed certificate for membership to The Goldfish Club caught their attention.

"Hey, I've heard about this. You only become a member if you successfully ditch your plane in the sea," Adam said.

"Really?"

"Yeah, some guy started it during World War II. It was originally just Defence Force, but nowadays it's any pilot."

"Yes, it says here that Annabelle…"

"Ah, you've found my claim to fame," Annabelle said, laughing as she joined them.

"That must have been frightening," Kat said.

"It all happened so quickly that I didn't have time to be frightened, and then when I was recuperating this arrived," Annabelle said, waving a hand toward the plaque. She handed Adam a flying lesson brochure and a piece of paper with the name Al Burton and a telephone number written on it. "It's a unique club to be a member of."

"I'll say," Kat said.

"Thanks for this," Adam said, taking the papers from Annabelle. "I take it Al lives nearby."

"Oh yes," Annabelle said. "He has a place over on Boundary Road."

"Well, thanks for the coffee," Kat said.

"My pleasure. I hope we'll be seeing you again soon."

They returned to the car, drove out onto the main road, and pulled over. Adam picked up his phone and searched for Burton's address.

"Was that useful?" Kat asked.

"Perhaps," Adam said. "I think we'll pay Al Burton a visit."

"But won't he be away if he's flown Mary McFarlane's plane to Normandy?" Kat said.

"Even more reason to visit."

Adam spun the car around and following the GPS on his phone, located Boundary Road. They drove along the country lane until they came to the property indicated on the map. Adam pulled into the driveway leading to a small cottage in desperate need of painting. The letterbox had the name 'Burton' stencilled on the side. A garage at the side of the house was open, and a small farm truck parked in front. They climbed from the car and walked towards the front door.

Children's high pitched voices sounded from behind the house. Adam was about to knock on the door when a football came bouncing around the corner, followed by a boy of around ten years old wearing a Liverpool football shirt. He stopped running and gathered the ball. He looked from Adam to Kat and back again.

"Hello."

"Hi, mate, is your dad about?"

"Nah, he's over at the airfield."

"Surrey Flats?"

"Nah, the other one."

"The old one over on Turner's Lane?" The boy nodded. "Okay, thanks."

Adam and Kat returned to the car.

"I take it you know where this other airfield is?" Kat asked.

Adam nodded. "It's a bit of a stretch to call it an airfield; it's more of a disused airstrip."

"How did you know that Mary McFarlane has an aircraft?"

"It was on the asset listing that your team put together," Adam said.

"Amazing that you remembered that," Kat said. "There were a lot of items on that list."

"It jumped out at me when I reviewed the file, and combined with the fact that I had just learned that Jake had been checking out airfields when he disappeared, I thought it was worth pursuing."

Kat nodded. "Makes sense. How far to this airstrip?"

"About ten minutes. It's no longer operational, although it appears to be used by agricultural aircraft, you know, crop dusting and that sort of thing. It's hidden away on a back road. I only found it because I was specifically looking."

Kat watched the fields and streams pass by as they drove, and found that she was enjoying herself. She glanced across at Adam. He too looked relaxed apart from the slight frown on his face, and she remembered that this just wasn't a drive in the country. But neither was it just work; it was personal. He was trying to find out what had happened to his friend.

Chapter 28

They approached the farmer's airstrip from the south. Adam pulled over to the edge of the country lane, parking beside a tall hedgerow. They climbed from the car and walked along to a break in the foliage.

"There," Adam said, pointing across a field of grazing sheep to where a small plane was parked in front of a tall corrugated iron shed. Two men were unloading boxes from inside the aircraft onto the flat deck of a farm truck. Their voices and occasional laughter carried on the breeze, but it was impossible to hear what they were saying. One man wore maintenance-type overalls, and the shorter of the two had trousers and a white button-down shirt. Next to the small hangar stood a single fuel pump attached to a cylindrical tank.

Adam pulled out his phone and snapped several photos before making a call.

"I've just sent you a couple of photos of two men unloading a small plane at the abandoned airfield on Turner's Lane."

He listened for a moment to the person on the other end of the call.

"Will do, sir," he said, ending the call.

Kat looked at him with a raised eyebrow. "Not Greenwood?"

"Not Greenwood," he said, turning his attention back to the

men.

"I wonder which one is Al?" Kat said.

"I would guess that he's the one in the shirt, dressed like a commercial pilot."

They continued watching the men transfer the crates to the truck for several more minutes until they heard another vehicle approaching.

"Come on," Adam said, jogging back to his car. He opened the boot as though looking for something. Kat joined him, and they peered over the raised lid as a black SUV approached from the north. It slowed further along the lane and turned into a gateway leading into the field. A man jumped from the front passenger seat and unhooked the gate latch and pushed it open. The SUV pulled through and stopped. The man closed and secured the gate, glancing in their direction before climbing back into the vehicle.

Adam and Kat watched as it drove across the field toward the plane, scattering the grazing sheep, who protested loudly at the disturbance. Adam closed the boot as the vehicle moved out of sight, and they hurried back to their earlier surveillance position. Adam took more photos. Al Burton climbed aboard the aircraft and passed the remaining cargo stowed in the hold, down to the other man. He crouched in the doorway, watching the vehicle approach. The SUV pulled alongside the plane, and a man and a woman alighted. They exchanged greetings before doing a circuit of the aircraft, and the woman checked the door of the hangar, which appeared to be locked. They seemed watchful and alert. Al jumped down from the plane, closed its doors, and exchanged a few words with the new arrivals before climbing into the passenger side of the truck.

"Come on, they're leaving," Adam said, turning back towards his car.

The truck bumped across the field towards the gate with the SUV following close behind.

Kat jogged after Adam and slipped into the passenger seat, sinking low. At the same time, Adam once again pretended to retrieve something in the boot. She watched as a man opened the farm gate and the truck passed through the open gateway, followed by the SUV, which paused long enough to pick up the gateman. Both vehicles turned onto the lane heading away from Kat and Adam.

Adam slammed the boot shut, climbed into the car, fired the engine and pulled out a short distance behind them.

"Okay," he said. "Let's see where they're going."

Adam kept his speed down and followed along the country lane until they came to a T-junction with a more significant road. Both vehicles turned right. Adam again hung back, letting a couple of cars pass before he too turned right.

They drove for a kilometre keeping the SUV in view. There was more traffic in both directions than on the quieter country lane.

"This road leads into Cobham," Adam said.

"I know." Kat's sharp tone made him glance at her. Her posture was tense, and she was frowning.

"Kat, I'm sorry. But we need to see where they're going."

"I know, keep driving."

Adam mentally kicked himself. It had seemed like a good idea to bring her along, given the events of the previous evening. Now he was second-guessing himself. He didn't want to traumatise her further, given what had happened to her in this area.

"Gabe's father has a place along this road," she said. "It's around the next bend."

"Kat," he began.

"Look," she said, pointing.

Both the truck and the SUV pulled off the road into the gateway of South Hill Manor. As Adam and Kat passed, they saw the gates swinging shut, and the two vehicles disappearing onto the property.

"I wonder what William Huntly-Tait had delivered by an airplane that required an escort?" Kat said.

Adam shook his head. "I'm not entirely sure, but we need to take a look at that plane." He pulled over in a farm gateway a little further on and waited for two cars to pass before executing a U-turn and heading back to the airfield.

Adam pulled his car over to the side of the lane, tucking it beside the tall hedge.

"I'm going to take a look. Do you want to come or wait here?" Adam asked.

Kat had already undone her seatbelt before he finished speaking. "I'm coming, of course." She slid across into the driver's seat and got out of Adam's door.

They hurried to the gate, climbed over, and jogged through the field to where the plane, a Cessna 172, stood. The white, fixed-wing aircraft balanced on its three wheels. A double red stripe decal cut along each side. They moved around behind the plane, partially obscured from the road, and Adam pulled two pairs of thin disposable gloves from his pocket and handed one set to Kat.

"Let's check the hangar first, then the plane," he said as he pulled on his gloves. He walked to one end of the tall corrugated iron shed, past the fuel tank and around behind the building. He returned from the other side a few seconds later, having completed a full circuit. Adam peered in the only window before pulling a small pouch from his back pocket. Kat joined him at the shed's sliding doors, which were closed and secured with a chrome padlock. Adam removed two thin wires from the pouch and began working the lock.

"You just happened to have a lock-picking kit on you?" she asked.

"I keep it in the boot of the car, you never know when it could be useful," he said, looking up and giving her a reassuring smile.

"What about needing a search warrant and all that?"

"True, but hear that?" He paused and cocked his head as though listening. "I'm concerned that someone inside could be in grave danger."

Kat smiled and shook her head. "Do you have an answer for everything?"

"Usually," he said as the lock gave a click and popped open. Adam returned the tools to the pouch, unhooked the padlock, and pulled one of the doors across. He peered into the interior. It was empty.

"Wait here," he said and slipped inside.

Kat looked around. Apart from the sheep, who were ignoring them and going about their business, they were alone. The scene would have been peaceful, had it not been for the strong sense of foreboding that tugged at her.

"See anything?" she called.

Adam returned a few seconds later. "Nothing. The little office is practically empty, just a desk, chair, and a few flight charts on the wall. I expect they store the plane here when they're not using it, which means they might be coming back, so we need to hurry."

"We'll see them coming, from the lane, right?" Kat asked.

"Yeah. If we do, make for the trees behind the shed and work your way back to the car."

She nodded. "I'm glad you've thought that through."

"You should always have an escape route."

After closing and re-securing the padlock, they approached the aircraft. Adam pulled the passenger door of the plane up and peered inside. He felt Kat come up behind him and look around him into the interior.

"Have you been up in one of these?" she asked.

He nodded. "As a passenger, not a pilot," he said. "I've flown in a lot more helicopters, though."

He moved to one side so that she could see further inside. The aircraft had two seats side by side. The passenger seat was tilted forward to allow easy access into the cargo bay, which was now empty.

"This type of aircraft normally has four seats," he said. "Removing them will allow the transportation of more cargo." He pointed to grooves in the floor and redundant harnesses hanging on the walls. Adam took a few photos on his phone and stepped back, crouching and looking under the fuselage.

"What are you looking for?"

"The unique aircraft registration number," he said. "It's an alpha-numeric sequence beginning with the letter G." He moved toward the tail and snapped a photo. "There," he said standing, and tapping his phone, sending the picture. "We'll see if Mary owns this beauty."

"So, what do you think was in the crates those guys just unloaded?" Kat said.

"Heroin, if I were to hazard a guess."

"Really? William Huntly-Tait doesn't strike me as a drug dealer."

"You'd be surprised the people who run these things."

"It's not a very large cargo space, even with the seats removed," Kat said, peering into the cabin once more. "How much would they transport?"

"In one flight? 50 to 100kgs," Adam said.

"That doesn't seem to be a lot for such a big risk," she replied.

"Kat, 100kgs of heroin powder would have a street value of around £10 million."

"Oh," she said. "And that's just one flight."

Adam nodded and reached into an inside pocket.

"So, what now? What else do you have in your bag of tricks?"

Adam held up what looked like a small piece of black plastic. He leaned over and slipped his hand beneath the tilted passenger seat and pushed it into place. He stepped back and lowered the door, closing it.

"Now let's get out of here," he said, removing the gloves and dropping them in his pocket.

"Not so fast. Hands where I can see them," a voice called.

<h1 style="text-align:center">Chapter 29</h1>

Adam swore under his breath. He raised his hands, turning towards the voice and stepping in front of Kat. The move would have irritated Kat, had she not seen the Glock being pointed at them when she spun around. Her mouth dropped open in surprise. Two men were standing in front of the hangar. Where had they come from? There had been no cars on the lane the whole time they'd been there. The larger of the two men held the gun, but it was the other man who spoke.

"What the hell are you doing?"

"Mate, we were just admiring the plane," Adam said, adopting an overly friendly tone. "I wasn't planning on stealing it or anything. I'm in the market to buy one. We were just over at the Surrey Flats Aerodrome talking with Annabelle and Harold about it."

The two men looked at each other with uncertainty.

"Move away from the plane," the shorter man spoke again.

Kat and Adam stepped out into the open from beneath the wing and moved towards the men.

"Why is she wearing gloves?"

"Oh these," Kat said, lowering her arms and turning her hands over. "It's for my prosthesis, makes both hands look the same."

The men looked confused. Kat moved closer to the unarmed one, and both men looked at her. "Here, I'll show you," she said. She raised her arm.

Adam took advantage of the gunman's momentary distraction and launched himself at him, grabbing his gun arm and twisting. There was a shriek of pain, and the gun clattered to the ground. Adam kicked it away under the plane's carriage as the man swung a massive fist at him. Adam ducked and tackled his much larger opponent, taking them both to the ground, where they rolled, trading blows.

Kat landed a solid kick to the unarmed man's knee, spinning and catching his nose with the heel of her right hand as his knee buckled, and he staggered forward. The man cupped his hands to his face as blood spurted from his broken nose. She kicked out again, catching the man in the groin. He groaned and collapsed onto the ground.

She raced to the plane and retrieved the gun, pointing it towards Adam and the man he was wrestling with shaky hands. "Stop, or I'll shoot."

Adam's assailant's eyes went wide, and he released Adam, who scrambled to his feet. He rushed to Kat and relieved her of the gun.

"Get their phones," he said.

Kat approached the two men who were still on the ground nursing their injuries and, she suspected in the case of the man she'd seen off, his pride. She held out her hand, and they gave her their phones.

"Let's go," Adam said, shoving the gun into the waistband of his jeans and taking the phones from her.

They jogged back across the field, scattering a few grazing

sheep.

"Where did they come from?" Kat asked, pulling off the gloves as they ran.

"Probably from my escape route," Adam said. "They weren't behind the building when we arrived, so they must have circled from the tree line."

"But how did they even know we were there?"

"I suppose there was a camera that I didn't spot," Adam said.

They reached the gate and were climbing over when the sound of a fast-approaching vehicle reached their ears. Seconds later, the black SUV from earlier rounded the bend and screeched to a stop.

Adam cursed.

All four doors of the car opened, and three men and a woman got out. The men used the car doors as cover and pointed guns at them.

"Drop any weapons," the woman instructed. She cut a menacing figure, dressed in black from head to toe. Her eyes were cold.

Adam raised his left arm and, using the fingers of his right hand, reached into the waistband of his trousers and removed the stolen Glock, holding it out in front of him before tossing it on the ground at the side of the road.

"You?" The woman turned her attention to Kat.

Kat shook her head. "I'm unarmed."

"Search them," the woman instructed with a flick of her head. Kat watched as one of the men holstered his gun and approached them.

He patted his hands down Adam's sides, reaching under his jacket and checking around his waist. He eased a mobile from an inside pocket on Adam's jacket and dropped it on the ground before crushing it with his boot.

"Oops."

Adam didn't react. The man removed the lock-picking kit and Adam's warrant card from his back pockets and tossed them to the woman before he crouched and patted down each leg.

"Keys," he demanded and held out his hand.

Adam retrieved his car keys from a front pocket and handed them over. The man tossed them to one of his colleagues.

"Bring his car, Rich," he said.

Rich caught the keys with a grin and sauntered down the lane toward the Ford Capri.

"Be careful with it," Adam called. "It has a dodgy clutch."

"I think that's the least of your worries at this point," the woman said.

The man frisking Adam stepped towards Kat. He gave her a leery grin before running his hands around her abdomen and down her legs. It took all her willpower to resist the urge to knee him in the face. He moved to stand behind, invading her personal space. He slipped his hand into her back pocket, retrieving her mobile, dropping and crushing it too.

"Get in the car," the woman instructed.

The man gave Adam a shove forward with one hand and grabbed Kat's right wrist bringing it around behind her back; he reached for her left one and let her go with a surprised noise.

She spun around and glared at him. "What, you're worried it's contagious?" she snarled, waving her left hand in front of his face.

The man looked uncomfortable for a moment.

"Kat," Adam said, his voice carrying a warning.

She looked over at him and registered the slight shake of his head. With a last glare at her assailant, she followed Adam to the car. They slid into the back seat with the larger man squeezing in beside Adam. The driver climbed behind the wheel, and the woman returned to her position in the front passenger seat.

"Where are you taking us?" Adam asked.

No one replied.

Kat shuddered, and Adam reached for her fingers, squeezing them and not letting go.

Outside, the sound of a propeller filled the air. They looked out of the car window to see the small airplane bumping along the makeshift runway before turning, gathering speed, and lifting off.

Adam cursed under his breath.

The woman in the front seat laughed. "Can't have anyone else coming to check the plane."

The driver started the car, did a U-turn, and headed back along the lane to the main road. Several minutes later, they drove through the gates leading to South Hill Manor with Adam's car following close behind. Both vehicles drove down one side of the property and around to a back entrance, where they pulled to a stop one behind the other. Across a large yard behind the house and at the edge of the forest was a long building with four roller doors.

"Take them upstairs," the woman said.

Kat and Adam were led to a back door by two of the men. They walked through the mudroom, along a corridor, and up a narrow staircase. Kat glanced around, getting her bearings. Although she'd visited South Hill Manor on several occasions when she was going out with Gabe, she hadn't been in every part of the house. It appeared that they were in the staff quarters at one end of the east wing.

Turning right at the top of the staircase, they were pushed along a narrow corridor to a room at the far end. One of the men opened the door and ushered them inside. The sparse furnishings included a wooden table, two chairs, and a sofa with several tears in its fabric. Curtains were drawn across the room's only window, but still let in some of the fading light from outside.

"Benny, you secure them, and I'll cover you. Don't want a repeat performance of the airfield."

Adam smirked. "At least you're learning."

Benny released Adam's arm and backhanded him across the face. "And it's time you learned to shut up."

Adam stumbled but kept his balance. He scowled and wiped the back of his hand across his mouth, and it came away with a smear of blood.

Kat pulled against the hand holding her, and the man pushed her towards Adam.

"Run and help him, then," he sneered and stood in the doorway with his gun trained on them.

Benny dragged two of the chairs from the table and placed them back to back in the middle of the room. The first man produced cable ties and tossed them to Benny, who pulled Adam's hands behind his back, tied his wrists, and pushed him onto the chair. He hesitated for a moment before pushing Kat onto the other seat and securing her right hand to the style of the chair. He avoided her prosthesis as though he were a little scared of it. He crossed the room to a wardrobe and removed a coil of rope, which he proceeded to wind around their middles, securing Kat's left arm to her side.

He stepped away to join his colleague in the doorway and admired his handiwork.

"Okay, Steve, let's go. You two make yourselves comfortable, and we'll be back later," Benny laughed.

Steve shoved his gun into his holster and pulled the door closed. Seconds later, Kat and Adam heard the lock engage.

"Are you okay?" Kat whispered as the men's footsteps retreated.

"Yeah, you?"

"I'm a bit scared. My last memories of this place aren't great, well at least the ones I can remember aren't," Kat said.

Adam wiggled his hands so that he could grasp her fingers.

"I would say that I won't let anything happen to you, but I'm not sure that I can promise that."

"Sugarcoat it, why don't you," she said with a weak laugh.

"They didn't tie your left hand, are you able to work it free?" Adam asked.

"I'll try," Kat said, attempting to pull her arm up by lifting her shoulder. "It's very tight."

Adam used his feet to turn his chair on an angle. "Try now."

Kat continued to wriggle and tried to lift her arm for a few minutes but to no avail. "The trouble is my hand is damaged, so it's not responding as it should."

"That's okay, keep trying," Adam said. "Suck in a deep breath and go again."

They both held their breath, and this time Kat managed to get her elbow between the layers of rope. She pushed down, but only succeeded in tightening the top bond.

"Take a break for a moment," Adam said, sensing her frustration. "Let's go over what we know."

"Okay," Kat said.

"So, we're being held at the country home of William Huntly-Tait, prominent barrister, who has been retained by CIP. Which makes him connected to Mary McFarlane, partner of CIP and owner of a small aircraft, possibly the one we just saw."

"And you think that someone is bringing heroin into the UK via small aircraft and using this place as the storage and distribution point?" Kat said.

Adam nodded.

"Do you think they know who we are?" Kat asked.

"They have my warrant card, so they know I'm a cop, which is a worry since it hasn't put them off. They must be serious about keeping things hidden if they are prepared to kidnap a police officer. Huntly-Tait will know who you are. You dated his son, and if we are to believe him, it was his father who arranged for your visitor last night."

Kat was quiet for a moment. "But what if Huntly-Tait isn't involved? I mean, someone else could be using his house."

"But he was here the night of your accident, the same night Jake went missing in this area."

"I don't think I'm a reliable source. I may be remembering different occasions and putting them all together," Kat said.

"Perhaps," Adam said. "What about Gabe?"

"Gabe?"

"Could he be the one behind this?" Adam said.

"No," Kat said. "Gabe is a sweet guy; a little easily led perhaps, certainly not a criminal mastermind."

"It takes all sorts."

Kat was silent for a few minutes digesting everything Adam had said. She wriggled her left arm again. The rope was cutting into it above her elbow and sending shooting pains into her stump. She redoubled her efforts, sucking in her breath and shifting her weight to the chair's right side. At the same time, Adam worked his chest and shoulders back and forwards, inching the rope higher. The pressure eased, and the top line went slack around their shoulders. Kat pulled her left arm free and lifted the rope off her neck. Twisting, she lifted it over Adam's head, and together they pulled so that the second coil around their middles loosened. Adam stood and stepped out of the rope. Hands still secured behind his back, he crossed the room to the wardrobe and began sawing the cable tie back and forth against the metal door handles. Kat stood with difficulty and shook the rope free so that it pooled around her feet. She stepped out, still connected to the chair by her right hand. Sitting down again, she began picking at the cable tie, trying to break it.

"I hope they're taking care of my car," Adam said.

"We're in this predicament, and you're worried about your car," Kat said, shaking her head.

"It's a genuine concern. It's a modern classic."

"What happened to the two mobiles we took off those guys at the plane?" she asked as a sudden thought popped into her head.

"You saw one get crushed on the road, and the other I dropped by the gate when the SUV appeared."

"And yours?"

"That's by the gate too."

"Smart," Kat said. "So, does that mean someone is coming to get us?"

Adam shook his head. "No, it just means that when I fail to check in at the end of the day, someone will hopefully locate my phone and our last location."

"Then help could be a long way off," Kat said.

"I'm afraid so."

Kat abandoned her attempt to break the cable tie and instead carried the chair with her to the window. She pulled the curtain aside a fraction and looked outside. The sun was beginning to set. The view was over the kitchen garden at the side of the house. The forest on the hill beyond the garden looked uninviting in the gloom.

"Do the windows have locks?" Adam asked from across the room, still sawing at the cable tie.

Kat moved the curtain a little further open. "Unfortunately."

"Damn, we'll have to go out the way we came in."

Chapter 30

Nathan entered the offices of Forensic Accounting Associates via a side entrance. He showed his credentials to the lone security guard and made his way up the stairs to the first-floor office.

Something about CIP had been bugging him. When he woke that morning, another line of inquiry had emerged in his thoughts. He just had to prove it. CIP's hidden Ponzi scheme appeared to operate like their other funds. Clients deposited their money to purchase units in the fund, which accrued dividends, interest, and growth to each client's account. When a client requested a withdrawal, the funds were paid out. Nathan and the team had been working their way through the clients invested in Fund 4. The early investors were individuals like Kat's father and his golfing buddies, but the later investors were all companies and trusts. It was some of these later investors that, Nathan had discovered late on Friday afternoon, existed in name only. The directors were ghosts, and the registered offices were fictitious. Nate would have continued working into the night, but Stevenson insisted that they all go home and get a good night's sleep. The investment funds had been deposited by electronic transfer from legitimate bank accounts in the name of these companies, so local and offshore banks had somehow been tricked into opening accounts for shell companies.

Nathan sat down at his desk and switched his computer on. He inserted his ear pods, selected his latest dance party playlist, cracked his knuckles, and got to work. Over the next, hour he submitted formal requests to DI Greenwood to obtain transaction details from the bank accounts of thirty-seven different entities going back four years. He logged into the firm's secure data storage. He opened a file downloaded from the CIP servers showing the transaction details of all the money paid out from Fund 4. He clicked to expand the detail of the fifty most recent withdrawals of more than one hundred thousand pounds from the various portfolios. He let out a loud exhalation of disbelief and sat back in his chair. Without exception all withdrawals, regardless of company name attributed to them, had been made to a single offshore bank account.

"This isn't a Ponzi; it's an elaborate money-laundering scheme," he muttered.

Nathan sat forward and began to work on the remaining data to see how far back the pattern went. He was so engrossed in his work that he didn't see the two men creep up the stairs or hear the splash of liquid from the cans they carried as they spread it around the room before creeping back down the stairs.

Just as the smell of fuel hit his nostrils, flames engulfed the room.

Chapter 31

The cable tie snapped, and Adam pulled his hands free. He rushed to join Kat at the window of the small room where they were trapped. "Here, let me help you," he said, dropping to his knees and pulling at the tie holding her right hand to the chair, with his teeth. After a minute, it began to split and fray, and he broke it apart.

"Thanks." Kat rubbed her wrist on her shirt for a moment. She reached out and touched Adam's cheek. "The side of your mouth looks sore."

Adam leaned into her hand and held her gaze. "As much as I'd like to indulge in your sympathy, we need to get out of here before they come back."

Kat nodded and dropped her hand, colour brushing the top of her cheekbones. She took a step back.

"Options, as I see them, are one, chair through the window, but someone would hear us, and we wouldn't get very far," Adam said.

"And we'd still have to jump one storey," Kat said.

"Then, it's option two."

"Which is?"

"Overpower them when they return."

"Which might be sooner than we think. Listen?" Kat said.

"Close the curtains," Adam said, lifting Kat's chair back into the centre of the room again, back to back with his. "Sit as though you're still tied up."

Kat sat facing the door and placed the rope back on her lap with her hands at her sides as the key turned in the lock. Adam flattened himself against the wall. The door opened, and Steve walked into the room, followed by Benny.

"What?" Steve began.

Kat launched herself out of the chair, kicking out and landing a solid strike just above his right knee. Benny fumbled for his gun, as Adam's fist connected with the side of his head, sending him sprawling into the open doorway. Adam followed through with the series of body blows taking Benny to the floor. Adam fell on him, pinning his arms. Benny bucked, twisting his legs around Adam's and throwing him off, but not before Adam had liberated his Glock.

Having taken advantage of Steve's imbalance to land a second kick on his left thigh, Kat slammed the palm of her right hand into his nose. As he raised his hands to protect himself, she grabbed his shoulders and kneed him in the groin. She stepped away as he doubled over and glanced at Adam, scrambling to his feet with Benny's gun in his hands. She let out a breath, feeling the adrenaline rush through her.

"Let's go," Adam said, propelling her through the door, pulling it shut and turning the key. Adam pocketed the Glock along with the key.

Steve and Benny began shouting and pounding on the door.

"Quick, this way," Kat said, leading them back along the corridor. Instead of going down the stairs, she took them through another door, which opened onto a second stairwell. It curved up and around several times. "This connects to the main part of the house if my memory is correct," she whispered.

Adam peered upwards to check that the stairwell was empty before they climbed to the second floor and cracked open a door leading to the central part of the house.

"This floor is mostly bedrooms. The main staircase leads down to the next floor, which has a study, library, and family lounges. The ground floor is more formal. I think there is another, smaller, less used set of stairs on the other side of the house, but we have to cross this long hallway to get to it," Kat said.

"It's probably worth the risk," Adam whispered. "We can't stay here."

They closed the stairwell door behind them with care and crept along the wide hallway, past a table filled with framed family photos and several half-closed doors. Voices floated up from the floor below, and somewhere in the house, a door closed with a bang causing them to jump and exchange a nervous glance. They came to the main staircase and paused, listening before hurrying across the landing. A little further on the hallway split, one part continuing straight, the other turning right at ninety degrees.

"Come on, nearly there," Kat urged.

A door opened on the floor below, and the voices became louder. Kat grabbed Adam's arm, and they slipped into a room and hid, with the door ajar. The small room was a bathroom painted blue and containing a claw foot bath and hand basin. It smelled fresh and clean. Snippets of conversation drifted up to them.

"They've somehow escaped."

"Oh, for God's sake. Find them; they can't have got far. Set the dogs loose."

The door closed, and the voices became muffled.

Kat let out the breath she'd been holding. "They're looking for us."

"Yes, but they think we're outside, so that gives us a few minutes," Adam said. "Come on, let's get moving."

They left the bathroom and hurried along the hallway, keeping close to the wall until they reached a door at the far end. Adam eased it open and found himself in an unadorned stairwell similar to the one they'd ascended on the opposite side of the house. They paused and listened for a few moments. There was no noise coming from below. Adam peered over the edge of the railing and turned to Kat, giving a flick of his head. Together they crept down the stairs to the first floor.

"Where does this staircase end?" Adam asked.

"One side of the house, I think, rather than the back," Kat said. "But I can't be sure."

They crept down one more flight. There were three doors on the landing; the one to their left, with a frosted glass panel, led to outside and one to their right led back into the central part of the house. The stairs continued down. Adam pointed down and raised his eyebrows in question.

"Wine cellar," Kat whispered. "Creepy."

Adam put his hand on the outside door handle just as loud voices sounded from inside the house. A man's voice rose above the others.

"Sounds like someone arriving," Adam said. He eased the gun from his waistband and cracked the door leading into the house.

Three men and a woman stood in the main foyer near the front entrance, partly obscured by a grand sweeping staircase.

The woman and one of the men held semi-automatic rifles.

"Wait here." Adam slipped through the doorway and rushed across the floor, taking cover by the bannister behind a large potted plant. Hearing a creak on the stairs above, Kat bolted after him, squeezing in with him behind the planter.

The conversation was more apparent in the foyer, and Adam turned to Kat with a look of shock on his face.

"I know that voice," he whispered.

Chapter 32

"What's going on?" the new arrival asked, his tone exasperated.

"We caught two people snooping at the airfield," the woman explained.

"Do we know who they are and what they were looking for?"

"It's strange," the woman said. "She's the ex-girlfriend of Gabriel Huntly-Tait, and he is…"

"A cop," the man finished for her. He swore. "How the hell did they find the airfield?"

"The woman was Kat Munro?" an older well-spoken man asked.

"Yes."

"How?" he began. "I thought…"

"You thought what?" the first man asked. "What have you done?"

"I, ah, Mary was worried," the older man stumbled over his words.

"What did you do?"

"I sent someone to take care of her."

"You what?" the younger man exploded.

"She was becoming a problem. I know she was running

Internet searches on me and following me. I mean, she even turned up at an art gallery opening that I sponsored, and then I find that she is in the middle of some investigation at CIP. I had someone break into her flat to find whatever it was that she was collecting about me."

Kat's mouth dropped open.

"You're mad, she's just an accountant, and Huntly-Tait, this is not just all about you," the newcomer added.

Kat's expression turned indignant. "'Just an accountant,'" she mouthed.

"My man ended up unconscious and in custody, so I think we underestimated her," Huntly-Tait said.

"She's not to be harmed. Is that clear?" There were murmurs of acknowledgement.

Kat touched Adam on the arm and looked at him in confusion. "Is that…?" she began.

He nodded, and she stared at him, incredulous.

"Where are they now?" the man asked.

There was a moment of silence before the woman spoke again.

"Well, sir, that's just the thing. They've escaped."

"Oh, this just gets better."

"They could be miles from here by now."

"If there is one thing I know about Adam Jackson, it's that he isn't the type of man to flee. He will still be around here somewhere. But, first things first, we need to move all of the stock now. They may have found a way to alert the authorities."

"We're only just unloading the most recent cargo," the woman said.

"It all needs to go from here, now. H-T, it's time for your

man at the Met to earn his retainer. We need the dispatches monitored and to be alerted as soon as anyone even moves in this direction."

He turned to the woman. "It's getting dark out, so get your men out into the grounds with night vision. Are the dogs loose? Good. Once I've checked the factory, I'll sweep the house for heat signatures. We need to find them before they do any more damage."

Adam signalled to Kat with a toss of his head, and they moved on silent feet to the back of the foyer, keeping the stairs between them and the others. They slipped through an archway beneath the grand staircase that led through to the rear of the house. Kat grabbed Adam's hand and pulled him down into a dark alcove below the stairs just as the group from the foyer strode through a matching archway on the opposite side of the stairs. Kat and Adam held their breath as they passed within centimetres of their hiding place. William Huntly-Tait was in the lead, followed by the woman and one of the men who had detained them at the airfield. A man, well known to both Adam and Kat, brought up the rear. Don Webster.

Kat shook her head in disbelief.

The four passed through a doorway, and the sound of their footsteps retreated.

"What the hell? Donny?" Kat whispered. "What's going on here? Is he undercover too?"

Adam frowned. "No. Colonel Wilson would have told me."

"But that means...no, not Donny."

"I don't know what to say, Kat. Don will have the contacts in Afghanistan to buy opium. They must be smuggling it out to somewhere in Europe and then flying it in, packaging it up here, before distributing it."

"If they're using Mary McFarlane's plane, perhaps they're using her place in Normandy as a drop-off and pickup point," Kat suggested.

"And we know there's a link between Mary and William Huntly-Tait. She's his client."

Kat sighed. "Okay, so what do we do? They're heavily armed, and they're looking for us."

"I'm going to check out this factory, which must be in that large building out the back at the edge of the forest. You find a phone and call this number." Adam recited a telephone number and had Kat repeat it back. "If they catch you, they won't hurt you. You heard Don."

Kat shook her head. "We should stick together."

"No, we'll achieve more this way. We need to get the police here before they leave with the drugs. "

Kat nodded. Adam started to rise, but Kat pulled him back down so that their faces were only inches apart.

"Be careful." She kissed him.

Adam slipped his arms around her and held her tight, returning her kiss. Kat relaxed into his embrace, and for a brief moment, the danger they were facing faded, and it was just them. With some reluctance, they broke apart, and Adam rested his forehead against hers for a moment. "Don't worry about me. Make sure that you don't do anything risky, okay?"

They both stood, still holding on to one another, and Kat unwound the thin scarf she wore.

"Adam, here take this. The dogs know my scent. I've played with them on numerous occasions, so this might buy you some time."

Adam took the scarf, slipping it into his pocket. He gazed

at her for a long moment and reached out to stroke her cheek. He leaned in to give her another quick kiss before slipping out of their hiding place as quietly as a thief in the night.

Kat put her fingers to her lips as she watched him disappear into the shadows. Kissing him again had been long overdue, and if ever there was an incentive to get out of this mess, she had it now. She thought for a moment. Where were there phones in this house? All she could think of was William's study, but the thought of going in there frightened her. She was paralysed by fear for a moment and took several deep breaths and forced down the rising wave of panic. She closed her eyes and made herself think. The bedrooms could have phones, but that would mean going back upstairs, and she figured it was safer to stay on the ground floor. There had to be one in the front room, and as long as she kept away from the windows, she would be fine.

She strained to listen for any sounds in the silent house. After several long seconds, she crept out from the nook, retraced her steps beneath the arch, and tiptoed into the foyer, keeping her body pressed against the side of the staircase. When she reached the large planter they'd hidden behind earlier, she stopped and peered around it. The door to the formal lounge room at the front of the house was twenty meters away across the spacious entrance hall. She craned her neck to peer up the stairs to the first floor. The stairs were empty, but she couldn't see up to the landing. Not giving herself any more time to second guess, she dashed across the foyer to the lounge's doorway and slipped inside.

The room was long with several sofas, armchairs, and elaborate side tables topped with expensive-looking lamps that bathed the room in a soft glow. The large fireplace was unlit. Heavy peach coloured curtains framed the four double bay windows along the front of the house, and the French doors at the far end. The walls were covered in ruby red wallpaper and displayed paintings of rural scenes, some of which Kat knew to be originals; there was a Turner and even a Gainsborough. She scanned the room. There, on a side table on the furthest side of the fireplace from where she stood, was a telephone. Movement outside in front of the house caught her attention. Kat ducked down behind the nearest sofa when a man wearing night vision goggles and carrying a semi-automatic rifle crossed in front of the windows. His head moved from side to side as he scanned the grounds. Breathing deeply, she waited until he had passed before moving out from behind the sofa. She crawled across the room on her hands and knees towards the table with the telephone. Her damaged prosthesis made the movement challenging, but she felt safer keeping close to the ground rather than standing up. She reached the far sofa and collapsed beside it, resting her back against the arm, out of sight of the windows. She could hear the voices of the guards talking outside as she reached up onto the table and retrieved the telephone handset. She punched in the numbers that Adam had her memorise, and after one ring, a voice answered.

"Yes?"

"It's Kat Munro, Adam said to call."

"Kat, thank God, where are you?"

She went to answer as the phone was plucked from her hand.

"What are you doing?"

She looked up into a familiar face.

"Gabe?"

Chapter 33

dam crept through the back of the house, past the entrance to an enormous kitchen where four people were seated around a large table, playing cards. He slipped through an open doorway and out a side entrance. He cowered in the porch as a man strode by, night vision goggles affixed to his eyes and a weapon in his hands. Adam briefly considered disarming him and taking his gun and glasses but dismissed the idea. It would take too long, be too noisy, and at the moment, he still had an element of surprise; they didn't know where he was. Adam calculated the distance across the back yard to the outbuildings at the edge of the woodland to be around five hundred meters. Several vehicles were parked along the way, which would provide him with good cover. He counted thirty seconds until the next guard passed, then thirty before the next. The security was tight, executed with military precision.

When he reached the corner of the house, Adam sprinted across the driveway to the first vehicle. He crouched with his back to the fence and listened. Like clockwork, the next patrol completed his circuit of the house, and Adam moved again on silent feet to the second vehicle. Peering around the front of it, he could see the long building, now less than two hundred metres away. One of the roller doors was up, and two men were standing in the opening, semi-automatics cradled in their arms, their eyes scanning the driveway.

Adam counted the seconds to the next security pass and was about to move from the truck to a large tree on the fence line when he heard a low growl behind him. He let out a breath and put a hand on the stolen Glock as he turned, coming face to face with a snarling Doberman.

"Hey there, boy," he whispered, avoiding eye contact with the dog as he extracted Kat's scarf from his pocket with his other hand. The dog continued to growl as Adam wrapped his scarf around his arm. He held it out, waiting for the dog's jaw to latch on. The dog stopped growling and instead sniffed at Adam's outstretched arm. Adam watched amazed as its tail started wagging, and it dropped down onto its belly and started head-butting Adam's hand. Adam took this as a good sign and scratched behind the dog's ears. A second Doberman appeared, and after sniffing Adam's arm, flopped down beside its mate.

"Anything?"

The voice startled Adam. It was Don, and he was close.

"No, sir."

"He's here somewhere, keep patrolling."

Footsteps retreated from his position.

"Where are the dogs?" Don asked.

"Monty, Rupert," Huntly-Tait called.

The two Doberman jumped to their feet and giving Adam a farewell glance, bounded away towards their master's voice.

Adam shoved Kat's scarf back in his pocket, silently thanking her, and waited for the next security pass. He once again snuck a look towards the entrance to the building at the back of the property. A small group of people were moving towards the house. He recognised Don and William Huntly-Tait amongst them.

"Load up and hose down. Leaving in ten," Don instructed.

Adam bolted for a large tree at the edge of the yard. He hunkered down just as a woman peeled off from the group and headed straight towards the vehicle he'd been hiding behind. He watched as she climbed in, started the engine and drove to the building's open doorway, turning the truck and reversing it into the space. He let out a shaky breath; that was close.

Adam crept along the tree line, keeping low behind the trees and shrubs until he came level with the far corner of the building. There was an open area to cross where he'd be exposed to both the security lights on the building and the night vision of the patrolling guards.

What he needed was a distraction. He crouched and felt around on the ground beneath him, selecting several large stones and weighing them in his hand in the darkness. Stepping out from behind the tree concealing him, he aimed and threw the stone across the driveway to a small car parked on the far side. The windscreen shattered, and an alarm went off, followed by the sound of shouts and running footsteps. Adam dashed across the open area and flattened himself against the end wall for a moment before he hurried around to the back of the building and crept up an external stairway. The door at the top swung open as Adam reached it, and a man stepped out, lighting a cigarette.

Adam brought the handle of the Glock down on the man's temple. His knees buckled, and he slumped unconscious against Adam, the unlit cigarette still clamped between his lips. His cap fell off as Adam eased him to the ground and lifted his semi-automatic rifle from around his torso. Adam searched the man's pockets, taking a cigarette lighter and a pocket knife, but couldn't find a phone. *Who doesn't carry a mobile phone?* he thought, annoyed. Adam picked up the cap and slipped it on his head, tilting the peak to obscure his features. He stepped over the unconscious figure and peered into the building.

He crept onto a metal mezzanine walkway and looked over the edge onto a production line with crates, such as those they'd seen removed from the airplane, stacked at one end. To one side, a man was packing scientific equipment from a table into a box: a microscope, beakers, tubes, and scales.

As Adam watched, another man, wearing a breathing mask and gloves, was scooping powder from an open crate into a clear plastic bag. The man weighed it, adjusted the contents, and placed the bag on a conveyer belt. Further along, a second man lifted a bag and sealed it using a heat-sealing machine before putting it back onto the conveyor. A third person added a label and packed it into a cardboard box. A small box containing at least fifty packets was sealed with tape. A heavyset man was loading the sealed boxes into a ubiquitous white van, reversed into the loading bay.

Two men armed with semi-automatic rifles wandered up and down behind the workers. Adam noticed that they had earpieces. It wouldn't be long before they tried to check in with their colleague that he'd just disarmed, so he needed to move fast. The catwalk where he was standing wrapped around two sides of the shed, with stairs at the far end leading down onto the factory floor. There appeared to be two rooms on the long side of the mezzanine. Adam could see through the window into each that they were empty apart from desks and chairs. There was nothing for it but to make his way to the far end. He turned and slid the bolt across the door to stop anyone entering from that direction surprising him. He tilted the cap forward and started walking around the mezzanine towards the stairs.

The woman whom Adam had seen earlier in the foyer approached the start of the production line.

"Pack up now; we're leaving," she announced. "Wash down the room, leave the conveyer, but everything else needs to go in one of the vehicles."

The workers nodded. Another man appeared with a bag trolley and heaved two unopened crates onto it. He wheeled them past the van to a small truck whose flat deck was just visible in front.

A plan took shape in Adam's mind. Hopefully, by now Kat had managed to make that call, and help would be on its way. What he needed to do was delay the departure of the people and the product. He slipped into the first office and closed the door, scanning the room. The desk had a few sheets of paper on it. Adam grabbed a waste paper basket, stuffed the documents into it, along with a calendar and a large map pinned to the wall and flicked the lighter that he'd liberated from the guard.

The paper caught and started to burn. Adam upended the basket onto the fabric seat of the chair and watched it begin to smoulder. He pushed the chair back under the desk and slipped out of the office, closing the door behind him. Adam repeated the process in the next office, setting fire to whatever paper he could find and then headed towards the stairs. He forced himself not to run, but halfway down, he glanced back. Smoke billowed under the door of the first office.

"Hey, what are you doing? Get over here and help load the truck," demanded one of the men on the factory floor.

Adam reached the bottom step as the glass in the window of the first office exploded outward.

"Fire," he shouted and started running towards the exit as pandemonium ensued.

Chapter 34

"What are you doing here, Gabe?" Kat said.

"You first," Gabe replied, disconnecting Kat's phone call. His usually tidy brown hair was ruffled, and a neat, clipped beard covering his jaw was a recent addition. He was wearing dress pants, a sweater, and a navy blue car coat.

"Please give me the phone?" Kat grabbed for it, but Gabe held it out of her reach.

"Not until you tell me what's going on."

Kat glared at him. "Where should I start? Perhaps with your father's people holding me against my will in a room upstairs?"

"No way."

Kat looked incredulous. "Do you even know what's going on here, Gabe?" Gabe didn't answer her. "Oh," Kat said after a moment of silence. "You're involved. I didn't see that coming." She dropped down onto the sofa.

"Involved? In what?"

Kat studied his face for a moment, uncertain whether his innocence was an act or whether he genuinely had no idea what was happening in his father's house. It was possible, she thought. He never used to come down to the country that much, preferring the excitement of London.

"Nothing legal," she said. Gabe's head dropped, and he sat down beside her. "So you do know something," Kat said.

"My father is always involved in some scheme or other, although he does seem to have gathered some fairly tough people around him in recent times. Kat, I have as little to do with him as possible outside of work, even inside work." His shoulders sagged, and he looked sad and defeated.

"Well, what are you doing here then?"

Gabe looked uncomfortable. He cleared his throat. "I was following you."

"What?"

"I saw a news report online that two women were attacked in their home in St. Albans and after warning you and knowing that's where Carl and Sara lived, I called her. When she confirmed what had happened, I went straight to your flat and saw you leaving with that guy. He's a cop, right?"

Kat nodded.

"I lost you after you left the Surrey Flats Aerodrome. So, I've been driving around a bit and decided to come here to use the bathroom before I headed back to London. I didn't know anyone was here, apart from the housekeeper, you have to believe me."

Footsteps sounded in the foyer, getting louder as they approached the front room.

"You can't let them find me here, Gabe," Kat said, springing to her feet.

Gabe hesitated, then jumped up and led her to the wall beside the fireplace.

"Quick, through here," he said, pressing a spot on the wall beside a large framed painting by Constable. A hidden door popped open in the wall. Gabe pulled it open, and Kat slipped through, leaving Gabe to close it behind her. He scooped up the discarded telephone handset from the sofa and replaced it in its cradle when his father entered the room.

"Ah, I wasn't expecting you tonight, Gabe," he said, looking startled and uncomfortable.

"Father, you're home," Gabe said, trying to sound surprised. "I dropped in to use the bathroom, and the front door was unlocked, but I didn't see your car out front."

"What are you doing down here?"

"I had lunch with an old friend in Cobham. I didn't realise you were coming down for the weekend," Gabe replied.

His father gave him a calculating look.

Footsteps sounded, and Don appeared in the doorway. He leaned against the doorframe and looked Gabe up and down. "Who's this?"

"This is my son Gabe," Huntly-Tait said.

"And what is he doing here?"

"I stopped to use the bathroom," Gabe said, stepping forward and returning Don's appraising stare. "And you are?" He inserted a proprietary note into his voice.

Don straightened, and a flicker of annoyance crossed his features.

"Don't let me hold you up," Don said, stepping aside and sweeping his hand towards the foyer.

Gabe glanced at his father, who gave a slight flick of his head.

"Okay, then." Gabe obliged, passing through the doorway and heading for the main staircase. "See you at work on Monday, Father," he called.

"Where are you going?" Don asked.

Gabe turned with one hand on the bannister and one foot on the bottom tread. "To use *my* bathroom." He held Don's gaze for a moment before continuing up the stairs to the second floor, ignoring the fear that crept into his bones.

Behind him, he heard Don ask, "What's he doing here?"

"Just what he says, I believe," Huntly-Tait said. "He had lunch with a friend and stopped in to use the bathroom."

"Mmm…" Don sounded unconvinced. "The trucks will leave through the forest track shortly, so make sure he doesn't go out the back. Does his bathroom overlook the yard?"

Huntly-Tait shook his head.

"Good. Now let's keep moving. Any sign of Jackson or the girl?"

"No."

* * *

Kat looked around. She was in a darkened dining room with the shutters closed over the windows at one end. The door leading to the main foyer was ajar, and a shaft of light cut across the threshold. Kat recalled that there was a butler's pantry adjoining the dining room. She started towards it when she heard heavy footsteps striding across the foyer. She ducked down behind a tall chair at the head of the massive twelve-seater dining table, but the steps continued past, and she heard Don's voice join those of Gabe and his father in the front room.

She crept across the rest of the room and cracked open the door to the butler's pantry. It was a long galley style room with benches either side and a sink in the centre of the far counter. This room was also in darkness, and she hurried to a closed door at the far end, listening intently before opening it. As she had hoped, it opened onto the stairwell that she and Adam had come down earlier. Without hesitating, she ran up the stairs to the second floor and crept out onto the landing, turning right and side-stepping with her back to the wall until she reached Gabe's bedroom. Kat slipped inside and looked around. In the gloom, it looked just as she remembered it. She picked up a framed photo from the top of a chest of drawers and took it to the window, where the light from the moon gave some illumination. The photo was of her, Gabe, Felicity, and a guy whose name she couldn't recall, smiling and laughing at an outdoor concert.

"They were good times."

Kat dropped the photo and spun around to see Gabe standing in the doorway. He switched on the light and pushed the door over.

"Gabe, you nearly gave me heart failure."

"I didn't mean to," he said, walking over and picking up the photo from where it had fallen. "I miss her laughter."

"Me too."

"I'm so sorry, Kat. I should never have been driving that night."

"It wasn't your fault," she said.

Gabe cocked his head and looked at her. "What do you mean? You've always blamed me for her death and your injury." He glanced at her prosthesis.

"I've remembered things," she said. "From that night."

"Such as?"

"We were run off the road. You didn't crash. They dragged you away and left Felicity and me there to die."

Gabe gasped and put his hands to his mouth. He sat down

on the edge of the king-sized bed and looked up at her. "I wanted to tell you, but my father insisted that I must have hit my head and not remembered correctly and that the men who pulled me from the car just happened to be passing. He said they helped you and Felicity too, but it was too late."

"Well, they didn't. I've remembered other things too. That night, I saw something I shouldn't have in your father's study. I was running away, and they followed us."

"What did you see?" Gabe whispered.

"Give me your phone," Kat said, crossing the room to stand in front of him.

"Not until you tell me what's going on. Who's that scary guy with my father, and where's your cop?"

"Let me make a phone call first, and then I'll explain what I can," she said.

Gabe sighed and retrieved his phone from the inside pocket of his jacket, handing it to her.

Kat keyed in the number that Adam had given her. It connected straightaway.

"It's Kat."

"Are you safe?"

Kat eyed Gabe. "For now. We're at South Hill Manor outside of Cobham. We need help. I don't know where Adam is, but I think they're transporting drugs through here. An army officer by the name of Donald Webster seems to be in charge, although William Huntly-Tait is here."

"You've done great, Kat. A tactical team is ten minutes out."

"The people here are heavily armed, like semi-automatic type weapons, and there are at least eight of them. I don't know if they've got Adam or not."

"That's useful. Stay on the line."

Kat could hear her information being relayed. The phone beeped in her ear, she pulled it away and looked at the screen. The low battery icon illuminated.

"Have you got a charger?" she asked Gabe.

Gabe looked stunned. "In the car."

Kat cursed and put the phone back to her ear.

"Hello?" she said.

"Kat?" the voice on the other end answered.

"This phone is about to die unless I can find a charger."

"Okay, stay hidden, and we'll be there soon."

Kat handed Gabe back the phone with a frown on her face.

"Why don't you go back to your car, leave and call the last number I was just talking to."

The door swung open, hitting the wall with a crash.

"There she is," Don said, his massive physique loomed in the doorway. "Where is he?"

"Who?" Kat asked.

Don cocked his head to one side. "My patience is running thin, Kat. You've caused enough trouble tonight. Where's Adam?"

"No idea," she said. "I wonder what my brother would think about his old mate smuggling drugs out of Afghanistan and selling them on the streets of England? He must be turning in his grave."

"Drugs, Dad?" Gabe said, rising to his feet, and looking from Kat to his father, who stood behind Don in the doorway. Don stepped further into the bedroom.

"Hello?" a singsong voice called.

Don closed his eyes for a moment, as though controlling his emotions. "This day just keeps getting better," he said.

"Oh, there you are, darling," a shrill voice sounded, and

Mary McFarlane slipped into the room, dressed as though she were attending a cocktail function and teetering on high heels. She leaned over to kiss William Huntly-Tait's cheek, before glancing around at those in the room. Her eyes came to rest on Kat. "What is she doing here?" She looked Kat up and down as though she were something nasty she'd trodden in.

"She was just leaving," Gabe said, taking Kat's arm and walking her across the room towards the door.

Don moved into the doorway, blocking their exit as Kat shook her arm free of Gabe's hand.

"Don't make me hurt you," she said, glaring at Don.

Don laughed and pulled a Glock from a side holster beneath his jacket. "Your little kickboxing moves don't work against one of these, kitten. Come on, this way. You too, Gabe."

"Now wait just a moment," Huntly-Tait spluttered.

"What did you think would happen?" Don gave him a withering look.

"It's okay, darling," Mary soothed. "Perhaps Don has a little sample going spare."

"For God's sake, Mary, you sound like a common junkie," Huntly-Tait said.

Kat smirked, and Mary stepped forward and slapped her. Kat stumbled against Gabe, who held her back as she lunged at Mary.

"Mary, you do not want to start anything with her," Don cautioned, laughing. He motioned toward the hallway with his gun. "Now, come on."

A single burst of gunfire from a semi-automatic sounded from outside.

"Sounds like they've ratted out the fugitive," Don said,

laughing.

Kat and Gabe marched ahead of Don down the stairs and through the archway beneath the grand staircase. They continued past the kitchen and walked out through the back of the house into the yard.

"What's happening?" Gabe whispered to Kat.

"Do you really not know?"

He shook his head. "I haven't been back here since that night…" He glanced down at Kat's prosthesis.

She looked at him with pity. "Oh, Gabe. They're running a drug operation in the outbuildings. Don brings the drugs in from Afghanistan; we think using Mary McFarlane's plane, and your father provides the facilities to store, package and distribute them."

"What?"

"Do you know that woman with your father?" Kat tilted her head. "I've been investigating her firm for compliance anomalies."

Gabe nodded, looking a little shell-shocked. "He's been dating her for the past year, on and off."

"Really?"

They were met at the back door by one of the guards.

"Sir, we have a problem," he said, looking past Kat and Gabe to Don.

Don swore. "What now?"

The smell of smoke hit them as they stepped outside. All four roller doors on the garage were up, and men were pulling boxes and equipment from inside, depositing them on the ground, and returning for more. Like that of an angry cobra, tongues of flame could be seen licking at the roof of the building.

"Move that truck," Don shouted, pointing to the vehicle parked at the building's entrance.

"Someone slashed the tires, and it won't start," someone yelled back.

"For God's sake, push it then."

Don turned back to them with a wild look in his eye. He grabbed Kat by the arm and pulled her into the middle of the yard.

"Jackson, I have your girl. You need to show yourself in 10, 9, 8..."

Chapter 35

From his perch in a leafy tree on the fence line of the property, Adam cursed. He looked down at the little group standing halfway between the house and the outbuildings. Security lights shining from both the back of the house and the shed spilled across the yard, casting shadows and illuminating the gathering. Don Webster stood in the centre of the driveway with one hand clasped around Kat's upper arm. She struggled and tried to pull away from him, but to no avail. A Glock dangled from Webster's other hand, and his face was contorted into a nasty scowl. Behind them, several paces closer to the house, stood William Huntly-Tait with Mary McFarlane hanging off his arm. A younger man, skinny and smartly dressed, stood next to them, looking terrified.

"7, 6…" Don continued.

Kat continued to struggle against his firm grip on her arm. She launched a kick at his shin, which he deftly side-stepped.

"Steady there, princess," he mocked. "Maybe he doesn't care after all."

"Or maybe he's already gone," Kat said in a loud, clear voice.

Don raised the gun towards Kat.

Adam knew she was sending him a message, telling him to

stay put, but he couldn't do that, not when Don had a gun pointed at her head.

Adam dropped to the ground holding the semi-automatic out in front of him. "I'm here," he said, walking towards them.

All around, the weapons pointed in his direction.

"Hold your fire," Don called, letting Kat's arm go and taking a step towards his old comrade. "Take his weapon."

A man approached Adam from the left and took the rifle from his hands. He patted Adam down and relieved him of the stolen Glock, the lighter, and pocket knife before pushing him forward towards Don.

"What the hell, Donny?" Adam said, positioning himself between Don and Kat.

"What can I say, mate? Do you like my operation?"

Adam shook his head. "What's wrong with you? You've seen the damage heroin does."

"If not me, then it would just be some other squaddie landing on a big payday. Come on, Adam, you can't tell me you weren't tempted. How many opium farms did we raid and burn? What a waste."

"Speaking of burning," Adam began before Don landed a hefty punch in Adam's stomach, doubling him over. He fought for breath before gasping out, "Haven't you got a fire to put out?"

"Nah, we're leaving anyway, and if we let that burn, it should destroy any evidence." Don laughed. "And by the time your lot arrives, it'll be a burned-out shed with a couple of bodies inside."

Kat felt the cold fingers of fear grip her and gasped.

"Donny, this isn't you," she said.

He looked at her with regret. "Sorry, kitten. This time, I

have to make sure that Adam stops interfering." He tilted his head as he turned his attention back to Adam. "The little explosion outside that pub in Rotherhithe was supposed to deter you."

"It was you," Adam said, looking at Don in disgust. "You could have killed someone."

"I know your aversion to all things that go boom after what happened in Afghanistan, so I thought a little gas leak would give you cause to redirect your investigation."

"Then you don't know me that well, after all, do you."

Several men pushed the truck with the slashed tires to one side, and the van drove out of the garage. It turned down the long driveway beside the building and disappeared from view. A second truck reversed into the garage, and the remaining equipment was tossed onto its flatbed.

The crackling of burning timbers was getting louder, and the smell of scorched wood drifted toward them.

"Come on." Donny grabbed Adam's arm and propelled Kat in front of him, pushing them both towards the burning building.

Movement in the darkness from the tree line caught Kat's attention seconds before two bright flashes of light lit up the yard, and a small explosion sounded.

"Go," Adam shouted as he broke free from a disoriented Don.

Kat ducked under Don's arm and reached for Gabe. Together they ran back to the edge of the house, dropping down behind a small hedgerow bordering a garden below the kitchen window.

"Stay down," she whispered to him.

"What the hell was that?" Gabe asked.

"Dunno, a stun grenade, maybe?"

"But who threw it?"

Grunts and the smack of fists on flesh sounded, but they couldn't see who was fighting as the yard was engulfed in a mist of thick grey smoke. Gunfire sounded from the direction of the outbuildings, and they clutched one another, squatting as low to the ground as they could.

Kat peered over the hedge and noticed a man on his back on the gravel several metres away, not moving. She rose, eased herself over the border, dropped to a crouch, and crept towards him.

"Kat," Gabe hissed.

When she reached the man, he was still breathing despite the blood pooling around a head wound, and the unhealthy angle of his leg. His right arm was thrown out to the side and clutched his rifle. Kat eased it from his hand and stepped back to their hiding place.

Gabe helped her over the small hedge, and she handed him the gun.

"Do you know how to use this?" she whispered.

"No idea," he said, handing it back to her as though it was a poisonous snake.

"Hopefully, we won't have to find out."

Together they peered through the gloom as the smoke began to lift. There were shouts and the sounds of running footsteps and vehicle engines starting up.

"Police. Drop your weapons and get down on the ground," a tinny, reverberating voice called. "We have you surrounded."

Kat watched as a second van and truck drove away at speed and vanished into the wood's dark fringe. Several seconds later, from within the trees, a barrage of gunfire sounded.

Shouts, doors opening and closing, and the crack of returned shots echoed through the crisp night air for a full minute, before silence fell.

Gabe put his arm around Kat and pulled her close. He was shaking.

"It's okay, Gabe, I think the police have arrived."

"I hope so," he said.

As the smoke cleared in the yard, they could make out the figure of Adam standing over Don, who lay on the ground panting. Adam had Don's Glock in his hand, pointing it at him. Camouflaged officers appeared out of the darkness on all sides.

"Kat Munro?" a voice beside them spoke.

Kat spun around with the gun in her hands, positioning herself in front of Gabe.

The person stepped into the light pooling from the kitchen window. The woman was heavily armed but wore a helmet and a bulletproof vest with the word 'Police' written across it. Kat laid the gun she was holding on the ground, and they rose to their feet.

The officer spoke into her shoulder-mounted radio. "I have her. South side of the house. She's safe." To Kat, she said, "I'll wait here with you until we get the all-clear."

Kat smiled at her, relieved. "Thanks."

Gabe bent forward and rested his hands on his thighs, letting out a long breath.

Kat watched as Don was hauled to his feet and handcuffed. Near the back entrance to the house, William Huntly-Tait stood still as another officer patted him down. Beside him, Mary McFarlane looked on with bemused detachment at the scene unfolding around her.

Sirens sounded close by, and a minute later, two fire engines drove into the yard, expelling firefighters who raced towards the burning building. A police officer spoke to a driver, and one of the engines moved around behind the garage. A minute later, a jet of water sprayed across the burning roof.

Adam shoved the Glock into the back of his trousers and turned around, looking for Kat. Spying her standing with Gabe and the police officer, his face broke into a grin as he strode towards her.

Kat stepped forward into his arms.

"Thank God," he said, hugging her.

"You're okay," came her muffled reply.

He released her, but keeping his arm around her shoulders, turned to the man beside her.

"Are you going to introduce us?"

"Gabe Huntly-Tait," Kat said. "Meet DS Adam Jackson."

Gabe hesitated for a moment before extending his hand. The two men shook hands.

"I am pretty sure that Gabe isn't involved in this, Adam," Kat said.

Adam nodded. "We'll let the officer in charge decide how he wants to proceed, but I expect you'll be questioned tonight. We'll need a statement at the very least."

Gabe nodded. "I had no idea. Can I talk to my father?"

"Not at this stage," Adam said. "Later."

Two officers approached, and Adam stepped away to talk with them.

"Gabe, you're to go with these two officers now," he said, returning a moment later.

Gabe nodded.

"Thanks, Gabe," Kat said, reaching out and squeezing his

hand.

He shook his head. "Too little, too late. I thought he was going to shoot you, and there was nothing I could do." He gave her a sad smile, and they watched as the officers led him to a waiting patrol car.

"I was never letting that happen, you know," Adam said, turning to her.

"I don't think you had much control over what Donny was doing."

"True. Let's sit down; you look like you're about to collapse," Adam said.

Kat leaned into him. "I'm exhausted."

"Come on," he said, leading her to where his car was still parked at the back of the house.

Chapter 36

Adam and Kat were seated in front of the large wooden desk in Colonel Wilson's office a couple of hours later, drinking coffee and eating sandwiches provided for them by his staff, while they waited for him to arrive. The cosy corner office had the blinds drawn over the bay windows, and side lamps provided soft lighting. The building and those around it were silent. The only activity in the small hours of a Sunday morning was from a street sweeper outside, making its way along the deserted streets of Westminster.

"It seems like a long time since we had breakfast at your flat," Adam said.

"I know, I'm starving," Kat said. "I'm sorry that I slept the whole way back to London. I was pretty crap company."

Adam laughed. "I've had better."

Kat gave him a tired smile.

They ate in silence for a moment.

"Where were you? What happened after we split up?" she asked Adam.

"You first," he said.

Kat swallowed another mouthful of coffee and put her cup down on the edge of the desk. "I made it to the front room, where I figured there'd be a telephone. I'd just called that number you gave me when Gabe interrupted and disconnected the call. He'd followed us from London but had lost us after we'd been to the aerodrome and had decided to stop by the house. Fortunately, I was able to persuade him to hide me when we heard his father and Donny approaching," she said. "I crept through the dining room and up the back stairs that we'd come down earlier and hid in Gabe's bedroom. I used his mobile to call again, but then Donny caught us and took us outside to the yard, and well, you know the rest." She reached for her cup again. "Where did you go?"

"After I left you, I made my way across the yard, disarmed one of their guys, and broke into the outbuilding from the mezzanine level. I saw them dismantling their factory into vans ready to depart," Adam said. "It was a much bigger operation than I had expected. I set a fire in an office as a delay. Then I got outside, disabled one of the trucks to slow their departure, and climbed a tree where I had a good view over the yard, waiting to see what would happen next, and then Don led you out of the house."

The door opened, and Colonel Wilson wheeled himself into the room.

Adam jumped to his feet, but Wilson waved him away.

"Sit, Jackson," he said, coming to a stop by Kat's chair.

"Ms. Munro," he said, holding out his hand to Kat. "I'm delighted to meet you at last."

"It was you I spoke to on the phone?" Kat said, recognising his voice.

"Yes," he said. "You were very brave."

"More coffee?" an officer asked from the doorway.

"Yes, please," Adam said.

"I didn't feel all that brave," Kat said.

"Kat was just explaining to me what happened after we split up," Adam said.

"Well, you're going to have to go back to the start and take me through it all again."

* * *

Wilson sat back and sighed. "It's worse than we thought."

Adam nodded. "It appears to be a long-standing, very well run operation."

"I would never have suspected a man such as Huntly-Tait of working with the likes of Webster," Wilson added.

"So you think Gabe had nothing to do with any of this?" Adam asked, looking at Kat.

"Gabe is one of those people who can't hide his emotions, and he was genuinely shocked. Coupled with the fact that Donny didn't know who he was, I'm almost certain that he wasn't involved," Kat said.

"Interesting. You would have thought he'd notice a heroin distribution centre operating out of the outbuildings at his family home," Adam said.

"I don't think Gabe's been down there since the night of our car accident."

The officer returned with a tray of freshly brewed coffee and more sandwiches and set it down on the desk.

"Thank you," Kat said, smiling at the young officer. She reached out for a cup and handed it to Wilson before helping herself to a fresh one. She glanced at Adam.

"Speaking of that night, has Donny said anything about Jake?"

Wilson raised an eyebrow at Adam. Kat registered the look.

"He didn't tell me, I guessed," Kat said. "I think perhaps I saw Jake at the house the night he disappeared."

"But you don't remember?" Wilson said.

"Not for certain. I'm sorry."

"Don't be sorry; you've nothing to be sorry for."

"So has he said anything?" she prompted Adam.

Adam looked angry as he shook his head. "He just laughed when I asked him."

"Colonel, when I spoke to you on the phone a second time, it seemed that you already knew where we were," Kat said.

"We pinged the GPS tracker on Adam's phone when he didn't check in and saw that the location was near the old airstrip, so we knew that you were in the area. The team had just located the discarded mobile when you called. Even though you were cut off, we were able to trace the number to a landline at South Hill Manor before you called again."

"Ah, so that's why you got there so quickly," she said.

"Did you find the airplane?" Adam asked.

Wilson nodded. "Yes, that tracker you planted was very effective. They moved it to a disused airfield at Wisley, where we found two more aircraft of interest."

"What about the vehicles that had already left by the time you got there?"

"One four-wheel drive was picked up exiting the forest about four miles from the property, loaded with equipment and heroin, and another two vehicles were apprehended in the woods. We believe that a further two left before we got there, but we have leads on those as we speak."

"Were you already investigating Donny?" Kat asked. "Is that what Jake was looking into?"

"Not Webster specifically, but there were suspicions from our personnel in Kabul that not all of the opium production in the Helmand province had been halted. A local informant suggested that someone in the British Army had a deal going with a local tribe to export opium to Europe and then Britain, but he was killed before we could get further information."

Kat nodded. "So, Jake was gathering intel."

"Jake had a role with the deployment force, which meant he regularly travelled back and forwards, so he was well placed to do some undercover work for me."

Wilson's adjutant walked into the room and bent his head to speak quietly to Wilson, who nodded.

"Hugo has arrived," he said.

Kat frowned. "Hugo, as in…"

"As in me," DI Greenwood strode into the room. The corners of his eyes crinkled as he smiled at them. He was dressed more casually than Kat had ever seen him in jeans and a jumper pulled across his portly midriff.

Adam jumped up to greet him. Greenwood shook everyone's hands.

"Well, you two have had an eventful weekend," he said, looking from Kat to Adam.

"Yeah, I'm about ready to sleep for several days to catch up," Kat said.

"We'll get someone to drive you home soon, but there are a couple of things that you might like to know first," Greenwood said, pulling up a chair to join their semi-circle in front of Wilson's desk.

Kat looked at him with interest.

"Mary McFarlane is coming down from her high and is talking freely," he said.

"But will any of that be admissible if she's stoned?" Kat asked.

"Probably not, but it's giving us useful leads," Greenwood said. "Huntly-Tait has lawyered up, but is co-operating."

"What about Webster?" Adam asked.

"Nothing at all from him, at this stage," Greenwood said.

"If you could arrange for me to have a few minutes with him, I'll get something out of him," Adam growled.

"Doesn't work that way, as well you know," Greenwood said.

"More's the pity," Adam said.

"Anyway, it appears that the clients of this operation are mostly very well-heeled. This is a high-end gig, with rich clientele."

"Such as Mary McFarlane."

"Yeah, it turns out she was an excellent customer, with a massive habit, but more crucially, she had the means to launder the proceeds. Along with a very wealthy client list who enjoy dabbling."

"But we didn't find anything unusual in her personal finances that would hint to either a big drug habit or laundering drug proceeds," Kat said.

"But you did find Fund 4," Greenwood said with a smile.

"Fund 4 is tied up with this?"

"Almost certainly. We think that clients paid for their drugs by purchasing units in the Fund. Those proceeds then paid for the next shipments."

"Hang on," Kat said. "You're saying that my father buys drugs from Donny and pays for them by purchasing units in a Ponzi scheme? That's ridiculous. Have you met my father?"

"I'm not saying that," Greenwood said. "The initial investors, such as your father, thought they were investing in one of CIP's legitimate funds. But instead, they provided the seed capital for this venture. Nathan has been tracing individual transactions through the scheme. It appears that it is now self-funding. So, whichever CIP partners were involved were starting to move those initial investors out of Fund 4 and into one of the firm's ordinary funds. Nathan and the team have traced money being deposited by individuals who appear to be paying for their drug habits by buying units in what amounts to a fictitious fund. He's also tracked payments made to an offshore bank account. The funds are almost immediately transferred to another jurisdiction and then disappear."

Greenwood fell silent and looked at his hands. The atmosphere in the room had changed.

"What are you not telling me?" Kat said, staring at him.

"There was a fire at your offices early this evening. Deliberately set while Nathan was working."

Kat clapped her hand over her mouth, eyes wide. "Is he…"

"He's in hospital under observation. He jumped from the fire escape; he has a broken arm and some smoke inhalation; he was fortunate, as was the weekend security guard who was knocked unconscious by the arsonists."

"I need to see Nate," Kat said, leaping to her feet. "Can I go now?"

"It's the middle of the night, Kat. The hospital won't welcome you storming in at this hour. You can see him tomorrow," Adam said.

Kat looked out of the window and sat down again. "I don't know what time of day or night it is."

"That's understandable, you've had a full couple of days," Greenwood agreed. "Don't worry about Nathan, he's going to be fine."

"What about Henry Smyth, was he involved?" she asked.

"It doesn't appear so. Mary told us that he didn't touch the stuff. It seems that he may have uncovered Fund 4 and threatened to go to the authorities. He was attempting to go into hiding when someone got to him, and he was killed."

"That's what he meant in the note to his parents that he had to leave," Kat said. "That's so sad."

"I will visit Smyth's parents tomorrow and update them before this all hits the papers," Adam said.

"That would be good," Greenwood said.

"Roger Chen must have been in on it all," Adam said. "Otherwise, why throw himself off a bridge?"

"Yes, I believe he was the one running the financial side of the operation. His digital signature is all over the transactions," Greenwood said.

"What about Eddie Doors?" Kat asked.

"Eduardo Diaz?"

Kat nodded as Wilson chuckled.

"Mary McFarlane is trying to paint him as the drug dealer, but I'm not sure. We'll need to substantiate that some other way," Greenwood said. "He appears to be the brains behind their trading strategies and wasn't involved in the client side of the business."

"That makes sense," Adam said. "He isn't the most person-able of characters."

Kat yawned and raised her hand to cover her mouth.

"Your prosthesis was broken tonight," Wilson said.

Kat nodded and held out her hand to him. Deep grooves showed across the back of her fingers. "It was dented last night actually at my brother's house. It's a pity as my good one was damaged a few days earlier, but I should get it back this week."

"You'll definitely need to get that one looked at," Adam said. "It looks like you chipped the nail varnish."

Kat grinned at him. "Another first world problem that I can't seem to escape," she said.

"Despite the damage, your hand has got good functionality," Wilson said. "I've seen a number of these that don't look or operate nearly as effectively. And you say this isn't your good one?"

"They're prototypes, a new type of technology, which on the whole is really, really good." She held it out to Wilson. "Touch it, it doesn't feel like plastic, it's light, but it's still super strong."

Wilson touched the back of her hand and looked surprised. "And it's warm."

"Once we've tested a bit more, I'm going to help the lab cost it out more effectively so that this tech can be made widely available. I'm hoping to arrange a joint venture between the military and industry, so we can limit the profit margins and make it more affordable for those who need one," Kat said.

"Let me know if you need some support doing that," Wilson said.

"Thank you; I will."

* * *

Adam drove Kat back to her flat at 4 a.m. through the quiet streets of central London. He parked opposite her building and got out of the car, reaching into the back for a small bag.

"Are you coming up?" she said.

"Yeah, I'll take the sofa if that's okay."

"Sure."

Adam nodded to the occupants of a car in front of the building as they passed.

"Who's that?"

"We've had someone watching your flat all weekend, just a precaution," he said.

Kat unlocked the door of the flat. Zelda came bounding across the floor to greet them. Kat scooped her up and nuzzled her. Zelda's purr rumbled across the quiet room. She watched as Adam checked each of the rooms as well as the balcony.

"It's all good, Kat, you can sleep without concern," he said, returning to her side and reaching over to tickle Zelda under the chin.

"Thank you," she said. "I still can't believe that the investigation into CIP is linked to your missing friend and my accident two years ago."

Adam nodded. "I had a hunch, but it was far more intertwined than I had imagined. I'd just like to know what happened to Jake and where to find him."

"Hopefully, Donny will do the right thing and tell someone where he is," she said.

"He won't. He won't admit to murder, even as an accessory."

"You think he's dead?"

"Yeah, after what I saw tonight, I do. We would have met the same fate."

Kat shuddered, and Adam put his arms around her, hugging her tight. She leaned her head on his shoulder and let out a long sigh.

"I'm so tired, I feel like I'm drunk," she said.

"You need to sleep."

Kat nodded and stepping out of his embrace deposited Zelda on the sofa.

"You can join me," she said.

Adam stared at her for a moment before clearing his throat and looking away. "That's probably not the best idea for tonight."

"I meant just to sleep. That sofa is very uncomfortable to sleep on."

Adam still looked torn.

"Up to you," Kat said, a false note of brightness entering her voice. "I'm going to have a quick shower."

When Kat stepped from her bathroom ten minutes later, wearing pyjamas with a towel wrapped around her wet hair, she found Adam stretched out on top of her bed. His boots sat neatly beside his bag at the end of the bed.

Adam watched as she opened a drawer in her bedside table and removed a soft sock which she pulled over her stump. She glanced at him.

"Does this bother you?" she asked, holding her arm out. A silvery scar ran from her forearm to her elbow.

"Not in the slightest," he said.

She gave a hint of a smile.

"There are towels in the bathroom cupboard, help yourself," she said.

Adam swung his legs off the bed and stood, grabbing his bag and headed for the bathroom. "Thanks, I will."

Kat pulled the towel off her head and draped it over the edge of the door. She ran the fingers of her right hand through her damp hair before climbing into bed and falling fast asleep.

* * *

When Kat awoke several hours later, she was tight up against Adam with her left arm resting on his waist. He had one arm around her, and one hand curled around her stump. She felt something that had been squeezed tight in her chest for so many months shifting, and loosening.

"Hey," he mumbled, his voice thick with sleep.

"Hey, you," she said, lifting her head and smiling at him.

"When we were creeping around that house yesterday, I didn't think today would start like this," he said.

"You and me both."

Adam rolled onto his side, still holding her so that they lay facing one another. They were silent for several moments.

"I could get used to waking up like this," he said.

"Yes, although I'm not sure I'm looking particularly glamourous this morning. Never a great idea to go to bed with wet hair," Kat said, smiling at him.

"You look gorgeous," he said, winding a lock of her hair around his hand and leaning in to kiss her.

The kiss was deepening into something more when his phone rang. He pulled back and sighed, planting a kiss on the tip of her nose. "I need to get that."

Kat watched as he slipped out of bed and retrieved the ringing phone from his jacket pocket.

He frowned as he glanced at the screen before answering. "Jackson."

He listened for a moment before interrupting the person on the other end.

"Now is not a good time. I'll call you later." Then. "What? Pregnant? Whose is it?"

Kat heard a raised voice through the handset.

"It can't be. We've been apart six months."

He listened while the other person spoke before sinking onto the end of the bed, shoulders slumped, eyes closed with his free hand pressed to his forehead.

"Okay, okay, we'll work something out. I'll pick you up after work, and we'll talk."

He ended the call and sat for a moment with his head in his hands.

Kat crawled forward on the bed and touched him on the shoulder. "Everything okay?"

Adam's head remained bowed, and his eyes were closed.

"Nancy's pregnant," he said, not looking at her.

Kat sat back. "Oh, I thought you were…"

"Yes, we're in the process of getting a divorce."

"But you must have…"

Adam sighed. "It was a stupid lapse in judgment on my part about three months ago. I went to collect some things and talk through the details of our separation, and one thing led to another." He cursed. "She wants to postpone the divorce."

"What do you want?"

Adam finally turned and looked at her. "I would have thought that was fairly obvious by now," he said.

Kat gave him a small smile.

"But, it's no longer just about me. There's a baby to consider. I need to do the right thing." He straightened his shoulders and turned away from her.

Kat nodded and sat back, feeling deflated.

Adam stood and pulled on his jeans and boots before looking at her again.

"I'm sorry, Kat."

"Don't be," she said, her voice heavy. She hoped she could hold back the tears that were brewing deep within her. "You need to do what's right for you."

He nodded and bent to kiss the top of her head. "We'll talk later, okay?"

She nodded, no longer trusting herself to speak. How was it they'd gone from being wrapped around one another to this, in minutes?

Adam walked to the bedroom door, his bag in hand, and paused. "Kat, the officers will remain downstairs for a few days, but you still need to be vigilant when you're out and about."

Kat nodded and slipped off the bed, following him along the hall and into the lounge. She unlocked the front door and held it open for him.

"Well, ah, bye," he said as he passed through.

Kat closed the door behind him, leaned against it, and swallowed the lump in her throat. Zelda padded up to her and meowed. Kat scooped her up and headed for the kitchen.

"Right," she said, letting out a long, steadying breath. "Coffee; I guess it's too early for anything else."

Epilogue

Kat stood with Nathan, Shamira, and Charles Stevenson at the top of the staircase leading to their charred and water-damaged office. A breeze floated through the cavernous space from the tarpaulin-draped windows. The red brick walls were scorched and the wooden floors damaged beyond repair from both the fire, subsequent water and the fire retardant used to put the blaze out. The aroma of smoke and chemicals hung in the air.

Stevenson unbuttoned his suit jacket and surveyed the damage with a heavy sigh.

Nathan's arm was in a sling, but he had been deemed well enough to be discharged from the hospital.

"What a mess," Kat said, shaking her head in disbelief. "Nate, you were so lucky to get out in time."

"I know, mate," he said. "I had my headphones on and my back to the stairwell, so I didn't hear anything. First thing I knew, I smelt smoke, and when I turned around, this whole side of the room was blazing, and the flames were racing along the ceiling towards me."

Shamira's eyes glistened with unshed tears, and she clutched at Nathan's uninjured arm.

"I just bolted for the fire exit and jumped off. Gave some

bloke walking past a hell of a shock," he said.

"Have they caught whoever set the fire?" Kat asked.

Stephenson shook his head. "No, not yet."

"So how much damage to the building overall?"

"The downstairs foyer, this floor and the one above will need completely renovating," he said. "The sprinklers all kicked in, and the fire brigade got here really quickly. It could have been far worse."

"It looks like the computers and files are all destroyed," Shamira said, looking at the twisted and shattered screens and burned out shelves.

Stephenson nodded. "Just as well we keep everything in the cloud. Being 90% paperless has turned out to be fortuitous."

"When will we be back in here?" Nathan asked.

"Three to four months," he said. "But in the meantime, I've managed to secure a floor in the building opposite. It's not as nice as this, but it will have to do."

"Lead the way, boss," Kat said. "I think we've got a fair bit of work ahead of us."

Stephenson nodded to the fire protection officer standing guard as they headed back down the stairs. They crossed the road, entered a plain modern steel and glass office tower and travelled to the fifth floor by lift.

Stephenson waved them into a meeting room, where there was an appetising spread of muffins and fruit laid out on a large conference table. The rest of the team were already seated around the table and rose to greet them. The reception-ist followed them into the room and took everyone's coffee orders.

"First things first, Kat, talk us through everything that's happened since last Thursday," Stephenson said, sitting down.

Over morning tea, Kat filled them in on the events of the previous few days, from the break-in at her flat, the intruder at Sara's, the trip to Surrey with Adam, and their eventual capture and escape at South Hill Manor.

"And this Don Webster is someone you knew?" Stephenson asked when she finished speaking.

"Yes, he served in Afghanistan with my older brother Joe before his death. He knows our family quite well. I still can't believe that he was behind all of this," Kat said.

"Does anyone know how he got involved with CIP?" Nathan asked.

"DS Jackson has been looking into his background, and he and Eduardo Diaz went to school together. Diaz introduced him to Mary McFarlane, and it went from there," Stephenson said.

Nathan shook his head. "Circles within circles."

"Right, people, we have a money laundering case to put together," Stephenson said, standing. "You all did a great job on this. I can see us working with the Financial Crimes Unit again."

"How's DS Jackson?" Shamira asked as she and Kat left the meeting room and walked across the plain open plan office to their new desks.

"He's fine."

"So why did you go down to Surrey with him?"

"He was concerned after what happened at Sara's, and he wanted to keep an eye on me."

"I bet he did," she said with a grin.

Kat stopped walking and turned to her friend. "He has a wife, and she's pregnant."

Shamira's mouth fell open. "Oh, Kat."

"I know," Kat said. "I don't want to talk about it, okay?"

"Well, if you change your mind, you know where to find me."

"Did the police work out who killed the security guard at CIP, and Henry Smyth for that matter?" Nate asked, joining them.

Kat nodded. "Mary McFarlane has decided to distance herself from the murders and has been co-operating," she said. "Apparently she'd become suspicious that Henry had discovered Fund 4 and was going to expose them. She saw him returning to the CIP offices as she was leaving, on the night he died. She panicked and called Donny, who sent a couple of his guys over."

Shamira gasped.

"The security guard interrupted them loading Smyth's unconscious body into the lift and confronted them. There was a fight and poor Popov ended up being thrown over the railing into the lobby."

"That's so sad."

"The men then drove Henry back to his apartment, administered the lethal dose and staged his death," Kat said.

"How awful," Shamira murmured.

"What about Adam's mate, Jake?" Nate asked. "Has he been found?"

Kat shook her head. "Huntly-Tait claims Jake was still alive when he kicked him out of South Hill Manor on the night I saw him, and Donny isn't talking," she said looking at her watch. "I've gotta go. I have another interview with the police soon. They have more questions for me. I'll see you later."

* * *

Kat exited the building, looking up and down the street for a taxi.

"Can I give you a lift?" a voice to her left spoke.

"Adam?" she said, as he stepped into view.

Kat chewed her bottom lip and found that she couldn't look at him. She scuffed the toe of her shoe in a small pile of leaves at the edge of the footpath.

"You haven't returned my calls," Adam said, after a moment of awkward silence.

"There's nothing else to say," she said.

"Can you at least look at me?"

Kat dragged her eyes from the ground to his face. His gaze drilled into hers for a moment before softening.

"Kat, there's plenty left to say, if you'll just let me."

"Adam, you have a family to think about now, you need to forget about me," she said.

Adam gave a heavy sigh. "I needed to check that you're okay. I left in rather a hurry the other morning."

Kat flashed a bright smile. "I'm fine, really. Let's just leave things where they are."

"I don't have a choice, do I?" he said.

"No." Kat looked past him to where a black cab was trundling down the road with its yellow hire light turned on. She reached out and squeezed his hand. "Bye, Adam."

She stepped around him and signalled to the taxi. It swooped to a stop and Kat opened the back door before climbing in. She gave her destination to the driver and sat back allowing herself one glance through the window. Adam stood still at the curb watching her drive away, his expression inscrutable.

Acknowledgements

First and foremost, thank you to my editor, Gary Smailes, for his sharp insight, guidance and encouragement. Many thanks to Julia Gibbs, copy editor extraordinaire and to my beta readers Sarah, Adie and Craig whose time and effort I hugely appreciate. Thanks also to Daryl and Deborah for patiently answering my police procedure questions. Any errors are entirely mine. The awesome cover is by Warren Designs.

My advance reader team has once again been massively supportive with their early reads and reviews. A big shout-out to Shannon, Michaela, Melanie, Judy, Eveie, Roger, Karen, Graham, Eileen, BJ, Suzanne, Susan, Helen, Kathy, Judith, Kathryn, Jackie and Milena.

Thanks to my husband Craig, father Jack and my gorgeous boys Jude, Zak and Scott for your encouragement and excitement about my books, particularly if it means a trip overseas to do 'research.'

Where would I be without the encouragement of my enthusiastic cheerleaders? Thank you so much ladies for the laughs and the serious discussions.

Thank you to the book bloggers and reviewers who help to share their excitement for my books. And finally, a big thank-you to you, my readers, without whom I wouldn't be doing something that I enjoy so much.

A Note from the Author

2020 has certainly been a strange year and no-one has been untouched by the pandemic that has swept the globe. I hope my stories provide you with a little light escapism when needed.

If you enjoyed *Death Count* and would like to help spread the word, I'd be so grateful if you could leave a review (as short or as long as you like) on the site where you purchased it and don't forget to tell your friends!

If you would like further information about me or my books you can check out my website (www.slbeaumont.com) or join my Reader's Group and be kept up to date about up-coming book launches, exclusive giveaways and competitions and receive a FREE copy of the prequel to The Carlswick Mysteries series.

Thank you so much!
S

Keep reading for a preview of my award-winning novel Shadow of Doubt.

Shadow of Doubt

Chapter 1

July 10

"For God's sake, get one of the others to do it," I said, exasperated, as I looked up from my computer at my boss who was leaning on the wall of my cubicle.

"No. It's your turn," Andrew replied turning away, signalling an end to the conversation.

I sighed and stood up, stretching my back. Three hours straight sitting at a desk wasn't good. I had been hoping to squeeze in a trip to the gym after work to loosen everything up, but it looked like my evening was going in entirely another direction.

Hesitating only for a moment, I followed Andrew down the row to his cubicle, not willing to give in quite so easily. Andrew was a heavyset man in his mid-thirties. His thinning hair was cropped close to his head, but did nothing to detract from his good looks. He oozed charm and ruled his team of accountants and analysts in the derivatives division of the investment bank, Dobson Stone, with a mixture of fear and admiration. To be on Andrew's good side was like being bathed in the warmth of sunshine, but do wrong by him and it felt like being exposed to the iciest of winters. Fortunately,

I had only ever felt the heat of summer, which gave me the opportunity to push the boundaries. And now was when I needed one of those opportunities.

"Come on, Andrew. You know that you're going to employ him anyway." I flashed my most winning smile at him. "Let's just skip this bit."

'This bit' was the tradition in the team of finally vetting any new recruit by taking them out to a local watering hole and doing a 'social' interview. The derivatives team was a close knit, play hard, work hard group and Andrew was a big fan of team players. Ever since the disastrous recruitment of an accountant named Peter, who had been hired without the social interview, Andrew had deemed it mandatory. Peter had passed all of the other interview stages with flying colours, but once he joined the team his lack of humour, aversion to socializing with his colleagues and propensity to back stab had caused major problems.

"Need to make sure he's not another Peter, Jess. And besides, William seems like the kind of guy who will appreciate a pretty face." Andrew grinned, knowing full well that the latter comment would annoy me and distract me from my argument.

Putting my hands on my hips, I scowled at him and practically hissed, "I can't believe you just said that. I will report you to the Diversity Committee. Maybe select me for my knowledge of the business or my social charm, but because of my looks? Give me a break."

Andrew threw back his head and roared with laughter. He had one of those loud laughs which made people stop what they were doing and look in his direction, in case they were missing something really good. Jimmy looked up from the next cubicle, catching the end of my rant. He and fellow Antipodean Dave were always quick with a quip and up for anything. They were usually behind the many practical jokes that went on at the office and they never, ever, missed an opportunity to wind someone up.

"Watch out, Scotty is about to blow," Jimmy called out to anyone in the team who was listening. Jimmy had an open, friendly face. At the tender age of twenty-four, he already had smile lines surrounding his mischievous eyes. He had the physique of the champion fighters in his family, but not the temperament. Andrew and I both glared at him. Still grinning, he held his hands up as if to protect himself and sat down again.

"Machiavelli's Wine Bar, seven pm," Andrew instructed and turned to pick up his ringing phone. I was dismissed with a wave of his hand.

I returned to my cubicle muttering about the appropriateness of the venue and picked up my mobile to call my husband Colin. He answered on the second ring.

"Make it quick, Jess. I'm having a crazy day."

"I have to work late, a recruitment interview in a pub of all things," I said.

"Which one?"

"Machiavelli's."

"Okay. Good. Gotta go." He was gone. I wasn't even sure that he had heard me.

Jimmy and Dave stopped by my desk as I was shutting down my computer at the end of the day. Dave was the opposite of Jimmy physically, short and slight with a mop of messy blond hair, but he shared his friend's sense of fun.

"Where are you meeting him?" Dave asked, picking up my

stapler and twirling it around.

"At Machiavelli's up by St. Paul's," I replied, taking the stapler from his hands and replacing it on the desk, only to have him pick up my hole punch instead. "I will know which kleptomaniac to come after if I come in tomorrow and there are stationery items missing," I warned him with a grin.

Dave simply laughed, putting the hole punch back in its place, and swiped my favourite pen instead. I shook my head at him. He was incorrigible.

"We'll be at The Tower if you wanna meet after," Jimmy said, naming the pub closest to the office as we walked towards the bank of lifts to take us down to the lobby entrance of the building.

"Okay, see you there in fifteen minutes," I said, only half joking. Seriously, I was going to get this over and done with as quickly as possible.

* * *

The rain had stopped and the early evening sun bathed the city in a soft glow. The old fashioned wrought iron streetlamps that lined the road towards St. Paul's Cathedral hadn't yet turned on. Machiavelli's was on a corner and had floor-to-ceiling plate glass windows wrapping around both street views. It was already busy for a Wednesday night, with groups of men and women dressed in business attire gathered around tables chatting and laughing.

I stepped off the street and entered through the open doors. The bar itself was brightly lit with strings of tiny lights draped from one corner of the room to the other and back again forming a crisscross pattern across the entire ceiling. The heels of my shoes beat out a loud rap on the polished wooden floor, as I walked towards the bar, my eyes scanning the room. Andrew had said that William Johnston was tall and dark-haired. "You should have made him wear a rose," I had suggested to Andrew as I was leaving the office, which had only earned me a glare; at this rate summer would be turning into autumn.

Ah, that had to be him, leaning against the bar, fiddling with his mobile phone. He was tall, as Andrew had described, with thick dark hair, which curled over his collar and hung across his forehead. He was well dressed in a dark blue suit. As if aware of my scrutiny, he straightened up and looked towards me with a questioning tilt of his head. Over-confident, I thought, deciding in that instant that I disliked him. I stopped in front of him.

"William?" I asked, returning his cool questioning gaze.

"You must be Jessica." His accent was English, well-educated. I shook his hand. "Call me Will. Can I get you a drink?"

"I think it's me that's supposed to offer that. What can I get you?" I asked.

"A Becks then, please, Jessica," he replied leaning back against the bar and studying me.

I signalled to the nearest barman. "A bottle of Becks and a skinny gin and tonic please."

We found a couple of empty armchairs in one corner and Will turned on the charm. First, he helped me take my raincoat off and laid it over the back of my chair, then he waited until I had sat down before taking a seat himself. Old manners, unusual in the politically correct equal opportunity business world, but still, I refused to be charmed. I wasn't here to make friends. Will adjusted the cuffs of his pale blue double-cuff shirt beneath his suit jacket. His cufflinks were gold dice; I noted the satirical choice for a career in investment banking, where so much was speculative.

"So, what's this then? Get me drunk and see if I will spill all my deep, dark secrets?" He smiled.

"Actually, it would save me a lot of time and money, if we can skip the drunken bit and you just tell me your secrets," I replied.

Will leaned forward and looked up at me with a glint in his blue eyes. "So, Jessica, what exactly *would* you like to know?"

I spluttered on my drink. Holy crap, this guy was super confident. Flirting with the interviewer didn't usually get you a job.

I sat back in my chair and tried to adopt a neutral expression and ignore the fact that he had my attention. "Well, why don't you tell me a bit about yourself?"

"Okay, I grew up in Sussex. Obtained my Maths degree from UCL and Chartered Accountancy with EY," he answered. "But I'm sure you know all that."

I had expected him to wax lyrical about himself, given that I had left him with such an open-ended question. The fact that he didn't, showed he was clever. There was more to him than just the charm. I finished my drink as we chatted a little about the work he had done and who we both knew at EY.

"Anyway, enough about me. How did a nice Scottish girl like you end up working in the cut-throat world of investment banking?" Will asked.

Okay, so maybe I was wrong. There was that awful charm again.

"Who said anything about me being nice?" I growled.

Will, to his credit, laughed and raised his empty bottle.

"Next round is definitely on me," he said.

I looked at my watch and acquiesced. It would be rude to end the interview after just twenty minutes, even if I did consider it a farce. "Okay, but just one. I have to get going."

Will nodded and made his way to the bar. I watched him go. He had broad shoulders and carried himself in a way that spoke of someone at ease in their own skin. He stopped and shook hands with a guy standing at a tall table and leaned over, kissing the cheek of the woman with him. As much as I hated to admit it, he would be a good fit in the team. Easy to get on with and charming enough to deal with the odd difficult trader. I didn't have to like him. Hell, I didn't really have to even work with him. My job here was done.

"So. What else are you supposed to glean from me tonight?" he asked with a grin as he placed my drink on the little table between our chairs.

I sat twisting my wedding and engagement rings around on my finger. "Nothing, I think I'm done. I guess you'll be hearing from Andrew tomorrow. Do you have any questions for me?"

Will tilted his head, a little smile playing around his lips. "Just one."

"Sure, fire away."

"Will you have dinner with me?" he asked.

I wasn't expecting that. "No," I replied, trying not to sound prim. "You do realize that I am married?"

Will nodded and shrugged his shoulders. "Just thought I'd ask," he replied.

* * *

I arrived at The Tower around eight pm. The doors of the old pub were wide open and Jimmy and Dave were holding court out front, surrounded by a group of people. From the peals of laughter coming from their audience, it sounded like they were trying to outdo each other with the funniest anecdotes; nothing new there. Jimmy caught my eye as I walked closer and broke away from the group to greet me.

"Hey, Jess, how did it go? William? Verdict?" he asked.

"He has the charm of a prince and the morals of an alley cat. He will be a perfect fit," I answered.

Jimmy looked stunned for a moment, before a grin spread across his face.

"Did he try to hit on you?"

I must have looked uncomfortable because he slipped a friendly arm around my shoulders and turned me towards the doors leading into the bar.

"Didn't you tell him about the strapping Scotsman that you have tucked away at home?"

I laughed. "No, it wasn't like that."

Jimmy signalled to the barman. "My friend here needs a G and T pronto."

The barman obliged, upending a blue bottle into a measuring cup just as a loud boom sounded and the pub shook. The cup slipped from the barman's fingers with a clatter. Bottles in the refrigerators behind the counter and those on the shelf against the wall behind the bar rattled. Empty glasses tipped over on an adjacent table and several bottles of spirits skidded off the end of the bar, splintering into shards as they hit the wooden floor. Clear liquid ran across the boards following the slope of the floor towards the door. With a shriek, I grabbed on to the edge of the bar for support.

There was an eerie silence for a moment as everyone looked at each other with a mixture of confusion and concern.

"What the hell was that?" Jimmy said. "An earthquake?"

"Jim," Dave shouted from outside.

Jimmy and I looked at each other for a second before rushing through the door to join Dave.

"Look." He pointed up the road to where an enormous cloud of smoke and dust rose into the dusky sky. The screech of brakes sounded as traffic pulled to an abrupt stop on the busy road. Then loud splintering crashes could be heard as brick, timber and metal returned to earth and the awful sound of human suffering rose above the din.

We started running up the road in the direction of the blast. Jimmy and Dave, not hampered by shoes with three inch heels, raced ahead of me, covering the two blocks in no time. By the time I joined them, the first survivors were staggering from what remained of the Kings Arms Hotel, covered in white powder from fractured concrete and plaster.

"What the—" began Dave.

We stood frozen to the spot and watched as two figures stepped from the rubble into the road, leaning on one another to stay upright. Both had blood running down their faces from cuts to their heads. Behind them, a woman took a few lurching steps before collapsing beside a broken wooden bar stool with a feeble cry for help. A dazed man stepped over her, crossed the road and kept walking, his gaze unfocused. Two young women stumbled out of the wreckage, clinging to one another, their clothes torn and dusty, each missing a high-heeled shoe, so that they appeared to be engaged in an elaborate twisting dance routine. A man pushed past them calling for help, blood squirting from beneath the hand he pressed into his shoulder where his arm would once have been. Another man remained seated at an outdoor table, his hand still wrapped around a half-full pint of beer. On his lap sat one of the pub's many colourful hanging baskets, the reds, blues and greens of the flowers and foliage in stark contrast to the chalky white powder which covered the man's hair and clothes. What remained of his drinking companions lay scattered around him, like a macabre human jigsaw. The man stared into space with a blank expression.

"Oh my God," I said, covering my mouth with my hand as I took in the horrific scene, struggling to comprehend the wreckage.

All around us people began rising from where they had taken cover moments earlier. There were desperate shouts as some hurried towards the wounded, whilst others held back, unsure what to do faced with such devastation. As I looked around, I noticed some people begin filming the carnage on their mobile phones.

Dave rushed forward and took the arm of one of the young women, while Jimmy went to the aid of her friend and helped them to sit down on the edge of the curb. They were shaking uncontrollably, so I took my raincoat off and draped it around the shoulders of the one nearest to me.

The wail of sirens from emergency responders racing to the scene began to get louder as they approached from all directions. A single police car pulled to a stop beside us and two young police officers alighted, donning their hats as they stepped out. Their faces displayed horrified expressions as they surveyed the chaos, but these were soon replaced by grim determination as they strode forward and took charge. One officer directed those of us helping the injured to lead them to an open outdoor square across the road from the scene, whilst the second officer tried to contain the spectators.

"Help is on the way," he called. "We need to make certain that there isn't a second device or a gas leak before going in." Jimmy, who'd been climbing into the rubble to assist the injured, now stepped back and looked around with a helpless expression. "I know," the officer said understanding his reaction. "But until we know what we are dealing with we don't want any further casualties."

"It was a car bomb," a man in the growing crowd called out, pointing to the almost unrecognizable mangled remains of a vehicle lying on its side up against the broken windows of a neighbouring building, which until a few minutes earlier had been a lunch-time sandwich bar. "I saw it light up seconds before the explosion."

"Okay, sir. Don't go anywhere. We'll need a statement from you," the officer replied before relaying the information through to headquarters on his shoulder-mounted radio.

"Jessica." I turned towards the voice. Will jogged across the road to join me. "Are you okay?"

"These poor people, they were just having a drink like we were earlier," I said, wringing my hands and watching as a team of fireman leapt from their truck, unwinding a hose to deal with a small blaze that smouldered at the rear of the site.

Will nodded. "I know."

I looked up at him. His brow was furrowed and he looked as distraught as I felt.

"Who would do such a thing? In the heart of London?" I asked.

Jimmy and Dave returned from helping the two young women to an ambulance that had just arrived. Dave handed me back my raincoat.

"Will, this is Jimmy and Dave, two of your new colleagues," I said.

"G'day, mate," Jimmy said as he hurried past us and back towards the remains of the pub. "Can you give us a hand with this guy?" he called over his shoulder.

"Sure," Will replied, following him and taking the other side of a solidly built injured man who had staggered from the pub. Between them, Jimmy and Will helped him across the road to the square where more ambulances and paramedics were beginning to arrive.

The smell of smoke and rotten wood intermingled with something sweet and sickly hit me as I helped an older woman away from the debris to relative safety. I wrinkled my nose and looked skywards; sunset was upon us. I noticed a police van arrive and several officers begin setting up spotlights on tripods pointed at what remained of the pub.

We were busy for the next twenty minutes, helping the walking wounded from the ruins across the road to the square to be triaged and assisting the small handful of police officers to set up barriers until more of their colleagues arrived. At one point I found myself moving odd shoes, bags, documents and other personal objects thrown by the blast into the street, to an area at the edge of the square. The bomb squad arrived and we were all moved back from the site. We were beginning to feel surplus to requirements when a police officer approached us.

"Anyone else is going to need either a stretcher or a body bag," he said with a grim expression. "Thanks for your assistance, but I'll need you back behind the barrier now. Leave your details with the officer over there as we'll need statements from you all."

We nodded and walked across to the officer holding a tablet, at the edge of the police cordon, and gave our names and contact details. I looked down at my white shirt; it had a blood stain on the sleeve and black marks across the front. I went to pull my raincoat on but noticed that it had drops of blood across the shoulders. I shuddered. I looked at my hands, they were blackened too. I hiccupped, the beginnings of a sob.

"Come on," Jimmy said, taking my arm. "Let's head back to The Tower, I need a stiff drink after that. Will, mate, join us?"

* * *

As we ducked under the hastily erected police cordon, a block back from the scene we noticed Aditi Sharma, the petite dark-haired BBC reporter, standing alongside the crews of several other television networks, awaiting the signal from her cameraman as he counted her in. We paused to listen.

"I'm reporting live from the scene of a devastating terrorist attack in the heart of London tonight." Aditi paused and looked behind her at the remains of the pub, a smouldering pile of brick and plaster, dotted with a number of white sheets, covering the bodies of the dead. "Eye witnesses tell me that a car bomb exploded outside the Kings Arms Hotel on Cheapside at 8.05 pm tonight. No one has yet claimed responsibility for the attack at one of the City's popular after work venues. There is currently no official death toll, but I understand that there are already eighteen confirmed dead and many more injured."

Aditi pressed her right hand to the earpiece in her ear as the news anchor in the studio asked her a question. A moment later she nodded.

"Another incidence of home grown terror? We're hearing those rumours here too. This is the third attack since the outcome of the Brexit referendum, but as yet there's been no official comment. Witnesses describe the two men who parked the van containing the bomb and walked away ten minutes before the explosion, as white and in their twenties. We understand that police teams are pulling the street CCTV footage as we speak."

She paused, listening before continuing. "At this point no one has claimed responsibility, so we have no idea as to the motive behind the attack, but there is some speculation that this incident may be related to the recent Trafalgar Square and Windsor bombings. However, it does seem that this was a much larger device, so authorities will be desperately hoping that this isn't an escalation of violence."